HOW MUCH I NEED

MIAMI NIGHTS SERIES, BOOK 5

MARIE FORCE

How Much I Need
Miami Nights Series, Book 5
By Marie Force

Published by HTJB, Inc.

Cover Design by Ashley Lopez
Print Layout: E-book Formatting Fairies
ISBN: 978-1958035047

The Miami Nights Series

Book 1: How Much I Feel *(Carmen & Jason)*
Book 2: How Much I Care *(Maria & Austin)*
Book 3: How Much I Love *(Dee's story)*
Nochebuena, A Miami Nights Novella
Book 4: How Much I Want *(Nico & Sofia)*
Book 5: How Much I Need *(Milo and Gianna)*

CHAPTER 1

MILO

In case you've ever wondered, being shot in the neck totally sucks. Before it happened to me, I never gave the first thought to what it would be like to have to keep my neck still for weeks while it heals from surgery to remove the bullet that came frighteningly close to my spinal cord and damaged bones in my neck. I'm thankful every day to still be able to move my extremities and to feel all the important parts. I owe my mobility—and my life—to my cousin Carmen's husband, Jason, a world-class neurosurgeon, who was right there when I needed him.

I hope I never need him like that again.

Until your neck is immobilized for four weeks, you don't realize how much you use it—for things like breathing, eating and talking, to start with—not to mention laughing, coughing and sneezing, which is the worst when your neck has been sliced open and put back together.

All that said, there're also a few upsides, such as the way my older brother, Nico, is falling over himself to take care of me because he's so relieved that I survived a bullet meant for him. I wouldn't go so far as to say I'm milking it, per se, but if I'm enjoying having Nico running around to get me all my favorite things and visiting multiple times per day, what can I say? I'm only human, and he amuses me.

Yesterday, he went way out of his way to go to Little Havana to get me my favorite pastelitos after I told him I was craving them. And he got the Cuban coffee I love, too. See what I mean? Taking a bullet for your brother turns him into your faithful servant. Our sisters, Maria and Dee, have a bet on how long Nico will keep up this level of fawning. Maria gives it another week. Dee says I've got a month left to enjoy it.

Don't get me wrong. I hate seeing Nico upset. That doesn't amuse me, nor does the reason behind the shooting. Sofia's abusive ex-husband wasn't happy to see her moving on with her life, so he decided to do something about it by killing her new guy. He took a shot at me, thinking I was Nico, and well, you know the rest. While I'll be forever grateful not to have been killed or paralyzed, I'm equally grateful that neither of those things happened to my beloved brother either.

The guy who did it—and his cousin—are locked up, and the cops who came to get a statement from me when I was coherent again told me they have video from the intersection where the shooting occurred. They shouldn't need my testimony, which is good, because I remember nothing after dropping off a group at the Departures area at MIA and then heading back to Little Havana to pick up a bachelorette party.

I'd already put in a full day at my regular job writing computer code. I volunteered to take Nico's rides with the car service he owns so he could keep an eye on Sofia during her waitress shift at Giordino's, my aunt and uncle's restaurant. Sofia's ex had been ramping up his threats to the point that Nico was afraid to leave her unprotected anywhere, even at the restaurant.

As my Nona likes to say, no good deed goes unpunished.

The next thing I remember is waking up in the hospital with my parents, siblings and grandmothers standing over me looking like they'd been to hell and back. From what I was told, it was touch and go for a while there. Jason couldn't give them any assurances before the surgery, so they'd put in a very long night waiting to hear if I was going to survive the surgery with everything still working.

I've never seen my dad look so ravaged, even when my mom was battling breast cancer, and that was an awful time for us. Apparently, this was worse than that for him, my mom and everyone who loves me.

Nico says our whole neighborhood is cooking for him and Sofia, which isn't fair. I hope they'll cook for me, too, when I get home, because the people in our subdivision can *cook*. He says everyone is asking for me, worried about me, sending love, wondering what they can do, which makes me happy because I've invested the time in getting to know most of them. Nico took over mowing Mr. and Mrs. Miller's lawn, which I'd been doing since Mr. Miller had hip replacement surgery. I'm glad Nico is taking care of things like that for me. I wouldn't want Mr. Miller to have a setback because he did too much too soon. I heard he even drove my Meals on Wheels route last week, and I can't wait to hear what my regulars think of him. I'm sure they'll have something to say.

The worst part of this whole thing, by far, is the halo screwed into my skull that's keeping my head from moving at all while my neck heals. I hate that freaking thing more than I've ever hated anything. Being stuck inside a cage is as maddening as you might expect, and Jason says it's going to be a while yet before I'm freed from my metal prison.

Since I can't do much of anything, I mostly spend my time in the hospital watching the door, waiting for the afternoon shift change, which has become the highlight of my day—five days a week, anyway. That's when my favorite nurse, Gianna, comes on duty. One of the other nurses told me they rarely have the same patients every day, but Gianna must've pulled some strings or something because she's always assigned to me.

I've grown to hate the days when she's off. They feel endless without her there to brighten my small world. Sure, my family is in and out on a schedule that must be planned to cover all my awake hours, but nothing can compare to the time with Gianna. When I'm not looking at the door, I'm watching the clock. She's two minutes later than usual. I hope that doesn't mean she wasn't assigned to me today.

How crazy is it that the only way this will be a good day is if she comes through that door in the next few minutes, with her silky dark hair pulled into a high ponytail that puts her lovely face on full display? I dream about her pretty face, her gorgeous smile, and plot ways to get rid of the sadness I see in her big brown eyes. I've got a whole list of ideas for when I get the hell out of this place.

I'm still mortified that she was the one who removed my catheter after the surgery. I can't even think about that nightmare without wanting to curl up in a ball and hide from the world. Except I can't do that for reasons I've already mentioned. Besides, she's told me at least ten times to quit making a big deal out of it.

"If you've seen one penis, you've seen them all," she likes to say.

That's highly offensive as I consider mine to be rather special. When I tell her that, she laughs, which makes me unreasonably happy. I get the feeling she doesn't laugh like that very often, so I try to make it happen as often as I can.

Ah, there she is, and right away I can tell she hardly slept. She confessed to battling terrible insomnia that makes her feel like a zombie at work. The dark shadows under her eyes are a dead giveaway. I wish I wasn't stuck in this stupid bed so I could help her get through her shift. Although, what could I do? I know nothing about medicine, except for what I've learned from weeks in the hospital.

I'm due to be released soon to a rehab facility that's part of the Miami-Dade complex, but I'm dreading that because I won't see Gianna every day. I can't even think about leaving her floor without a blue funk descending, which is odd. I tend to be a positive, optimistic sort of person, but thinking about moving on without her feels all kinds of wrong to me.

And, yes, I'm aware that I sound like a crazy weirdo for having developed such a fierce crush on my nurse. While awake in the middle of the night, I wondered whether it's merely a case of proximity and boredom. But the second she comes into the room, every part of me feels better than it did five minutes ago. That's got nothing to do with boredom and everything to do with her.

"Hi there." Her cheerful tone never fades, even when she's exhausted. "How'd you sleep last night?"

"Fine. How about you?"

She shrugs as she scans her badge and logs into the computer stand in my room. "The usual bleep show."

That she never swears is another thing that amuses me about her. She says she swears off the job, but I'm not sure I believe her. "Isn't there anything you can take for that?"

"Not without messing me up the next day. Melatonin helps, but I'm maxed out on how much of that I can take. But we're not here to talk about me. How're you feeling? Is the itching at the incision site still bad?"

I'd much rather talk about her. "Yeah, it's making me crazy."

"If the topical cream isn't working, we can give you something for that, but it's apt to make you sleepy."

"It's fine. I'm coping." I don't want to be asleep while she's on duty.

"The itching usually only lasts a few days, and it's a sign of healing, which is good news." She types some more. "More good news is that Dr. Northrup has cleared you for release to rehab. You'll be transferred as soon as they have a bed available."

I want to cry, even though I'm glad to be doing well enough to move on to rehab. I want to get back to full strength, mostly so I can show Gianna what I'm like when I'm not stuck in a metal cage. But what will happen when I don't see her every day anymore? Will I become just another ex-patient to her, or do I stand a chance of seeing her away from this place?

The thought of not seeing her every day is devastating, and no, I'm not being dramatic. I mean it. "Will you visit me at the rehab?" Do I sound as pathetic as I feel asking her that?

"I'd love to," she says with a smile. "You're my star patient. I have to see you over the finish line. And, I'm moving to the morning shift after this week, so I can see you after work."

Is that all I am? I want to ask her. *Your star patient?*

After a few more clicks on the keyboard, she sets the rolling desk aside. "Is there anything I can get for you?"

I try to think of something I need to keep her there longer, but my family has seen to it that I have everything I could ever want and then some. "No, thanks."

"Okay, then. I'll check on you in a bit."

"I'll be here." *Counting the minutes until you return.* It's official. I'm pathetic and getting more so by the minute.

GIANNA

Everything is harder when I haven't slept. I'm like a zombie moving through my day, checking and double-checking everything I do so I won't make a terrible mistake that kills someone. Thank God for caffeine. As I refill my coffee cup in the break room, my phone buzzes with a new text.

I pull it from my pocket and see yet another message from the wedding venue, threatening legal action if the outstanding balance isn't paid for my canceled wedding by the end of the month. Thinking that was handled a long time ago, I was shocked to learn recently that isn't the case, thus my worse-than-ever insomnia. I forward the message to my ex-fiancé, Jared, the one who canceled the wedding. He promised me he'd take care of paying the venue, but he also promised me a lifetime of love and happiness.

We all know how that worked out, so I'm starting to feel a bit panicky about having to pay those fees.

It's no wonder I'm not sleeping. Or eating. Or functioning. We owe them *thirty thousand dollars*. I'm the one who signed the contract, so I'm on the hook for the money even though I wasn't the one who canceled the wedding—or even wanted the big white wedding. That was all him. I wanted something small and simple, but he wasn't having that.

Good times.

Jared responds a few minutes later. *I'm working on getting this taken care of. Sorry for the delay.*

They're going to SUE me if it's not paid. I'm freaking out.

I told you I'll take care of it, and I will. Not sure what else you want me to say.

When will you pay them?

Soon.

Call me crazy, but I don't trust him. Not anymore. Which is why my stomach is in knots so tight I can barely choke down a protein shake a few times a day to keep myself alive.

Thirty. Thousand. Dollars.

Since the wedding was canceled *on* the big day, we're required to pay the full total of the contract. What the hell was I thinking agreeing to a big over-the-top wedding in the first place? I thought I was in love and got carried away, especially after he set the budget at forty thousand for everything.

How is it my fault that he offered to put up that kind of

money? None of this is my fault, but I'm the one they're going to sue if he doesn't pay up and soon.

I rub my hand over my stomach, which is in a constant state of upset.

The only bright spot in my day is my most delightful patient ever, Milo Giordino, and his lovely family. They've been feeding the entire 5 East floor while he's been in residence. I'll miss him when he leaves, which is so weird. I rarely miss my patients when they move on to rehab or go home to recuperate.

I hope for the best for all of them, but I don't miss them.

I'll miss Milo.

I'm thankful to him for giving me something else to think about besides the gloom and doom that has been my life since I lost my parents suddenly four years ago and had to finish raising my two younger brothers, who wanted nothing to do with me as their guardian. I almost think they would've preferred being put in foster care to being "stuck" with me. When they turned eighteen, both went as far away to college as they could get. I took that personally.

I did my best for them after the shocking loss of our parents, giving up my own college life to come home to care for them. Not that college life was so awesome, what with a good friend going missing my first year there. But that's something I try not to think too much about, or I'll go crazy wondering what happened to our beloved Skylar.

After a very rough few years, was it any wonder that I latched on to the first man who was nice to me during all that madness? I was desperate for someone to share the burden that'd been sitting on my shoulders for years at that point. I was a fool, and I know that now, but knowing it doesn't solve my most pressing issue.

"Gianna?"

I turn to find one of my best work friends, Annie, sticking

her head into the break room. How long have I been hiding out here? I have no idea. "Mrs. Ellis is robo calling."

"I've got her."

"Thank you."

She's my most annoying patient. I won't miss her when she leaves.

But Milo Giordino?

I'm going to miss the hell out of him and his ridiculously handsome face.

CHAPTER 2

MILO

"What's eating you today?" Nico asks as he devours a cheeseburger while I pick at the chicken sandwich and fries he brought me.

"Nothing. Why?"

"You seem super gloomy."

"For someone who got shot in the neck, you mean?"

"No, I mean for you. You're never grumpy or out of sorts, so it's freaking me out that you are now. What's wrong?"

"Nothing other than they're moving me to rehab. Maybe tomorrow."

"Isn't that a good thing? One step closer to getting out of here."

"It is, but…"

Before I can reply, Gianna comes back into my room and wipes every other thought from my mind.

"Oh, you're eating," she says. "I can come back."

"That's okay." I stuff the rest of my lunch into the bag it came in and set it aside for later. "What's up?"

"Time for some exercise."

They make me get up and walk around several times a day. Usually, I've done a lap or two by now. "I thought you'd forgotten."

"Nope. I just got busy. But I'm here now. Shall we?"

"Sure." I don't want to because every time I get out of bed, I realize how weak and feeble I've become since I was shot.

As always, she helps me to sit and then stand, holding me just right to keep me from falling. I'm thankful to be wearing pajama pants and one of several button-down shirts Nico brought me from home, so I don't have to deal with the hospital gowns. I slide my feet into slippers and take a minute to get my bearings and catch my breath.

Have I mentioned that this totally sucks?

"I'm going to hit the bathroom first."

"I'll go with you," Nico says, which is a relief.

I hate when Gianna helps me in there. Nothing says sexy like a game of "let's see if I can hit the bowl without looking." Ugh, the indignities never end.

My brother holds the belt that Gianna has put around my waist, since they're still treating me like a fall risk. "Do you need me to aim it for you?" Nico asks without an ounce of the usual ball busting I expect from him.

"I've got it." I take a leak and mostly hit the bowl, or so I think. It's hard to tell when you can't look anywhere but straight ahead and side to side thanks to the erector set holding my neck immobilized.

I shuffle to the sink and wash my hands and gasp at my reflection. "I look like shit. Why didn't you tell me?"

"You look like you've been shot and are recovering right on schedule."

"Tomorrow, I want you to bring me a new razor." Since I look like death warmed over, I'll probably never see Gianna again after I leave her ward.

"Can you shave in that thing?" Nico asks.

"I can try. And you can start being normal again."

"What does that mean?"

"You're being too nice to me. It's freaking me out."

"I'm never going to stop being nice to you after you took a bullet for me."

"We need to get past that."

"I'm not there yet," Nico says as he guides me toward the bathroom door.

"Get there, will you? I'm craving some normal."

"Talk to me about that when you're back at home where you belong."

"I will." Before he can open the door, I stop him with my hand up. "Do me a favor? Let me go for the walk with Gianna by myself."

"I knew it. I told Mom yesterday that you were crushing on her."

"Whatever. Stay here."

"Yes, sir."

I can't deal with this easygoing version of Nico, who's never been this agreeable with anyone except his fiancée, Sofia, and her son, Mateo. He'd do anything for them, and now I guess he'd do anything for me, too. Although I always felt like he'd be there for me no matter what, even before I took a bullet that was meant for him.

Nico turns me over to Gianna and takes a seat to finish his lunch as I shuffle toward the hallway. She'll make me do at least two laps around the floor, after which I'll be completely exhausted.

"Your brother is very devoted to you."

"Because he feels guilty about me getting shot."

"Ah, that's right."

"It's hard to believe that his fiancée's ex would do such a thing. I'm just glad he didn't succeed in killing either of us."

"I'm glad for that, too."

"So's our mom."

"I'll bet. Her nerves must be shot." She laughed. "Whoops. Poor choice of words."

I control the urge to laugh because that'll hurt. So I chuckle when I'd much prefer to laugh. As we shuffle along, I try to find the words to ask her if I'm really going to see her again when I leave her floor without sounding pathetic. Fine line there, as my entire situation is somewhat pathetic. See Exhibit A: needing help in the bathroom.

"We see so many gunshot wounds these days," she says. "It may not seem like it right now, but you got so, *so* lucky."

"I know. When I think about what might've happened..."

"Don't do that."

"I can't do much else but think."

"Think happy thoughts. You got lucky for a reason. What're you going to do with your second chance?"

"Funny you should ask. I'd like my second chance to include you."

"Milo," she says with a laugh, "you're too sweet."

"I'm not being sweet. I'm serious. I like you. I like talking to you. I don't want to stop talking to you just because I'm not here anymore."

"My life is complicated."

"Okay."

"It's just that it might be better—for you, that is—if you don't see me anymore after you leave here."

I stop walking and turn to face her, even though I can barely see her face until she looks up at me, madly vulnerable and wounded. I can see all that in her expressive brown eyes. "It wouldn't be better for me if I didn't get to talk to you anymore."

"It's not uncommon for people to develop an... infatuation... with their nurse while in the hospital."

"That's not what this is."

"How can you be so certain?"

"Because I've never felt so upset by the thought of not seeing someone anymore."

"You're upset about that?"

"Very. I don't want to go to rehab because you won't be there."

She gives me a nudge to get me moving again. "That's silly. Rehab is one step closer to home."

"It's a big step away from you, and I don't like that. It's got me seriously bummed out to be leaving the hospital."

"You're the only patient I've ever had who wasn't itching to get out of here."

"It's all your fault. Seeing you has become my favorite part of the day."

"Milo…"

"Are you blushing? I can't see from up here."

"Yes! And I can't blush at work. It's not professional."

"Then you'd better agree to see me after this, so I won't have to keep embarrassing you."

"You're sure about this?"

"Positive."

"Okay, then I'll promise to come visit you at rehab. We'll go from there."

I feel like I can breathe again for the first time since she told me I'll be leaving her floor soon. "That'd be great, but you know what would be even better?"

"What's that?"

"If you gave me your number so we can text."

"I can do that, too."

"I promise you I'm not a weirdo who'll make you regret giving me your number."

"I know you're not. Why do you think I said yes?"

As we pass the nurses station for the second time, I can tell by my level of exhaustion that we're getting close to the end of our walk. But I'm not ready to be done with our conversation. "Should we do another lap?"

"I'm down if you are."

"I'm definitely down." I just hope I don't embarrass myself by falling or stumbling as I move on legs that feel like they belong to someone else.

Whatever it takes to have more time with her.

GIANNA

As I drive home from work, I decide to skip a planned trip to the twenty-four-hour Publix because I'm so tired. It'll be a soup-and-grilled-cheese kind of night, which is about all I'm capable of after barely sleeping last night. I'm desperate enough to take something to help me sleep tonight so I don't have to struggle through another workday on an empty tank.

The potential for error gets higher the longer I go without sleep.

Several of my colleagues asked today if I'm okay, and I can't have that. If something goes wrong, they'll be able to say they could tell I was off my game. I can't afford to lose my job, especially not with the threat of litigation hanging over me.

I pull into the parking lot at home and into my assigned space. I gather my work bag and lunch cooler and am getting out of the car when a man approaches me. For a second, I'm too surprised to react or to grab the bottle of pepper spray hanging from my keychain.

He shoves something toward me, and I have no choice but to take it, so he won't knock me over. "You've been served," he says as he walks away, leaving me reeling from the near assault and the realization that I'm being sued.

Somehow, I manage to get myself inside with hands shaking so hard, I can barely function. I tear open the envelope and read the first page of the enclosed document that confirms the wedding venue decided not to wait until the end of the month to sue me. I withdraw my phone and do something I absolutely do not want to do. I call my ex.

His voicemail picks up.

The sound of his voice makes me sad and angry at the same time.

"This is Gianna. I've been served with lawsuit papers from the wedding venue. You promised me you'd take care of this." I sound distraught, but who wouldn't be? It wasn't my idea to have or cancel the big wedding, and now I'm being sued? If I sold everything I own, I couldn't come up with half of what I owe them. The house I live in was left to me and my brothers by our parents. It's not mine to leverage. "Will you call me, please?"

I hate having to ask him for anything after he broke my heart and humiliated me by calling off our wedding. I found out it wasn't happening when I arrived at the church. Humiliation on top of humiliation. For an awkward few days afterward, I sat in stunned disbelief with my brothers and closest friends on hand as they tried to find some way to comfort me.

At least they tried.

My brothers left the second they could, and who could blame them for wanting to get away from my train wreck? They text every now and then to make sure I'm still alive, but other than that, they're off living their lives, while I'm still dealing with the nightmare Jared left for me to clean up.

I try calling him again, but again his phone goes right to voicemail. I don't bother leaving another message. He probably shut off the phone after he got the first one.

In the kitchen, I pour a huge glass of wine and bring it with me to the sofa. I pull a blanket over myself, hoping to stop the shivering, but that doesn't do a thing to help since the shivering is from fear, not the cold. An hour after I arrive at home, I've worked up the courage to read the document sent from the venue's lawyers.

They're suing me for forty-five thousand dollars plus court costs and lawyer fees. They've tacked on interest for the year they've been awaiting payment. I have about two seconds' notice before I'm running for the toilet to vomit up the wine and the tiny bit of food I've had today.

Forty-five thousand dollars.

The number echoes through my mind like a nightmare I'll never escape, and the most ironic part is that I wanted a small, simple wedding. After losing my parents so tragically, every sort of "celebration" is a trial for me, including my graduation from nursing school, my brothers' graduations from high school and every birthday and holiday we've endured without them. The last thing *in the world* I wanted was a big flashy wedding when the most important people in my life wouldn't be there.

But Jared insisted. "We're only going to do this once, babe," he'd said, imploring me with a look he knew I couldn't resist back when I still loved him. "Let's do it up in style."

His insistence on doing it up "in style" included a costly dress I'll be paying for over the next three years unless I'm able to sell it for a fraction of what it's worth. I should list it on the local swap site, since it's a gorgeous dress that someone else will love as much as I once did. I'll get around to that one of these days. In the meantime, I pay $157 a month for the dress I wore for just over two hours.

I was such a fool to fall so deeply in love with a man I thought would eventually fill all the empty places inside me. Instead, he only made everything worse than it already was, which is saying something. Things have been rough for the last four years, and now I'm facing financial ruin on top of everything else.

I'd laugh if I wasn't so terrified.

My mind shifts to Milo and how sweet he was earlier when

he said he doesn't want to leave the floor because that means leaving me, too. He's a lovely guy, but I thought Jared was, too. Milo is tempting. Even with the metal halo holding his neck in place and the physical challenges of his recovery, he always makes me feel better when I see him. At any other time in my life, I'd be tempted to accept the things he's offering me, but now… I just don't know.

I don't want to be so desperate to fill those empty spaces that I jump from one man to another, hoping maybe *he* can fix what's wrong with me.

No one can do that but me, and with a lawsuit hanging over my head, the last thing Milo needs is me and my drama when he's got to put all his effort toward recovering from his injury.

I'll keep my promise and visit him in rehab, but that's all I can do, even if the thought of not seeing him every day is just another thing to be sad about.

CHAPTER 3

MILO

She's way off today. Even more so than she was yesterday. The circles under her eyes have turned a dark purple, and her hands are shaking as she types on the computer.

"What's wrong?" I ask her, relieved I wasn't moved before she came on duty.

She glances up from the keyboard. "Nothing. You're getting out of here today. We should be celebrating."

"Gianna... Tell me the truth. I could see that something is terribly wrong the second you came in the door."

Her deep sigh confirms my suspicions. "It's nothing you need to worry about."

"I'll worry if you don't talk to me."

She sets aside the computer stand and sits on the edge of my bed.

I'm dressed in a T-shirt and track pants for the move to the rehab facility that adjoins the hospital, but I'm not going anywhere until I find out what's up with her.

"It's unprofessional for me to talk about my problems with a patient."

"The hell with that. We're friends now. At least I feel like we are."

"I feel like we are, too."

I take a chance and put my hand on top of hers. "Then tell your friend what's wrong. Maybe I can help."

"You can't, but it's sweet that you want to."

"Tell me, Gianna."

After another deep sigh, I'm stunned to see her gorgeous eyes fill with tears. "I told you how my wedding was canceled, right?"

"You did, and I'm so sorry that happened."

Shrugging, she says, "The wedding venue is suing me for breach of contract."

"Oh no."

"Yeah, so, I'm trying to figure out where I'm going to come up with forty-five thousand dollars plus lawyers for both sides, and my ex, who promised to pay for the whole thing, has gone silent. I thought he took care of it a long time ago, until they started calling me again recently. Now they've gone ahead and sued me."

I'm feeling more infuriated on her behalf by the second. "Why isn't he on the hook for it?"

"Because I signed the contract. I'm an idiot, and I know that now, but I didn't know it then. The best part is I wanted a small, uncomplicated thing, and he wanted the big white wedding. Funny, huh?"

"Not funny at all. No wonder you haven't been sleeping."

"Yeah, they've been threatening this for weeks, and I got served last night when I got home. At first, I thought I was being attacked in the parking lot. I guess a lawsuit is better than an assault."

"I wish I could hug you."

"I wish you could, too."

"I will as soon as I can. I promise."

"I'll look forward to that. In the meantime, do you know a good lawyer?" She tries for a teasing tone that falls flat due to the devastation that's plainly obvious.

"As a matter of fact, I do. My mom is a lawyer. I'd be happy to ask her to call you." I hand her my phone. I beat myself up all last night for letting her leave yesterday before we exchanged numbers. "Put your number in, and I'll have her get in touch."

"You don't have to do that, Milo."

"You need a lawyer. She's an awesome lawyer and will fight like hell to make this right for you."

She eyes the phone for a long moment before she takes it and punches in her number. "Tell her she's under no obligation to get involved."

"The minute she hears what you're dealing with, she'll want to help." I'm certain of that. "Try not to worry. I'll have her call you tonight, okay?"

"If you're sure she won't mind."

"I'm sure." And I'm gratified to watch as her entire disposition seems to get lighter now that she knows help is on the way.

Not to mention now I have her phone number and can keep in touch with her.

She seems to realize all at once that we're still holding hands while she's on duty. "Don't tell anyone around here that I unloaded on you, okay?"

"I never would."

"This is certainly a first," she says with a nervous laugh.

"What is?"

"Telling a patient my problems."

"I'm not just a patient. We agreed we're friends now, and friends help each other. That's the whole point of friendship."

"Thank you. I feel lucky to have met you and your amazing family."

"I feel lucky to have met you, too."

Our time together is interrupted when Dr. Jason Northrup and his group of residents come into the room.

Gianna quickly pulls her hand free and gets up to return to the computer.

"How's my star patient today?" Jason asks. "Ready to move to rehab?"

I glance at Gianna. I'm not ready at all, but I tell Jason what he wants to hear. "Sure thing, boss."

"Excellent." He does a perfunctory check of the halo and the screws holding it in place and puts me through a now-familiar neurological exam. "Everything is healing up great. Now we'll focus on getting you back to full strength so you can return to your life."

That ought to be my top priority, and of course it is, but I'm devastated to be leaving the ward where I got to see Gianna every day. The roller coaster of emotions makes me feel silly and immature when I should be counting my blessings. Jason told my parents after the surgery that I got incredibly lucky to still have full mobility.

To be moving on from in-patient care to rehab is a big step forward that I'm thankful to be making, but after the last few minutes with Gianna, I'm more determined than ever to keep her in my life and do whatever I can to help get her out from under the nightmare her ex has left her to clean up.

One of Jason's residents, a young doctor named Emma, is put in charge of overseeing my move to the rehab facility.

Before he left last night, Nico packed up all the stuff that's accumulated during my time in the hospital. We gave the last of the flowers to the nurses, and the rest of my things are packed into two bags that are ready to go with me to my new home away from home.

"Can I have just a minute?" I ask Emma when I'm loaded into a wheelchair for the ride.

She glances between me and Gianna, who stayed to help. "Um, sure."

After she leaves the room, I gesture for Gianna to come over to where I can see her. "I know it may not seem like it right now, but everything will be okay."

"If you say so."

"I say so. My mom is a Doberman on behalf of her clients. That's what my dad calls her. She'll make this go away for you."

"I sure hope you're right."

"I am. You can count on it. I'll text you after I talk to her. In the meantime, try not to worry."

"Thank you, Milo."

"I should be thanking you. You've made what should've been one of the worst things I've ever been through into one of the best."

"Stop it," she says with a laugh. "That is not true!"

"Yes, it is. And the minute I'm out of this contraption, I'm going to take you to dinner to thank you for taking such amazing care of me."

"You don't have to do that."

"I know I don't have to. I want to. I'll talk to you in a little while, okay?"

"Okay."

"And you're not going to worry, right?"

"I'll try not to."

"Excellent."

Gianna rolls me into the hallway and hands one of my bags to Emma while the other sits on my lap.

As we go by the nurses' station, I say goodbye to the others who've become familiar to me since I arrived on the ward after the surgery. I'm thankful to all of them, as well as to Jason and his team, for the second chance I've been given. We sure got lucky when Carmen fell in love with him and made him part of our family. That he was right there when I needed him is another thing to be grateful for.

I've never been someone who feels the need to wait around for some sort of disaster to strike to live life to the fullest. But you can't go through something like this without feeling differently about everything. Imagine if I'd died without knowing what it was like to be truly in love. What a tragedy that would've been. I'm not saying I'm in love with Gianna or anything like that, but if my desire to fix everything that's gone wrong for her is any sign, I could be.

I absolutely could be, and I can't wait to see what happens next.

~

Rehab sucks. From the minute I arrived, they've had me up and moving and running through exercises that make my muscles quiver from exertion. I'm sweating and nauseated within half an hour, and it goes downhill from there. By the time I return to the room I was in for five minutes before the sadists showed up, I'm so exhausted I can barely keep my eyes open. I'd give anything for a shower, but that's not possible with the halo and the vest that covers half my chest. I'll need help with getting cleaned up, so I'll wait until the nurse returns.

I sit on the bed and move painfully to get my feet up and find a comfortable position for my head. I miss Gianna. She knows how to make me comfortable in this stupid contraption. I can't wait to be free of it. I can't wait for a hot shower, another thing I'll never again take for granted. While I understand why the halo is necessary, it's like being inside a prison in some ways. I had no idea how many times a day I moved my head in one direction or another until I couldn't move it at all.

That's the last thought I have until much later, when I open my eyes to see that it's gotten dark while I napped. I try to sit up and moan as my tortured muscles fight back. It's ridiculous how weak I am. I work out every day at home and thought I was in good shape until I spent weeks in a hospital bed.

It takes a few minutes, but I fight my way out of bed, relying on abdominal muscles that ache as much as the rest of me does from doing more than their share of the work lately. I go into the bathroom and remove the button-down shirt—the only kind I can wear thanks to the halo—and the rest of my clothes, determined to do this much myself going forward. Using a washcloth, I manage to clean all the important parts. The nurse will help me remove the vest later and clean the skin under it.

I reach for a towel, moving carefully so I won't do something stupid like fall and set myself back even further. By the time I struggle into a change of clothes, I'm completely drained again, but at least I'm covered when my parents knock on the door.

I wave them in through the window in the door.

They're so happy that I survived the shooting I could probably ask them for anything, and they'd give it to me. Not that I'd ever take advantage of them, but their joy at seeing me is unmistakable every time they come in.

"How's it going, son?" my dad, Lorenzo, asks.

"Pretty good. Rehab is no joke, though. I liked the hospital better."

"This is a good sign that you're on your way home," my mom, Elena, says as she kisses the back of my hand. She hates that she can't kiss my face because of the halo. "Nico asked us to bring a razor."

"Just put it on the bedside table." I'm too tired to even think about shaving.

"And we brought dinner. Mom made delicious manicotti and salad. Are you hungry?"

I wasn't until I caught a whiff of the manicotti she knows I love. "Starving."

"Then we got here just in time," Mom says.

I sit on the bed with the tray table across my lap to eat, covered in paper towels so I won't make a mess of my clean clothes.

"I brought you more clothes that Nico washed for you," Mom says.

"When is he going to forgive himself for this and stop acting like my butler?" I ask them.

"Not any time soon," Dad says with a frown. "He's out of his mind over it."

"I told him to cut that out. All that matters is that I survived it and I'm not paralyzed or anything permanent. We got lucky."

"And he knows that, but he still feels responsible," Dad says.

"He didn't pull the trigger."

"Still," Dad says. "How would you feel if this had happened to him because of something tied to you, even indirectly?"

"As awful as he does, I suppose. But I miss ball-busting Nico. This kinder, gentler version of him is creepy."

My parents laugh.

"Hopefully, he'll be back to normal soon," Mom says, "but he's as upset as we've ever seen him."

"He doesn't need to be. This wasn't his fault. I don't blame him. No one does."

"We'll keep telling him until he gets it through his thick skull," Dad says.

"This is delicious, Mom. Thank you."

"I'm glad you're enjoying it."

"She made it just for you. I got leftovers."

"Oh stop," Mom says. "You're having manicotti tomorrow."

"Yay."

"Mom, can I ask a favor for a friend?"

"Sure. What's up?"

"Remember my nurse Gianna from the hospital?"

"Of course. She's a lovely young woman."

"Yes, she is, and we've kind of become friends. Her ex-fiancé called off their wedding *at* the wedding."

"Lord. How does someone let it get that far along if they're not planning to go through with it?"

"I don't know." It makes me so angry that anyone could do that to her, especially after she lost her parents the way she did. "He promised to pay what they owed the venue, but he never did it, and now they're suing her because she signed the contract."

Mom's brows furrow in the look that used to terrify my siblings and me when we'd done something wrong. "Do you have her number?"

"It's in my phone." I point to it, plugged into a charger across the room. That was the only plug I could reach when I checked in.

After Mom brings me my phone, I find the number Gianna gave me earlier and share the contact with my mom.

"Got it," Mom says. "I'll call her from the car on the way home."

"Thank you so much. She's incredibly upset."

"I can only imagine. We'll take care of it for her."

"I'm always thankful for you guys, but never more so than recently."

Mom blinks back tears. "We're thankful we didn't lose you in this senseless act of violence." She shudders. "For as long as I live, I'll never forget the horror of that night."

Dad reaches over to take her hand. "Nor will I."

"I'm sorry I put you guys through that."

"Certainly not your fault, but we do appreciate you surviving," Mom says with a forced smile.

"A while ago, Gianna told me she doesn't have any family to speak of, except for two younger brothers in college out West. They lost their parents when she was in college." I'm not sure why I feel the need to tell them this, but once they know it, I have no doubt that they'll treat her like family. That's how they are.

"That poor girl," Mom says. "That's terrible, and then her fiancé did this to her?" She shakes her head. "I'll take care of it. Don't you worry."

I almost feel a little sorry for Gianna's ex. My mom will make him wish he'd never been born by the time she's finished with him.

"Thank you, Mom."

"Any friend of my kids is a friend of mine."

"Did I get the feeling you might be a little sweet on that pretty nurse, son?" Dad asks.

"Maybe. I really like her. But it's hard to do anything about it while I'm stuck inside this damned cage."

"Did Jason say how much longer you'll need it?" Mom asks.

"At least another couple of weeks. I'll go mad by then."

"You're doing great," Mom says.

They stay for another half hour, getting up to leave when they see that I'm fighting to stay awake. "Sorry to be such a drag."

Standing next to the bed, Mom carefully reaches inside the halo to smooth the hair back from my forehead. "You're not a drag, and I can't wait to be able to kiss your cheek again. Sleep tight, my love."

"You, too."

"I'll sleep better when you're out of here."

"I'm fine. Don't lose any sleep over me."

"That's like telling her not to breathe." Dad pats me on the shoulder. "Love you, buddy."

"Love you, too. Thanks for dinner and for calling Gianna and everything else."

"You got it," Mom says. "We'll see you tomorrow."

I love the way our family steps up for people in need. Nico met his fiancée, Sofia, when she came to work at the family's restaurant. Our grandmothers "adopted" her following her son's emergency brain surgery. The surgery was donated by Jason, who discovered the child's tumor during a volunteer tour at the free clinic where my sister Maria works. That's my family for you. They see a young, single mother in crisis and do everything they can to make things easier for her.

I hope the Giordinos can work their magic on Gianna's behalf, too. I feel much better knowing my mom is on the case.

I send Gianna a text. *Hey, it's Milo. I gave my mom your number, and she's going to call you shortly. She's already infuriated on your behalf, so here comes Elena with all guns blazing.* I add a laughing emoji. *Rehab is no fun, especially since you're not here.*

She writes back a few minutes later. *Thank you SO MUCH, Milo. I can't tell you what this means to me. I'll be by to see you after work tomorrow. Let me know if I can bring you anything.*

Just your company would make my day. I stare at the text for a long moment, hoping it doesn't sound too needy or pathetic, before I press Send.

You got it!

I fall asleep smiling as I look forward to seeing her tomorrow.

CHAPTER 4

GIANNA

My phone rings when I'm on the way home. I take the call on my Bluetooth. "Hello, this is Gianna."

"Hi, Gianna. It's Elena Giordino. Milo told me about your situation, and I want to help."

"Thank you so much for calling, Mrs. Giordino."

"Call me Elena, honey. Start from the beginning and tell me what happened. I'm in the car with my husband, and the call is on the Bluetooth, just so you know. If you'd prefer that I call you back when I'm alone, I can do that in about thirty minutes."

"It's no problem." The cancellation of my wedding is the last topic I wish to revisit, but I know it's necessary to fight the lawsuit. I tell her about Jared proposing two Christmas Eves ago and how he wanted a big wedding. "He gave me a budget of forty thousand dollars and said to do with it whatever I could. He was busy at work—even busier than I am—so he left it all to me to plan."

"Do you have that anywhere in writing? A text or an email?"

"I might. I can go through the texts and see if there's anything."

"That'd be great. We might have to sue him to cover the damages from the venue's lawsuit."

"Ugh."

"I know, but he made promises to you, and I'm going to make sure he keeps them. We might be able to void the lawsuit if I can convince him to do the right thing. Can you send me photos of the summary pages of the lawsuit as well as his name and phone number? I'll call him in the morning and outline the situation to him."

Wow, this woman doesn't mess around. I love her already. "I'm driving, so I'll send them to you when I get home."

"Perfect. Sometimes all it takes in cases like this is a call from a lawyer letting someone know that things are going to get ugly for him unless he does the right thing—and quickly."

"I appreciate this more than you'll ever know."

"I'm happy to do whatever I can to help."

"I'll send you my address, too, so you can forward any bills for your time."

"There won't be any bill, sweetheart. We're so thankful for your care of Milo."

"That's my job, though."

"Let me do mine for you. It's a fair trade."

"Thank you again, Elena. I might just sleep tonight for the first time in weeks."

"You rest easy, and I'll call you tomorrow after I talk to what's-his-name."

That makes me laugh for the first time in longer than I can remember. Except when I'm with Milo. I laugh a lot with him. "I'll look forward to your call. If I don't answer, it's because I'm at work. I'll get back to you as soon as I can."

"Sounds good. I'll be in touch."

I'm so relieved to have her on the job that I feel like I can breathe for the first time since that process server all but attacked me yesterday. It's been a very long time since anyone went to bat for me the way Milo and his mother are. I've been so alone since my parents died, even when Jared and I were together, which should've been a red flag. Hindsight has been a bitch since the haze of grief over my canceled wedding and failed relationship has lifted.

When I get home, I scan copies of every page of the ten-page lawsuit and send those to her. *Jared's last name is Allen, and I've enclosed his contact info. I'm Gianna Lombardi. Again, I'm so, so grateful for your help.*

Elena writes back a few minutes later. *Got it. I'll call him in the morning and make his day. Will keep you posted. Let me know if you have anything in writing about his willingness to pay for the wedding. That will help.*

I'm going to look tonight. Will send you anything I have.

She responds with a thumbs-up.

Now I'm glad I didn't delete every message I've ever gotten from Jared, as I was tempted to do when he tearfully told me—in the vestibule of the church where our wedding was supposed to have been happening—he couldn't go through with the wedding and thought we should take a break from each other to "contemplate our futures." I was completely blindsided. Before he said those things, I'd had no idea that he was having second thoughts or cold feet or whatever it was that caused him to pull the rug out from under me *at* our wedding.

The humiliation was compounded by the fact that everyone I knew was on the other side of the closed doors waiting for me to make my grand entrance. Four of my closest friends paid five hundred dollars each for dresses they got to wear for an hour, not to mention the cost of the shower and bachelorette party they had for me in South Beach. When I think of that, I feel sick to my soul. In the weeks following that awful day, I returned all the expensive gifts they and others had given me at my shower, as well as the wedding gifts that had begun to arrive in the days before the implosion.

I send another text to Elena. *He also told me he'd pay for any dress I wanted ($5000) and my four bridesmaids were out $500 each, as well as what they spent on my shower and bachelorette party. If you wanted to add that to the tab.*

Will do. Let me know if you think of anything else.

That was it. The florist was another three thousand, but she insisted on payment in advance, so he'd already paid that.

Elena sends another thumbs-up.

It would be amazing if I could reimburse my four friends, two of whom I work with at Miami-Dade, for the money they spent on their dresses. When I think about the hideous and embarrassing task of canceling and returning everything, I imagine my grandmother and great-aunts in New York talking to each other about poor Gianna who got dumped by her fiancé practically at the altar.

My father's mother and her sisters, all of whom live on Long Island where I was born, are a catty bunch on a good day. They must've had a blast discussing my romantic disaster after they left the church when the wedding was called off. No wonder my parents moved south shortly after they got married. My mother had lasted a year dealing with that madness before she told my dad to get her out of there or she'd see him in divorce court.

He wisely moved her to Miami, where my brothers were born. We saw his family once a year, if that, which was more than enough for us. After my parents died, I got a belly full of my grandmother and great-aunts and give thanks every day for my mom giving him that ultimatum. I invited them to the wedding out of respect for my late father and came to regret that, too.

Thank God for my grandparents on my mother's side, who were an incredible source of support to me and my brothers after we lost our parents. They live in Ohio and did whatever they could for us from afar. They even offered to bring the boys to live with them, but with them in ninth and eleventh grades, they hadn't wanted to change schools on top of everything else. Which left me in charge of two grieving teenage boys who refused to grant me any authority over them even though I was their legal guardian.

That was fun.

Not.

Speaking of not fun, I scroll through my old texts with Jared, starting with the engagement photo we sent to family and friends. Seeing that for the first time in months is like a punch to the gut. I want to tell that naïve girl to trust no one, not even him. I want to tell her to run for her life from him, but she wouldn't have listened. She was so certain she'd found the person who was going to make her feel whole again, and the thought of living without Jared would've been impossible for her to fathom in the afterglow of his romantic, heartfelt proposal.

The day after our engagement, we exchanged several texts about the wedding.

Something small would be fine with me, I told him.

No way! We're only doing this once. I want the big deal for you.

I don't need that.

I remember thinking at the time that while he thought he was being nice by saying that, he was also forgetting how hard it would be for me to host a big wedding without my parents there. With hindsight, I've realized that my tremendous loss never got much attention from him. He treated it like something that'd happened in the past, before we met, and didn't affect the present or future. Jared still has all four of his grandparents and has never lost anyone close to him, so I gave him a pass on how he all but ignored my grief, which was another big mistake.

Love made me stupid. I'll never let that happen again.

After scrolling through a week's worth of texts with Jared, I find what I'm looking for—me asking him what he wanted to spend on the wedding and telling him with my brothers in college or about to be, I couldn't contribute much of anything to the budget.

Let's keep it between 30 and 40K, he replied.

I remember being astounded by those numbers. *For real?* I wrote back. *Wouldn't we be better off putting that toward a house or condo?*

We can do that, too.

I knew he did well in medical sales, but I'd had no idea he made that kind of money.

Are you sure that's what you want? I asked him. *I'd be fine with something simple.* In fact, I'd wanted to say I'd prefer it since the two people I loved the most couldn't be there.

I'm sure, he replied. *You deserve the best, and I want to give it to you.*

I have no idea how we went from him saying that to telling me he'd decided he couldn't go through with the wedding. I was so shocked and blindsided that I failed to ask *why*. What did it matter? In one ten-minute conversation, our relationship was over, and I was more humiliated than I'd ever been.

After scrolling further, I find the conversation where we agreed on a wedding venue and the message in which he told me to go ahead and sign the contract while he was on a work trip to Vegas.

I take screenshots of all the relevant conversations and send them to Elena.

This is exactly what we need. I know it couldn't have been easy to revisit those texts, but they'll help us get this taken care of. More to come tomorrow!

I'm weak with relief to have her on my side, and I need to tell Milo how much this means to me. I decide to call him.

"Hey," he says, sounding sleepy. "This is a nice surprise."

"Did I wake you?"

"Nah, I was just dozing while watching *SportsCenter*. What's up?"

"Your mom is amazing, and so are you."

"She's the best, right? I was thinking earlier that I *almost* feel sorry for your ex with her coming after him."

I laugh at the way he says that. "I think she's exactly what he deserves, and I'm so deeply grateful to have her help with this. Thank you again for connecting me with her."

"I'm happy to have been able to help you. Let me guess, your story made my mom furious, right?"

"It did."

"I figured it would. She would tell you that this is the stuff she loves about her job, helping to right terrible wrongs."

"I feel so relived just knowing she's on it, and she's refusing to let me pay her."

"Not surprised," Milo says with a chuckle. "Did she tell you that any friend of mine is a friend of hers, especially since you took such amazing care of me in the hospital?"

"Almost verbatim."

"There you have it. That's the way my family is. They see someone in need, and they do what they can to help."

"That's rather amazing. Everyone who works on the ward is sad that you've moved to rehab, because they all liked you so much, but they also loved the food your family brought in."

Laughing, he says, "It's okay to say they'll miss the food more than me."

"They might, but I won't. You were my favorite patient ever."

"Wow. That's quite an honor. You must see a lot of patients."

"I do, and not all of them are as nice to me as you were. And the families… Yours was the best, too."

"I can't believe anyone would be nasty to you when you're caring for them the way you do."

"Believe it. Nurses take a lot of abuse from patients and their families. Some of them aren't satisfied no matter how much we do."

"I'm sorry you have to deal with that."

"It's fine. Goes with the job. We had a weekend workshop in nursing school that covered patient and family relations, so I was somewhat prepared. Sometimes it's difficult to deal with, though, especially when you're doing everything you can for your patients."

"I have no doubt you give them all a hundred percent."

"Some of them only get seventy percent," I say with a laugh. "But don't tell anyone I said that."

"Your secrets are safe with me."

The warmest feeling of peace comes over me when he says that, which has me immediately sitting up straighter and shaking it off. Look at what happened the last time I allowed a man to become too important to me. This man is different. I already know that, but I won't be a fool again, not even for someone as wonderful as Milo. "I should get going to bed since your mom has seen to it that I'll actually sleep tonight."

"I hope you can get some rest."

"Me, too. Thank you again. It means so much to me that you wanted to help. I'll see you tomorrow after my shift."

"If you're too tired, don't worry about me."

"I'll be there."

"Good night, Gianna."

"Night, Milo."

As I end the call, I remind myself that even with a nice guy like Milo, I'm never safe to let down my guard.

ELENA

I sit at the table with my first cup of coffee and send a text to Milo, asking if he slept at all. The halo makes everything difficult for him, especially sleeping. He doesn't respond right away, so I hope that means he's getting some much-needed rest. Even weeks later, my nerves are still shredded from that awful night. I'll never forget the phone call from our daughter Dee, telling us that our sweet Milo had been shot.

Of all things.

Just when you think you've seen everything as a parent to four adults, something happens to make you realize you haven't seen anything yet.

Lorenzo and I have never prayed harder than we did for our youngest and sweetest child. Parents aren't supposed to have favorites, and neither of us would ever admit to such a thing, but we believe our three eldest kids would agree that Milo is everyone's favorite. The thought of life without him is simply unfathomable.

As is the thought of life without our Nico, for whom the bullet was meant. He committed the "crime" of loving another man's ex-wife. I shiver at the thought of how close we came to utter catastrophe. And we'd thought my breast cancer diagnosis was catastrophic. Compared to losing one of our precious sons to senseless violence... I can't bear to think about what a close call we had.

Lorenzo comes up behind me and massages my shoulders. "Why are you thinking about the bad stuff when our boy is doing so much better?"

After thirty-five years of marriage, I'm not surprised he knows exactly what I'm thinking about. "I wish I could forget it."

"You will. In time."

"I don't think I'll ever forget this one."

"Milo wouldn't want us upset and dwelling on what might've happened. He'd want us focused on the future and helping him get back on his feet."

"I'm doing that, too. And so are you. I feel you tossing and turning at night."

"I dream about it. Doesn't end well in my dreams."

I reach up to place my hand on top of his. "I'm sorry, love. It's a terrible thing to have weighing on you."

"It is indeed, but I need to take my own advice and focus on the good news. Our boy is making a splendid recovery thanks to Jason and the other medical staff. He'll be home soon, and we can dote on him to our heart's content."

"I can't wait for that. In the meantime, I'm going to fix this mess for his new friend, Gianna."

"He's awfully sweet on that pretty nurse."

"He sure is. I'm looking forward to making this call to her ex."

Laughing, Lorenzo bends to kiss the back of my neck, making me shiver the way he has from the start. "I'll leave you to that, my bloodthirsty Doberman, and I'll say a prayer for mercy for your victim."

I laugh along with him. He bestowed that nickname early in our careers and gave me a stuffed Doberman for Christmas one year that still sits on our bed. "Don't bother praying for him. He doesn't deserve it."

"All right, then. I won't. I'm going to the office for a few hours to check in, and then we can take dinner to Milo?"

We run a legal and accounting practice together, but we've recently taken a step back from the day-to-day management of the firm as we prepare to retire in the next few years.

"That sounds good. I'm working from here today."

He leans in to kiss my cheek. "I'll see you in a bit, then."

After he leaves, I refill my coffee and return to my post at the kitchen table. As I put through the call to Jared Allen, I experience the jolt of adrenaline that comes with doing the job I've loved for thirty years.

"This is Jared."

"Hi, Jared, my name is Elena Giordino, and I'm an attorney representing Gianna Lombardi."

"An attorney representing Gianna?" he asks in a slightly high-pitched tone.

"Yes, that's what I said. You may not be aware that the venue where your wedding was set to be held is now suing her for breach of contract."

"I, uh, I didn't know that."

"That's odd because she's left several messages for you after being served with the suit. I was going through your text messages with Gianna about the wedding—"

"Those are private! She had no right to share them with you."

"She's being *sued*, Jared. For forty-five thousand dollars plus legal fees after you talked her into a big wedding she didn't want and then called it off the day of the event—and by the way, who does that? I'm sure you can image that Gianna is extremely upset and afraid of being ruined financially since she was the one who signed the contract for the wedding that didn't happen."

After a pause in which he has nothing to say, I press on. "You should know that we're preparing to sue you since we have evidence that you agreed to pay for the wedding. Your decision to cancel it at the last minute doesn't change anything. The lawsuit paperwork is being drawn up by my associates as we speak." That's not true—yet—but he doesn't need to know that. "You can expect service by the end of next week at the latest. Oh, and don't bother trying to hide from my process servers. They can find anyone. You have a good day now."

I end the call before he can say anything else. I've put the ball in his court. Hopefully, he'll do the right thing and take care of the bill from the venue to end the legal machinations.

After a sip of coffee, I dash off a text to Gianna. *Morning! I spoke with him and let him know we're going to sue him imminently unless he settles with the venue and ended the call with that. Let's see if he takes care of it today. If not, we'll follow through with the lawsuit in the next week or so. Either way, he's on notice that you're being sued, you've retained counsel and you're prepared to sue him to hold him to his promise to pay for the wedding. The next move is his. If he reaches out to you with outrage (fully expected), I would ignore him. Let me speak for you going forward.*

I'm in a videoconference meeting about another case an hour later when Gianna responds.

I'll never have the words to thank you for this, Elena. He did reach out, and he's furious. As if this is somehow my fault. I took your advice and ignored his messages and calls.

Do we need to be concerned about your safety?

I don't think so, but I also didn't expect him to call off the wedding. I'll be careful.

Please do. And don't hesitate to call the police if he tries to confront you.

I won't.

I'm hoping you'll hear that the tab with the venue has been settled and the lawsuit dropped. I'll reach out to their counsel to let them know I'm representing you. Your job is to breathe and focus on your work and not worry about any of this. You've never been through this before (I assume), but this back-and-forth is perfectly routine in situations like this. Usually, the threat of being sued spurs someone who made promises he didn't keep to do the right thing. I'll let you know if there are any updates, but try not to worry. Hearing from a lawyer tends to move things along.

Wow, you're amazing. All this would be very interesting to me if it didn't involve me being sued.

Hahaha. It's probably safe to be intrigued. With those text messages to prove he agreed to pay for the wedding, he knows he's screwed. I expect him to do the right thing.

Hearing that takes a hundred-ton weight off my chest.

Hang in there. I'll be back to you with any updates.

Thank you again.

No problem! Happy to help.

I mean that. I love helping people like Gianna who find themselves in situations like this one through no fault of their own. I hate injustice and bullies and people who try to screw other people for sport. The most satisfying aspect of my career has been the pro bono work I've done mostly for women escaping difficult domestic situations.

I'm so thankful that my future daughter-in-law, Sofia, is now divorced from the man who later shot my son. That monster is in jail pending trial for multiple felonies tied to Milo's shooting.

I hope he rots in prison.

It's not like me to be vindictive, but no one deserves to rot in jail more than Joaquín Diaz does.

Though we wouldn't have wanted Milo injured so grievously for any reason, we're glad to know that Joaquín will likely spend decades in prison where he belongs so he can't hurt anyone else, while Nico raises the man's son as his own.

CHAPTER 5

GIANNA

For the first time in weeks, I'm not crippled with anxiety. Even Jared's hateful texts have no impact now that Elena is representing me. I have four patients today, so my shift passes in a blur of nonstop activity. I run myself ragged managing four very complicated cases in consultation with doctors, family members and my nursing colleagues.

By the time I finish entering all my notes from the day into the patients' charts, I'm an hour late leaving the ward. I take an elevator to the first floor, cross the lobby and then grab another elevator to the fourth floor of the hospital's second tower, which houses the rehab facility. I'm exhausted, dying for a shower, some food and a big glass of wine, but I'd never disappoint Milo by failing to keep my promise to visit.

In the elevator, I admit to myself that I missed him on the ward and looked forward to seeing him all day. That's a dangerous confession for a girl who's decided she's had enough of love and relationships that always end up the same way, with my heart broken.

Jared is the third man to break my heart. This time was much worse than the others, however, because he professed to love me and made promises he didn't keep.

But I don't want to think about him. Not anymore. I'd much rather think about handsome, sweet, sexy Milo Giordino, even if my guard is up against being hurt again the way Jared and the others hurt me.

My gut is telling me I have nothing to fear from Milo, but I thought that about Jared, too.

What's interesting is that my brothers never liked him. Greg said he was slimy, and Leo called him a phony. I accused them of not having given him a fair chance, but they said ten minutes with him told them everything they needed to know. Thankfully, neither of them said the dreaded "I told you so" after he called off the wedding.

If anything, they seemed relieved to have seen the last of him.

I should've listened to them. They're not babies anymore, even if I'll always think of them as my baby brothers. Despite our differences in the past, they never would've dissed the man I loved if they hadn't had real concerns.

As I approach Milo's room in the rehab ward, I hear someone breathing hard and quicken my pace, expecting to find him in some sort of distress. Rather, he's standing next to his bed, shirtless, eyes closed as he does bicep curls. The dark-framed glasses he normally wears are off. His chiseled abdomen glistens with sweat, and I can only stare at him, wishing I could see his chest, too. But that's covered by the halo brace.

Of course, I've seen his body as his nurse, but I didn't realize he was that ripped until now. I should say something, let him know I'm there, but I don't want to interrupt his groove.

I'm not sure how long I stand there watching—or does this count as gawking?—before he opens his eyes.

His gaze connects with mine in a moment so charged, it steals my breath for a hot second.

"Hey," he says, gruff and sexy. "Come in."

I'm frozen in place, deeply aware of him as a man and not just a former patient I grew fond of. This is nuts. The last thing in the world I need right now is another man in my life when I'm still trying to get rid of the last one.

He rubs a towel over his chest and abdomen to mop up the sweat. "Gianna? Are you okay?"

Am I okay? I don't think I am. "Y-yes. Sorry. When I heard you breathing hard, I thought you were in distress. I was worried."

"I'm fine, if you call barely being able to lift ten pounds without wanting to die fine," he says, sounding frustrated as he works his way into a button-down shirt.

I step into the room and take a seat in one of the visitor chairs even as my heart continues to beat erratically. My nipples tingle when I recall his sexy chest and abdomen. I hope he can't see that. "It's a start, and you shouldn't be hard on yourself. You're coming back from a major injury. It'll take time to get back to where you were before."

He lowers himself carefully into the recliner and rests the halo against the back of the chair. Then he feeds the glasses through the halo cage and puts them back on. Have glasses ever been so sexy on a man? Not that I can recall. "This thing is making me crazy," he says of the halo. "I want to rip it off and throw it across the room."

"Don't do that."

With a small grin, he says, "I won't. But I want to. Enough about me. How was your day?"

"Thanks to your mother, I had the best day I've had in weeks after actually sleeping last night."

"I take it she's on top of the situation."

"Is she ever! I'm so impressed by her and thankful to her—and to you for asking her to help me."

"I'm sure she's very happy to help. She's spent her entire career focused on taking care of people who've been wronged in some way. She loves cases like yours."

"What it must be like to be able to do that for people…"

"Look at what you do. You take care of people during the worst times in their lives and make them feel better just by being there. That's no small thing either. I mean, I write code for a living. Who does that help?"

"Um, everyone who uses computers and apps to run their lives?"

Milo gives a small shrug, which is all he can manage with the halo. "It seems shallow compared to what you and my mom do."

"I had a teacher in high school who used to tell us we all had different talents, and every one of them would contribute to society in some special way. He told us not to be pressured to go to college if we wanted to be plumbers or mechanics or hair stylists. He said we should follow our hearts and our passions because we had to work for a lot of years, and we should be passionate about what we do. Do you like writing code?"

"I do. I'm good at it."

"Then there you have it. That's your thing, and you shouldn't diminish your contributions to society just because you think other people's talents are more important."

"They are more important," he says with another of those sexy smiles that make him even more handsome than he already is. "And you're not going to change my mind about that. You're saving lives. I'm helping people use technology to make money."

"Which they need to care for their families. It matters, Milo."

"We can agree to disagree on this topic."

"If we must."

"Did you always want to be a nurse?"

"I wanted to be a doctor until I hit high school and got a clue about how many more years of school it would take to get there. I was impatient to get on with it, so I decided nursing school would be better for me."

"Are you glad now that you made that change?"

"So glad. I'm much happier on the front lines of patient care. I have more of an opportunity to really get to know my patients than the doctors do. I like working with patients and their families. It's satisfying work."

"You're very good at it."

"Thank you."

"Have you made many friends among your patients?"

"I hear from a few from time to time, but no close friends. Like, for instance, I've never visited a patient in rehab before."

"Is that right?" he asks with the biggest smile yet. "So I'm special, huh?"

I roll my eyes playfully. "When did I say that?"

"You said it. I heard you."

Before I can respond, his parents come in carrying multiple bags. The scent of something yummy has my mouth watering.

"Oh, hi, Gianna," Elena says. "So nice of you to visit."

"I'm the first patient she's ever visited in rehab," Milo tells his parents as he gives me a meaningful look. "That makes me special."

He's so cute and funny—and sexy as hell. This guy could be serious trouble if I allow him to be. Do I want that? Am I ready for it after thinking I was going to marry someone else just over a year ago?

Elena gets busy unloading the bags she brought and serves up plates of chicken marsala for all of us. She's given me a plate and silverware before I have time to tell her she doesn't need to feed me on top of everything else she's doing for me. But the food smells so good, and I'm starving for the first time in weeks. So I accept the meal graciously.

Not only is Milo lovely, but his family is, too, and it's so tempting to glom on to their warmth like the family-starved orphan I am. Now there's a cheery thought. I try not to think of myself as an *orphan*, even if I am. I hate that word, so why would I think that? Ugh, my brain needs to shut the hell up and let me enjoy this delicious meal.

"Tell me the truth, Elena," I say after a few bites of tender chicken that melts in my mouth. "You're some sort of superhero, right? Pulling off complex legal maneuvers as you cook up a feast."

"She's a superhero for sure," Lorenzo says with a warm smile for his wife. "My Elena can do it all. She never missed a beat while going through treatment for breast cancer."

"I missed a lot of beats then," Elena says.

"Not that we noticed," Milo says.

"You're too kind, sweetheart. We all know the chemo knocked me on my ass, but the important thing is I got back up."

"You're doing well now, right?" I ask her. The thought of anything happening to someone so formidable is unfathomable to me.

"I'm doing great. I have a routine checkup later this month. Those are stressful, but so far, so good. We just pray it doesn't come back."

"It won't," Milo says. "You showed it who's boss, and now it's scared of you like your children were as kids."

"Oh stop," Elena says with a huff of laughter. "You were not afraid of me."

"Yes, we were," Milo's sister Maria says as she arrives with her baseball player husband, Austin Jacobs, and his daughter, Everly.

"Don't listen to them, Gianna," Elena says. "I was the sweetest mother ever."

"Yes, you were," Maria says, "but we were also afraid of you."

Lorenzo rocks with silent laughter.

"We blame Nico for that," Milo tells me. "He was always testing the boundaries, so he taught Mom to be suspicious."

Maria points to Milo. "Truth. He ruined it for the rest of us."

"Are you two done talking about me like I can't hear you?" Elena asks.

"Never," Maria says.

"Brats," Elena replies. "I raised four brats."

"You love us," Maria says.

"What choice do I have?"

I adore these people. They are so fun and funny and loyal and loving. Maria, who's also a nurse, has gone over to take a closer look at Milo. "Are you sleeping? You look rough today."

"Gee, thanks, sis. And yes, I'm sleeping fine. Rehab is brutal. It wears me out."

Elena has brought enough food to feed Maria's family as well as Milo's sister Dee and her fiancé, Wyatt, when they arrive a short time later. Before I know it, we're having a party.

"It's so nice of you to visit Milo," Maria says quietly to me while Milo talks to Wyatt and Austin.

"Oh, well, I'm happy to visit him."

"He's the best of us all," Maria says with a sideways glance at her younger brother. "I can't say enough about how amazing he is. When we almost lost him…" She sighs. "We never would've survived that."

"He's doing great." I'm moved by her obvious love for him, knowing all too well that sibling love can be complicated. In this family, it seems rather simple and genuine as well as comical at times. "Pretty soon, he'll be right back to normal."

"He likes you."

"I like him."

"He *likes* you."

"Oh, well… He's very sweet."

"Yes, he is, and he's thoughtful and loyal and kind. One of his neighbors had a hip replacement, and Milo has been cutting his grass since the surgery. After he woke up in the ICU, one of the first things he wanted to know was if Nico had cut Mr. Miller's grass. If you want to know who he really is, that ought to tell you."

"Maria, what are you saying to her?" Milo asks, shifting in his seat so he can see around Wyatt.

"Nothing. We're just talking. Butt out."

"Whatever she's telling you is probably a lie," Milo says to me.

"So you weren't worried about whether Nico had cut Mr. Miller's grass after you nearly died and had a massive surgery?" Maria asks him.

"I was worried about Mr. Miller's grass. Why are you telling Gianna that? Leave her alone."

"Butt. Out."

"You butt out. Come over here, Gianna, where she can't get to you."

"Mari," Elena says to her daughter, "come eat your dinner."

Amused, I move over to sit next to Milo, which seems to make him happy.

Nico and Sofia arrive with her son, Mateo, who's thrilled to see Everly. The two children hug like they haven't seen each other in years. Mateo has obvious deficiencies from his own brain surgery, but they don't stop him from running in circles with Everly and talking up a storm to her.

"They're so cute," I say to Elena.

"They're best friends."

"Have you heard any more from he-who-shall-not-be-named?" I ask her.

"Not yet. I'll give him a few more days, and if he doesn't pay the venue, I'll serve him with a lawsuit. Either way, you're not paying that bill."

"It's such a relief to have you on my side."

"Aw, that's nice of you to say." She pats my arm. "I love this stuff. It's no problem at all." Leaning in, she lowers her voice. "It's apt to get ugly before it's over. If we sue him, he'll get mean, even though he knows he's on the hook for that tab. I just want you to be prepared for anything."

I swallow hard at the thought of more ugliness with Jared. There's already been more than enough to last me a lifetime. "I understand. With student loans and my brothers in college, it would take me the rest of my life to pay that bill."

"You'll never have to pay that bill if I have anything to say about it. He made promises to you. We're going to make sure he keeps them."

It's been a long time since I had someone like her on my side. Without my parents, I've often felt adrift in a sea of people to whom I have no connection. There's no one I can go to when I'm scared or worried or upset. Not like there once was, anyway. Elena has no idea what she's giving me, in addition to peace of mind. I can see where Milo comes by his innate kindness.

When everyone has eaten, I help Elena gather paper plates and use paper towels from the adjoining bathroom to wipe down the small table where Everly and Mateo ate.

"You don't have to do that, Gianna," Austin says.

"It's no problem." To Milo, I say, "I should get going and let you visit with your family."

"Don't leave on our account," Dee says.

"I have to work early," I tell her. I'm moving to days, which will be a shock to my system after working second shift since I started at Miami-Dade.

"Wait." Milo moves carefully to get up from the recliner. "I'll walk you out."

I want to tell him he doesn't have to do that, but since he went to the trouble to get up, I say good night and thank you for dinner to his family and walk with him to the elevators.

"I hate everything about being stuck in this place and in this cage, but mostly, I hate that I can't take you to dinner like I promised you for a while."

"There'll be time for that after you're well again."

"Do you promise you won't meet someone you like better in the meantime?"

"Milo…" He makes me nervous and excited at the same time. None of the men I've dated has ever been as direct or as sweet as he is. "I won't meet someone better. I promise."

His smile is well worth me being flustered. "Come see me again?"

"I will."

He pushes the Down button for me. "Good."

"I hope you can get some sleep."

"I'm tired, so I will. I hope you can, too."

The elevator arrives with a ding that startles me and makes me realize we've been staring at each other.

"I, uh, that's my ride. Take care, Milo."

"Drive safely, Gianna."

I leave him with a smile and a wave, already suspecting that in the whole wide world, there's no one better than him.

CHAPTER 6

MILO

I've never been more enthralled or frustrated in my entire life. Gianna is smart and stunning and funny and sweet and sexy and everything I've ever wanted, and there's not a goddamned thing I can do about it for weeks.

Ugh.

I bring that cheerful thought back into the room full of family members. They're silent and looking at me when I come in. When is my family ever silent? "What?" As I lower myself into the recliner, I begin to regret adding the weights to an already active day.

"That's what we want to know," Maria says. "What's up with Gianna?"

"We're friends."

"That's it?" Dee asks.

"What else am I capable of at the moment when I'm stuck inside a cage in a hospital?"

"There's a lot you can do from here," Nico says.

"Like what?"

"Send her flowers? Have coffee or lunch delivered to her and the other nurses on her ward during their shift. To start with."

The suggestions have the immediate effect of raising my spirits considerably. "I like those ideas."

"Tell me what you want to do," Nico says. "I'll take care of it for you."

"That's very nice of you, but I can still use an iPhone. I can handle it."

"Let me do it. I want to."

To my parents and sisters, I say, "Will you guys please do something about him feeling like this is all his fault and he has to wait on me hand and foot?"

"We've tried," Dad says. "I'm afraid you're stuck with new Nico for a while."

"I can't stand him."

"There's no way he can keep this up indefinitely," Maria says. "He'll be back to normal soon."

"It's not funny!" Nico says, his face red with outrage. "He nearly *died* because of me! Whatever he wants, he gets. Forever. That won't ever end."

Sofia takes his hand and whispers something to him that seems to calm him while the rest of us try to figure out what to do with this new version of my brother.

"I'm sorry, Nico," Maria says. "It's sweet of you to want to do everything for him, but you're being too hard on yourself."

"No, I'm not. He took a *bullet to the neck* that was meant for me, Mari. What would you do if that happened to you with Dee? Would you handle it any differently than I am?"

"Well, no, I don't suppose I would, but—"

"No buts." Nico's eyes fill with tears that are so unlike him, I can only stare in disbelief. "Do you *know* how close we came to losing him? Do you have *any idea*?"

"I do," Maria says softly, "but we didn't lose him, and we

don't want to lose you to this unreasonable guilt. It's not your fault. We're going to keep telling you that until you hear us."

"I've been trying," Sofia says. "He's not listening."

"I'm listening," Nico says testily, "but you've got to let me do what I need to so I can deal with this, all right?" His gaze takes in the entire family. "Please," he adds in a softer tone.

"It's fine." The others will follow my lead. "I'm more than happy to make you my bitch indefinitely."

Everyone else laughs, which immediately eases Nico's tension. That's a relief to me. I'm concerned he's going to have a stroke or heart attack from the stress of his guilt. If tending to my every need keeps that from happening, it's a small price to pay.

"I'll bring lunch to her and the others on the ward tomorrow from you," Nico says.

"I'll Venmo you."

"I've got it."

"Then it's not from me. It's from you."

"You're out of work," Nico says.

"They're still paying me, so let me pay you."

"Fine. Whatever."

"Fine."

"Well," Dad says, "now that we've worked that out, we should get going so Milo can get some rest."

They say their goodbyes and promise to be back to see me tomorrow.

Nico, Sofia and Mateo are the last to leave.

"You sure you don't need anything else to eat tonight?" Nico asks.

"I'm good. Thanks."

"What should I get the nurses for lunch?"

"Salads and subs maybe?"

"Will do. I'll let you know when it's delivered."

"Thank you again for doing that."

"Thank you for letting me."

"Yes, Milo," Sofia says with a small smile. "Thank you for letting him. This has been... It's been awful for us. I hope you know..." She shakes her head when tears fill her eyes.

Mateo hugs his mother. "Don't be sad, Mommy."

She puts an arm around her son. "I'm okay, baby."

My heart goes out to her and Nico. "I can't imagine what this must be like for you guys, but I need you to forgive yourselves and let go of any blame you're taking for something you had nothing to do with."

"We're trying," Nico says. "Harder to do than you might think."

"I'm sure it's awful, but I'm doing great, and thanks to getting shot, I've met a wonderful woman who has me seriously dazzled. So it might turn out that you guys did me a big favor."

Nico gives me a side-eye look that's much more like the real Nico than the sad-faced pout he's been sporting lately. "That's insane logic."

"Maybe so, but I'm really glad to have met her."

"She likes you, too," Sofia says.

I pounce on that statement. "How can you tell?"

"She watches you like a woman who likes what she sees."

This is the best news I've had all day. "Really?"

"Uh-huh," Sofia says. "I wouldn't worry if I were you. She's interested, too."

God, it's such a relief to have someone whose opinion I trust confirm that for me.

"Did they say how long you need to stay here?" Nico asks.

"Ten days to two weeks. They want me to be stronger before I leave. I can't believe how my body has gone to absolute shit after being in the hospital."

"You'll bounce back fast," Sofia says.

"Yes, you will," Nico adds. "We'll see to it."

"We should get Mateo home to bed," Sofia says to Nico.

He reaches out to do the bro handshake we made up years ago. "See you tomorrow."

"You can take a day off, you know."

"No, I can't. I'll see you tomorrow."

I let him have the last word because he needs it more than I do. None of us has ever seen Nico like he's been since I got shot, so we're not quite sure how to deal with him. I hate that he's suffering over this when he would've gladly thrown himself in front of that bullet to save me if he'd been there.

He's always been like that with me. He's six years older than me, with Maria and Dee between us, and from what I was told, when he heard he had a brother, he was instantly smitten and declared himself "in charge" of me. My mom said he barely let our sisters near me when they brought me home from the hospital.

It's funny because Nico isn't really like that with anyone else, except Sofia and Mateo now that he's fallen in love with them. But before that, I had no doubt I was his most loved person in the whole world, which was pretty cool. It's not like we ever talked about our deep bond or anything. It was just a fact of my life—and his. Which is why the shooting has been so awful for him. Me being shot would've been bad enough for him. Add that the bullet was meant Nico, and you've got a recipe for emotional disaster for him—and Sofia, who was once married to the man who shot me.

I feel terrible for them. It's an awful spot to be in, no question. But I want them to get past it so they can stop feeling so bad about things outside their control. For a time, I worried it might come between them, that Sofia's ex-husband shooting Nico's beloved brother might be the death knell for a relationship that makes them happy. I'm glad that hasn't happened. If anything, dealing with the aftermath of disaster seems to have brought them closer together.

Nico waited a long time to fall in love. I'd hate to have anything to do with messing that up for him, even indirectly.

I force myself up and out of the chair with every muscle protesting the simplest of movements. By the time I get changed into pajama pants and yet another button-down shirt, take a leak and brush my teeth, I feel like a newborn baby with muscles quivering and my neck aching like a bitch from the wound and from not moving for so long.

I'm in bed when the nurse on duty comes to check on me. She's an older woman who reminds me of my aunt Viv. "All tucked in?" she asks.

"I guess so."

She hands me a cup with the meds that prevent infection and something else to help me sleep inside the cage around my head.

I take them one at a time with sips through a straw she holds for me. "Thank you."

"Can I get you anything else?"

"I'm good. Thanks."

"Sleep well." She lowers the lights and closes the door behind her.

The primary difference in rehab is they don't check on me throughout the night like they did in the hospital, which is a relief. I don't think I've slept more than two hours at a time since the shooting, even with the knockout pill they gave me every night.

As I close my eyes and hope for sleep, my mind is filled with thoughts of Gianna and how much I can't wait to get out of here and spend time with her away from the hospital.

NICO

After we get home, Sofia gives Mateo a quick bath and tucks him into bed. Then she comes to find me in the bedroom we now share. "He's asking for you."

"Coming." I get up from the bed and cross the hall to say good night to the little boy who, along with his mother, has become the center of my world in recent weeks. Having them living with me is the best thing to ever happen to me. If only the worst thing hadn't also happened because of our relationship. I shake that off to focus on Mateo. "Are you snug as a bug?" I ask him, like I do every night, as I press the covers down on either side of him.

His giggle is adorable. "A bug can't be snug."

"Yes, it can."

"No, it can't. I asked my teacher."

He's too cute and too smart for words, and I love him. I lean in to kiss his forehead. "Night, buddy."

"Nico…"

"What's up?"

"Milo is going to be okay, isn't he?"

"He sure is. It's just going to take some time until he's back to his old self."

"Kinda like me, after I had surgery."

"Just like that. But you're both doing great, so don't worry."

"Can I ask you something else?"

"Anything."

"Is it true that my dad was the one who shot Milo?"

Oh shit. I didn't expect that, and for a second I'm paralyzed with indecision about what I should say.

"It's okay," he adds. "You can tell me if it was. I know he's not a good guy."

"How do you know that?"

"I saw him hurt Mama."

This is way too much for a kindergartner to have to deal

with. "It's true that your dad was the one who hurt Milo, but he won't be able to hurt anyone else."

"Because he's in jail?"

"Yeah."

"Okay."

"Mateo, I hope you know how much I love you and would do anything for you. My whole family loves you and your mama, and we're so glad you're with us now."

"I'm glad, too."

"Sleep well, buddy."

As I get up to leave the room, he says, "Nico?"

I turn back to him.

"I love you, too."

My heart. Damn, this kid kills me. "I'm so glad. I'll see you in the morning, okay?"

He nods.

I shut off the light but leave the door open so we can hear him if he wakes during the night. In the hallway, I'm surprised to find Sofia standing there with tears rolling down her face. I take her into my arms and note once again how perfectly we fit. I've never been with anyone who fits me the way she does.

"I take it you heard that?"

"Yeah."

I hold her for several minutes and then take her by the hand to lead her into our room. We sit on the bed and reach for each other again. As much as we both hate what her ex-husband did to my brother, I can't deny that our shared grief over the shooting has brought us even closer. Thank God for that, because I don't know what I would've done if it had driven a wedge between us.

I feel like I'm only holding it together thanks to the strength I draw from her, and I know she feels the same about me.

"I hate him so much," she whispers. "For what he did to Milo and for how this will always be part of Mateo's story."

"We'll help him write a story that makes this a footnote."

"What does that word mean? Footnote?"

I love how she works so hard to master English, which she only started to learn as a young adult. "It means a small part of the bigger story."

"Oh, I see, and that would be good."

"The best thing about him being so young when this happened is that he'll barely remember when Milo got shot or that his father was responsible. He'll only know me as his father, and I'll give him everything I've got."

Once again, Sofia's eyes fill with tears. "We're both so lucky to have you and that you still love us after everything we've put you and your family through."

I tilt her chin up so I can see her gorgeous face. "You heard what everyone said earlier. They don't blame us. They know neither of us would've ever done anything to hurt Milo."

"I just worry that your parents will forever associate that with me and us."

"They won't. They love you almost as much as I do, and they're so glad you're free of him, no matter how it happened."

"I feel… un… unworthy of their kindness."

"Please don't say that, Sofia. They'd never want you to feel that way. Somehow, we have to find a way to live with this. No one who matters is blaming us. Maybe they're right, and we need to be kinder to ourselves."

"It's very hard to do that when your sweet brother is still in the hospital and trapped inside that awful thing."

"He's doing great and getting better every day. You heard him say he wants us to stop feeling so guilty. He's said that to me more than once." I'm realizing that my guilt is feeding hers, so maybe I need to do what Milo asked and dial it back a bit.

"He's the best. We're so lucky he doesn't blame us."

"He is the best, and we are lucky. We need to focus on all the many ways we're lucky." I move closer to kiss her and feel relieved when she kisses me back. I worry all the time about her taking Mateo and disappearing because she thinks that's what would be best for me. After what we've had these last few months, I'd die without her. "I don't want you to worry about anything, okay?"

Her tearful snort of laughter makes me smile. "Sure. Whatever you say."

"I mean it. The worst is behind us. Milo is on the road to recovery. Asshole is in jail, where he's going to be for a long time. We've got each other and Mateo and a wedding to plan and so much to look forward to. That's what I want you thinking about. No more bad stuff."

She reaches for me, and I'm more than happy to hug her as tightly as she wants. There's nothing I love more than holding her, hugging her and making love to her. She's changed my life in every possible way. After years of going through women like a drunken sailor, everything stopped the second I first laid eyes on her, and nothing has been the same since.

Her love is the greatest gift I've ever received, and I'm determined to give her and Mateo the happy, peaceful life they both deserve.

When I pull back to kiss her, she wraps her arms around me and takes the kiss from innocent to dirty in a matter of seconds.

Message received.

Sex with Sofia is the only thing that can get my mind off the crushing guilt I feel about Milo's shooting, and I'm thankful for the respite I find in her arms. Being with her is like coming home, and as I kiss and caress her, I'm full of gratitude for her and Mateo, for Milo's recovery and for the bright future that's hopefully ahead for all of us.

CHAPTER 7

GIANNA

I'm dealing with a difficult patient and her demanding family the next day when my friend Annie signals for me to come to the hallway.

"What's up?" I ask her.

"A massive catered lunch just arrived with a note for you attached."

I follow her to the reception desk and see covered platters with sandwiches and salads along with a plastic bag full of different kinds of chips and a huge box of cookies as well as a box of pastries from Vicky's, one of the best bakeries in town.

"There're even pickles," Annie tells me as she hands the note to me.

My coworkers watch as I open the envelope and withdraw the handwritten note.

Gianna, I hope you and your colleagues enjoy lunch on me. Thank you for all the wonderful care on 5 East. Come see me later? xoxo Milo

"Who's it from?" Annie asks.

"Milo Giordino, to thank us for the wonderful care."

"Ohhhh," Annie says with a knowing smile. "Cutest patient ever. You're a lucky girl."

I feel my face heat with embarrassment. "Please," I tell the others. "Dig in and enjoy."

Medical professionals are like seagulls when the word gets out that a feast is available on 5 East. Suddenly, we have "friends" from all over the hospital "stopping by," which is fine because Milo sent enough for a hundred people. Once I get my patient settled, I return to see what's left of the lunch. I fill a plate with salad and half of a turkey sandwich and duck into the break room to eat.

"This is amazing, Gianna," Trudy says. "Tell your friend thanks from all of us."

"I will."

"My patients are never this appreciative," she adds with a laugh as she leaves the break room.

Annie plops down next to me with her plate. She puts bottles of water on the table for both of us.

"Thanks."

"This is quite the thank-you note from an ex-patient," she says between bites.

"It was nice of him."

"That's it? 'It was nice of him'? I didn't take care of him when he was here, but I do have eyes, and that man is sexy, even with a halo. I'm sure you must've noticed that, too."

I shrug, reluctant to give anything away, even as the image of his ripped abs glistening with sweat pops into my mind to remind me that Milo is, indeed, a very sexy man.

"Please don't tell me you're still mourning that jackass Jared."

"I'm not."

"No one does *this*," Annie says, gesturing to our plates, "unless they're interested in someone as more than just a nurse, Gianna. Tell me you know that."

"I get it."

"So what are you going to do about it?"

"I don't know. He's still in rehab for another week or two."

"And then?"

"I don't know, Annie." I deeply resent the tears that fill my eyes. "I just don't know."

She places her hand on top of mine. "Listen, I know what happened with *him* was awful and unexpected and traumatizing." As one of my bridesmaids, Annie knows better than most just how awful it was for me after Jared canceled our wedding. "But maybe that dick did you a favor if this is what's waiting for you on the other side of heartbreak. Everyone on the floor loved Milo—and his family."

"I liked him, too. I mean, I like him, present tense."

"Have you seen him since he left here?"

"I stopped by the rehab to see how he's doing."

"And when was the last time you did that for an ex-patient?"

"Never."

She gives me a knowing look. "Hmmm."

"I just don't know if I'm ready to move on with someone else, and after all he's been through, I don't want to jerk him around."

"So he's expressed interest in letting you jerk him around?"

"Stop," I say with a laugh. "And yes, he's expressed interest."

"Gianna, honey, this is just what you need. A nice, thoughtful, sexy man and a hot rebound, since you've been in hermit mode since the meltdown with jackass."

"I couldn't do that to him. He's not that kind of guy."

"Girl, *every* guy is that kind of guy."

"Milo is different. He's… He's very sweet and sincere. He's not the kind of guy you use for a rebound. He's the kind of guy you marry."

"Interesting that you've already got that figured out about him." She gives me a side-eye look. "You know it's okay to like him, right?"

"Yes, I know that, and I do like him. It's just everything is such a mess for me right now." I haven't told her that the wedding venue is suing me, because I worry she might murder Jared if she hears about that. She's been fiercely protective of me since everything happened. "The timing isn't right."

"Fuck the timing, Gianna. You just said he's a nice, sweet guy who obviously likes you and wants to spend more time with you. Do not let what that dickhead did ruin this chance for you. Don't you dare do that."

"It's not about Jared. It's about me. I was so desperate for someone to make things better for me that I ignored the red flags with Jared until it was too late. I don't want to make another mistake."

"A man who sends lunch to you and your colleagues is not a mistake. Jared never would've done something like that."

"No, he wouldn't have."

"You don't have to go all in with Milo, but I think you'll regret it if you don't at least give him a chance."

"I know," I say with a sigh. "I've already had that same thought."

"So why are you so down in the mouth about a nice, sexy guy showing interest in you?"

"I'm not down in the mouth."

"Yes, you are. You look like you did right after Jared called off the wedding."

"I do?"

"Yep."

"Well, I don't feel the way I did then." I hope I never again go through anything as devastating as that was. It wasn't as bad as losing my parents, but nothing will ever compare to that trauma —I hope.

"Look, I understand that you've had way more than your share, starting in college when your friend went missing, your parents dying and then the shit with Jared. I give you so much credit for surviving all that. I know you're leery after the disaster with Jared, but don't be so afraid of getting hurt that you never take a chance again. That would be truly tragic."

"I hear you. Thank you for the pep talk."

"Any time."

The intercom on the table buzzes. "Annie, your patient in 3A needs you."

"I'm coming," she says. "Back to the grind. Thanks for lunch."

"Glad you enjoyed it."

After Annie leaves the break room, I think about what she said. She's right, and I know it. I can't lump Milo in with Jared or any of the other men I've dated. I already know he's different, and perhaps that's what scares me the most. If I give him a chance, I'll probably fall in love with him. That's what I do. In recent years, I tend to fall fast and hard because I'm trying to fill the gaping hole inside that resulted from losing my parents so suddenly. I know this about myself, and I'm trying to be more cautious, especially after Jared disappointed me so profoundly.

I take my phone out of my pocket and compose a text to Milo. *Thank you so much for lunch. Everyone loved it. You didn't have to do that, but it was very nice of you! I'll stop by after work to see how you're doing.*

I reread the text twice before I send it and return to work, taking thoughts of him with me as I go.

MILO

I'm on a break from PT when my phone chimes with the text from Gianna. I'm glad to hear the lunch was a hit. I'm sure Nico went all out since he's full of guilt. I wish he wasn't, but I do appreciate his help with my campaign to make sure Gianna is thinking of me until I can get out of here and see to it myself.

My lead therapist, Derek, says I'm doing great and should be able to go home in another week, which would be awesome except that will take me even further away from the place where Gianna works. Will I ever see her again when I leave the hospital? God, I hope so.

I haven't felt this way about a woman in a long time. The last time was in college when I dated Michele for two years and assumed we'd get married after we graduated. She had other plans, and by the time I found that out, I already had a ring and a plan to propose. It took me a long time to bounce back from that disappointment, and I haven't dated anyone seriously since her.

I could be serious about Gianna. That much I already know for sure, and no, it's not because of the heightened emotions surrounding a serious injury that have caused me to develop a huge crush on my nurse. That's not it at all. It's *her*. She's easy to talk to on top of all the other things that have me thinking of her more than I've thought about anyone in years. I feel like a caged tiger stuck in rehab inside this stupid halo that's keeping me from her.

That's why I'm doing extra workouts every night, hoping that the more I do, the quicker I might get out of rehab and the halo so I can see her away from this place. I'm already feeling so much stronger than I was when I got to rehab.

Part of me wonders if my attraction toward her will still feel magical outside the hospital. How could it not? I've never been this dazzled by a woman, so I have to believe that will last long beyond my hospital stay. I can't wait to find out what's next with her or to be able to convince her to give me a chance as a fully functioning man and not this injured, feeble version of myself.

I'm back in my room resting after another punishing session with the PTs when my Nona shows up, carrying a tote bag and bringing the smell of something that has my mouth watering.

"How's my sweet grandson today?" Nona asks, kissing the back of my hand.

"Hanging in there. How are you?"

"I'm fine if you are. Don't you dare ever do something like this to me again, you hear?"

Smiling, I say, "Yes, ma'am."

"You took five years off my life, and at my age, that's not time I have to waste."

"You're going to live forever."

"Ha, don't I wish? But while I'm still here, my grandchildren aren't allowed to scare me the way you did."

"What's this I hear about Nona's boyfriend showing up at the hospital? I said that can't be true because my Nona doesn't have a boyfriend."

Before my eyes, my grandmother blushes. "Stop it."

"You stop it and tell me all about him."

"Are you hungry? I brought your favorite meatball sub from the restaurant."

"I'm starving, and that sounds awesome, but quit trying to change the subject."

She gives me a playful scowl as she cuts the sub into small pieces that'll fit through the halo.

I take a bite and moan from how good it is. There's nothing in this world I love more than a meatball sub from Giordino's. "Fess up. What's his name and how'd you meet him?"

She returns to her seat next to my bed. "His name is Chris, and he's teaching me to fly."

"Actually or metaphorically?"

"Milo! Stop being saucy with your Nona."

I laugh like I haven't laughed in days. She's so cute.

"He's teaching me to fly *airplanes*, you fresh brat."

"I hear he's a little bit younger than you."

"Ugh, yes, like fifteen years younger. I have no idea what he wants with an old lady like me."

"Who are you to call my Nona *old*? She is timeless and, like a fine wine, aged to perfection. Anyone would be lucky to date you."

"You always were such a charmer," she says with a chuckle. "But thank you. I keep thinking of the expression that there's no fool like an old fool."

"Does he make you happy?"

She seems startled by the question. "Yes, I guess he does. We laugh a lot."

"I'm happy for you, Nona. Truly."

She gives me a skeptical look. "You don't think I'm an old fool?"

"Never. I'm glad to see you finding some happiness after working so hard for so many years."

"It's been great having Dee managing the restaurant. She's made it easier for all of us to take some time off and enjoy life a bit."

"You certainly deserve to smell the roses. You've all worked so hard to make that place such a big success."

"Vincent is all about quality of life these days, and I can't deny he might be right."

"Are you thinking about retiring completely?"

"Oh God, no. I'd go mad without something to do every day, and besides, work keeps me sharp, which is helpful while dating a younger man."

I laugh at the grimace she makes. "He's lucky to have you, and I'm sure he knows it."

"He was right there for me when this happened." She waves her hand toward the halo. "I couldn't believe when he showed up at the ER that night."

"I heard there was quite a stir."

"Which was the last thing I wanted when all our focus needed to be on you."

"I'm sure it provided some much-needed distraction for everyone."

"You know how our family is with a scoop like that. Bunch of dogs with bones."

"I can only imagine," I say with a chuckle. "I'm sorry I missed it. When can I meet him?"

"Oh, well, I don't know."

"I can't believe my Nona blushes."

"I do not!"

"Do, too."

"I don't remember you being so feisty before you were shot."

"Haha, you blush, and I want to meet him."

"Fine. I'll see what I can do."

"Excellent."

"I came here to see how you're doing. How did we end up talking about me?"

"Your stuff is much more exciting than mine."

"That's not what I hear. What's this about a lovely nurse who would have our boy's head turned all around if it wasn't anchored in place by that contraption?"

"You heard about that, huh?"

"Same way you heard about me. Nothing stays secret in this family. Spill the tea. Tell me all about her."

I love that my grandmother knows about spilling tea. "Her name is Gianna, and since you met her a few times, you know she's gorgeous, funny, smart, easy to talk to. I have a huge crush on her that's all about frustration because I can't do much about it from here."

"I helped Nico with the lunch delivery to her and her colleagues. I think it's safe to say she's thinking of you after what we sent over."

"Oh jeez, did you guys go overboard?"

She gives me a "duh" look that makes me laugh. "What's the Giordino family motto?" she asks. "Go big or go home."

"Thank you for helping Nico with that. Put it on my tab."

"Nico put it on his, which shouldn't surprise you. He's been suffering over what happened to you. Now would be a good time to ask for anything you want."

"All I want is for him to stop suffering. I hate that. It wasn't like he shot me."

"No, but he feels responsible the same way you would if the roles were reversed."

"I guess, but I wish he'd let it go. All that matters is that I survived it."

"He'll come around to that eventually, but it's going to take a while. I've never seen him like he was that night, Milo. Not ever. He was inconsolable when he realized you'd taken a bullet that was meant for him."

"I hate that for him."

"He'll be all right. On the plus side, this has brought him and Sofia even closer than they were before. They've been sick over what happened to you and why it happened."

"I'm just glad that monster is locked up so he can't torment her or Mateo anymore."

"We're all glad about that. His mother has reached out to Sofia to say how sorry she was about what happened to you. That he's not the boy she raised. He broke a lot of hearts that night."

"Yeah, that's got to be awful for his mother."

"I can't imagine what she's going through."

"There's no chance he'll get out, is there?"

"He's being held without bail because it's an attempted murder charge."

"At least I won't have to testify, because I don't remember anything about it."

"Thank God for that."

"Yeah, for sure."

She shudders. "I'll never forget hearing you'd been shot."

"Sorry to put you through that."

"Don't be sorry. It's not your fault. We're just so thankful that you're going to make a full recovery."

"Any time now."

"Have patience, my love. These things can't be rushed. I'd better get back. We've got a big party tonight. I need to make sure everything is ready." She gives my hand a squeeze. "I can't wait until I can kiss your cheek."

"I'll look forward to that and hugging you."

"Love you more than you'll ever know."

"Ditto. Don't forget to bring your boyfriend to see me."

"He's not my boyfriend. I'm too old for boyfriends."

"Lover, then? Is that better?"

She turns bright red. "Oh *my Lord*. I'm outta here."

I'm still cracking up when she stalks from the room. She's the absolute best, one of my all-time-favorite people, and our bond has always been tight. She'll often say that a Nona isn't supposed to have a favorite, but oh, how she loves me. I can't bear to think of the ordeal I put her and the rest of my family through the night of the shooting.

"Knock, knock," a familiar voice says thirty minutes after Nona leaves.

"Come in."

Dr. Jason Northrup steps up to my bedside, alone for once. "How's my star patient doing?"

"I'll be much better when you get me out of this contraption."

He takes a closer look at the pins holding the halo in place and then removes the bandage covering the surgical scar. "How's the itching?"

"Better than it was."

"Glad to hear that."

"How does it look?"

"Excellent. It's healing perfectly and ahead of schedule."

"That's good news."

"It is great news. That and the report from the physical therapists are very encouraging. I'd say one more week in the halo, and then we'll transition you to a neck brace."

"Another *week*?" I ask, moaning.

"I know it sucks, but we want to be sure everything has healed inside before we remove it."

My deep sigh says it all. "I hate to complain when you saved my life and my mobility, but..."

Jason laughs. "I get it. Believe me. Everyone hates the halos." His gaze shifts to the sandwich on my table. "Are those Giordino's meatballs by any chance?"

"They are. Help yourself. Nona brought me an extra-large. I'll never eat it all."

"Are you sure? I'm starving."

"Go for it."

"Thanks." He takes a seat next to my bed and quickly devours two sections of the huge sandwich. "Damn, that's good."

"*So* good. How are things with you and Carmen?"

"Great. We're excited about the baby and looking forward to everything."

"Must be nice to have your life settled like that." My wonderful cousin has been so happy since she met and fell in love with Jason, years after losing her first husband tragically.

"It's a huge relief to have found her. She's amazing, but I don't have to tell you that."

"No, you don't." I glance at him, hoping it's not a mistake to ask him what I want to know. "What do you think of Gianna? The nurse on 5 East?"

"Gianna Lombardi? She's an awesome nurse. One of my favorites. I always ask for her to take care of my patients when they're on her floor. Why do you ask? Was everything okay with her?"

"It was great. I really liked her." I give him a meaningful look —or as much as I can from inside the cage. "A *lot*."

"*Oh*, I see." He scratches at the late-day whiskers on his chin. "You know about what happened to her, right?"

"With the fiancé or the parents?"

"Both. She's had a rough go of it."

"I know."

He gives me a side-eye look. "Are you going to change her track record?"

"I'm gonna try like hell."

CHAPTER 8

MILO

The next two weeks are brutal—and yes, you heard that right. *Two* weeks. Ugh. Jason added a week "just to be sure" to the halo schedule, which was crushing. I work harder than I ever have in my life to successfully complete rehab so I can get the hell out of here.

Gianna comes by every night for at least an hour, which has become the brightest part of my days. I also have frequent visits from family, coworkers, neighbors and other friends. I'm blessed beyond measure to have survived such a major injury and to have the support of so many loved ones.

But I want out of here, and I want out of the halo that Jason extended for one more week when a scan of my neck showed I needed a little more time immobilized.

I had another scan yesterday, and I'm waiting for him to come by to let me know the results and hopefully free me from the cage. Even though I'm very happy to be alive and all that, I'm going mad inside this damned thing.

Jason arrives with the usual gaggle of residents in tow. It

took being his patient to realize how big of a rock star my cousin's husband is around here. "How's my best patient today?"

"That depends on whatever news you're bringing."

"The news is good, my friend. Today is get-out-of-jail day."

"Thank you, Jesus."

"It's Jason, but you can call me Jesus."

"Haha. Is he always a comedian?" I ask the residents.

"Quite frequently," one of them replies.

Jason asks two of the residents to deal with the pins holding the halo in place. "This shouldn't hurt, Milo, but try to remain still as they remove them."

I don't feel pain so much as pressure as the pins are removed and the halo is gently lifted over my head.

"You can scoot back to sit against the pillow," Jason says.

I use my arms to adjust my position and sigh with relief as my head connects with a pillow for the first time in weeks.

"Better?" Jason asks.

"*So* much better."

"The next step is a much less restrictive neck brace."

One of the residents produces the item and hands it to Jason.

"I'm going to need to sit you up for this." He pushes the buttons on the bed to get me where he wants me, and then he positions the brace around my neck. Even though it's not the most comfortable thing I've ever experienced, it's light-years better than the halo.

"How does that feel?"

"Fine. How long will I have to be in this thing?"

"At least two weeks, maybe longer. We'll see how it goes, but you're in the home stretch now, so take it easy and don't try to do too much. We don't want any setbacks."

"That's the last thing I want either."

"I'm going to send you home at the end of the week with outpatient PT for another month."

Home.

I'm at once thrilled and nervous. While I can't wait to get out of here and get back to normal, I've got to figure out a plan to keep seeing Gianna as much as I can after I leave here.

"How long until I can go back to work and drive?"

"At least another month. Maybe two. We'll see."

I guess it could be worse. "Sounds good."

"I know it's so hard to rest and relax between therapy sessions, but that's what you need to continue healing. Too much too soon is what causes setbacks."

"I hear you. No setbacks."

"You've got my number if you need anything."

"I do. Thanks again, Jason. For everything."

"I'd say it was my pleasure, but…"

"Yeah, I know. I'm so glad you were right there that night and knew what to do."

"I'm always thankful to know what to do, but never more so than with someone who means the world to my wife and me."

Smiling, I shake his hand and say goodbye to the residents, who've become familiar to me after so many weeks under his care.

After they leave, I reach for my phone to send a text to our family group chat. *I'm out of halo jail, and Jason is springing me at the end of the week.* I attach a photo of myself wearing the neck brace with a smile and a thumbs-up.

I receive a flood of texts in response, full of excitement.

Looking forward to having you back where you belong, bro, Nico says.

Shouldn't he come here where people are home all day? Mom asks.

He's coming HOME to our house, Nico says. *I'll take care of anything he needs.*

I can help, Mom replies. *Since you have a business to run.*

That's fine, but I want him here.

I just sit back and watch them fight over me. I have no doubt I'll have everything I need and then some with them on the job.

While they go back and forth, I compose a text to Gianna. *Got out of jail today and going home at the end of the week.* I enclose the selfie in the message I send her.

Then I sit back to watch TV while waiting and hoping to hear back from her.

GIANNA

I'm late leaving work and have to go to the grocery store, so I don't stop to see Milo, even though I've been thinking of him all day, especially since he sent the message about getting out of the halo and being released soon. I'll call him when I get home. I rush through the store and am home an hour after I left the hospital. After I've put everything away, I pour a glass of wine and take my phone to the sofa to call him.

"Hey," he says.

"Hey, yourself. No more halo and going home soon, huh?"

"Yep. It's so nice to be free of that thing."

"I can't imagine. Sorry I didn't come by after work. I left late and had errands I had to do."

"No worries. I figured you were busy."

"We had a crazy day on the floor today. One thing after another."

"That must be stressful."

"It can be."

"When I go to work, no one's life hangs in the balance."

That makes me laugh. "We don't think of it that way."

"Well, you should. What you do is heroic."

"You write the code that keeps the systems we rely on working."

"I suppose so, but I still say your thing is way cooler than mine."

"I like it, most of the time. What's your plan when you leave rehab?"

"Going back to the house I share with my brother and his fiancée and her son, although I probably ought to get out of there since Sofia and Mateo are living there now."

"Is that a recent development?"

"Fairly recent. Nico moved them in when the threats from the ex-husband accelerated. He's insisting on me coming home to our place when my mom wants me there. They're fighting over me."

"I'm sure you're in hot demand."

"For now, anyway. They're driving me kind of crazy, honestly. I can't imagine what it'll be like when they have me captive at home, but enough about me. I keep meaning to ask if you've heard anything about the lawsuit."

"Not a thing, so your mom is going to file the countersuit against him tomorrow." My stomach turns at the thought of the ugliness that's apt to generate.

"You're not afraid of him, are you?"

"Not physically, but he's going to be pissed."

"Too bad. He made promises to you. He needs to keep them. The wedding he wanted shouldn't wipe you out financially."

"You're right about that."

"Damn straight I am, and I'm sure my mom will get this resolved for you."

"I hope so. Tough way to learn a big lesson—don't ever sign a contract you're not personally capable of fulfilling."

"That's a lesson you never should've had to learn. Not that way, anyhow. He asked you to marry him and said he wanted the big wedding. Why would you think he wouldn't go through with it?"

"I was completely blindsided when he backed out, and even

then, it never occurred to me that he wouldn't take care of the expenses."

"That was the least he should've done after backing out. I'm so sorry that happened to you, Gianna."

"Thanks. It was awful, especially having to tell people and stuff like that."

"He was a fool not to realize what he had with you."

"How do you know that? For all you know, I'm a shrew away from work."

"Are you?" he asks, laughing. "I can't for the life of me picture that."

"Most of the time, I'm not, but I have my moments."

"I'm looking forward to witnessing all your moments."

I have no idea what to say to that.

"Too much too soon?"

"No..."

"Do you have any idea how frustrating it is to be stuck in here after meeting you and wanting to get to know you better?"

"Um, well, no, I guess I don't."

"Pretty damned frustrating, especially knowing you're going through this thing with the lawsuit and all that."

"Your mom is saving my sanity."

"I want to help you with that and anything else you need."

"That's very sweet of you, Milo."

"I'm not being sweet. I mean it."

"I know you do, and it's very sweet. I've realized a lot of things since he called off the wedding... Things I should've paid closer attention to at the time. I'm leery after that. I don't trust my own judgment."

"You can trust me. I swear you can."

"I know that, and that's why I'm leery, because I was so sure with him, too."

"If I had a chance to make you happy, Gianna, I'd never let you down."

. . .

MILO

The statement replays in my mind over and over the next day, during two grueling PT sessions.

If I had a chance to make you happy, Gianna, I'd never let you down.

I cringe every time I think about saying that. Her last relationship ended in thermonuclear fashion. The last thing she probably wants is some smooth-talking dude saying stuff like that to her—even if it's the truth.

I'd love the chance to show her that not all guys are assholes.

That's kind of been a problem for me with women, because they all seem to want the bad boys who put them through the wringer and treat them like shit. That's not me. That could never be me. If I care about someone, I'll do anything for them. I guess that makes me boring to some women. I dated a woman recently who told me life was too slow with me.

What the hell does that mean? Just because I wasn't constantly trying to make her jealous or doing stuff to upset her, life was too slow? Since she said that to me, I've wished I was more like Nico, who's never had a shortage of women interested in him, because he was the one always causing drama with his woman of the moment. And he seemed to like it that way until he met Sofia and his entire outlook changed.

I just want to live a peaceful life with a woman who loves me as much as I love her. Is that too much to ask for? So far, it has been for me. But now I wonder if my luck might be changing. I've never been as immediately attracted to anyone as I was to Gianna the first time I saw her, standing by my bedside after surgery. Even in the fog of confusion, pain and medication, I thought she was the most beautiful woman I'd ever seen.

I still think that.

At first, I thought I was dreaming when I saw her there and was relieved when I realized she was real. That's how much of an impact she made on me from the beginning.

When eight o'clock comes and goes, I give up on her popping in—and who could blame her? Most of my enormous family is here, keeping me company and feeding me to the point of bursting. I'm going to have to rein that in when I get home, or I'm going to get heavy like I was as a teenager.

I've worked hard to lose the extra weight. In the last year, I finally lost the last twenty pounds and worked out every day until the shooting. I can't let all that hard work go to shit while I recover.

My uncle Vincent and aunt Vivian are getting ready to leave with their daughter, Carmen, when Gianna appears in the doorway.

"Is this a party or is anyone invited?" she asks with a smile that lights up her gorgeous face.

"You're definitely invited." I wave her in. "The rest of these characters are the crashers."

"We were just leaving," Mom says as she jumps to her feet. "You come right in, Gianna."

"Subtle, Mom," I murmur.

"You hush." Mom bends to kiss me and stroke my hair. "It's so nice to kiss your cute face again, my love."

"All right, Mom. Dad... Do something."

"Let's go, El."

She wrinkles her nose at me. "Don't be mean to your mother."

"You're so happy I'm alive that I can be mean to you forever."

To my regret, her eyes fill with tears. "That's absolutely true."

"Elena."

"I'm coming. Love you, Mi."

"Love you, too, Mama. Thanks for coming, everyone."

"Love you," Vivian says when she kisses me, too.

After they leave, I roll my eyes at Gianna. "Am I covered in red lipstick?"

Smiling, she says, "Just a bit."

"Get it off me! They're crazy now that the halo is gone and they can kiss the shit out of me."

Laughing, she gets up to retrieve a wipe. As she stands over me, I look up at her, transfixed as she wipes the lipstick off my cheek. "There," she says. "All better."

"Thank you."

"You're welcome."

"I thought you weren't coming."

"I almost didn't."

"Why not?"

She tosses the wipe and returns to her seat, facing me. "Because I looked forward to seeing you all day."

If I've ever heard a better sentence than that, I can't recall when. "Is that right?" I ask with my most charming grin.

She nods. "That's a dangerous thing for someone coming back from a bad breakup."

"It's not dangerous. Not with me it isn't."

"So you say," she says with a timid smile. "And I'm tempted to believe you."

"What can I do to tip you over the edge?"

"Just be you. That's more than enough."

She can't possibly know how much it means to me to hear her say that, when being just me has never been enough for others.

Feeling bold, I reach out my hand, hoping she'll meet me halfway. When she does, my heart skips a happy beat as I link my fingers with hers. "I really like you, Gianna, and not just because you removed my catheter with as much finesse as you possibly could."

She snorts with laughter. "That's very romantic, Milo."

"I thought you'd like that. I've got nothing much to do but sit around and think of ways to make you laugh and smile. That's become my hobby since this happened."

"Whatever will you do with yourself when you get out of here?"

"I'm really hoping to work on perfecting my new hobby."

CHAPTER 9

GIANNA

The warm fuzzies from my visit with Milo stay with me at work the next day. I keep trying to tell myself to chill out and stop being so giddy over him, but I can't help it. I really, really like him, even if I know it's probably too soon after the mess with Jared to be wildly crushing on someone new. Even though a year has passed since our non-wedding day, the trauma still feels fresh at times. But lately? I don't think as much about that as I do about Milo.

"Are you humming?" Annie asks as we inhale lunch while standing up in the break room.

I turn from the microwave to face her. "Was I humming?"

"Sounded that way to me. And I'm glad to hear it. I've missed happy Gianna."

"Sorry to have been such a drag."

"No one could blame you." Annie eats half a sandwich in three bites and chases it with a bottle of water.

I remove leftover stir fry from the microwave and take it to the table, determined to sit for a least a minute.

"Did you see your favorite patient last night?"

"I talked to him."

Annie smiles. "How's he doing?"

"Much better since he was freed from the halo."

"I'm sure. Those things suck."

"Yep." I take a bite of the stir fry I made from my mother's recipe. "I'm in serious crush, Annie."

"I love that! It's just what you need after the dickhead. A nice, sexy rebound."

"I told you that's not what this is. He's not that kind of guy."

"I still say he'd love to rebound you. Trust me on that."

I'm not sure why that makes me feel uncomfortable, but it does. We're called back to work a few minutes later, and we don't have a chance to talk again before our shift ends. I'm still thinking about what she said when I get home to find Jared sitting on my front porch.

Part of me wants to turn and run away, but the other part of me that's been made strong by loss refuses to run from him. Being no fool, however, I make sure the pepper spray on my keychain is hidden in my hand.

"What're you doing here?" I ask, feeling slightly unnerved to have him show up after weeks of not talking to him except through Elena.

He holds up an envelope. "You're *suing* me, Gianna? Seriously?"

I'm glad the process servers finally found him after he dodged them for days. "Yes, seriously! The venue is suing *me*. What else am I supposed to do after you promised to pay for a wedding I didn't even want?"

He's tall, muscular and handsome in a way that once appealed to me. Not anymore. As I wait for him to tell me what he wants, I can't for the life of me remember what I ever loved about him.

"Why are you here?"

"I want to work this out separate of lawyers."

"Unless you're planning to pay the venue, there's nothing to work out."

He runs his free hand through wavy dark blond hair. "About that... I was thinking... It's insane to pay full price for something we never got to enjoy. Maybe if we were to reschedule, we could work something out with them."

I gasp. Did he really say that? "Reschedule the wedding?"

"Well, yeah..."

I start to laugh. I laugh so hard I can barely breathe. Even as he becomes visibly annoyed, I can't stop the laughter. "Are you out of your goddamned mind?" I ask him the minute I can speak again. "You want to *reschedule* the wedding you canceled *the day it was happening?*"

"It's better than eating forty grand for nothing."

I hold up my hand to stop him from saying anything more. "So rescheduling a wedding to someone you didn't want to marry a year ago is better than losing forty grand? That's a hell of a reason to get married, Jared."

He shifts from one foot to the other, seeming as uncomfortable as I feel. Good. He ought to be uncomfortable. "That's not the only reason."

I raise a brow in disbelief while I wait to hear what he's going to say.

"I miss you."

This is unbelievable.

"And there's the honeymoon to consider. The cruise is in a week." We'd put off the trip until our first anniversary due to Jared having just started a new job.

"I'm aware."

"We shouldn't let that go to waste either."

"It's not going to waste."

"You're still going?"

"Of course I am. I saved for a year to pay for that trip." A trip

I had no interest in, I might add. "I wouldn't miss it for anything."

"Who're you going with?"

"That's none of your business."

He moves toward me.

I take a step back. "Don't come any closer to me. I want you to go."

"Can't we at least talk about this?"

"Do you remember me asking you that same exact question when you told me you couldn't go through with the wedding and that we needed a break from each other? You said, and I quote, 'There's nothing to talk about.' That's my answer, too."

"I'm sorry, Gianna. I never meant for any of this to happen."

I'm in utter disbelief as I stare at his face, which is both familiar and unfamiliar at the same time. Did I ever really know him? "What did you think would happen when you canceled our wedding and walked out of my life? Did you think I'd be so despondent that I'd take you back no matter what? That's not going to happen—now or ever. In fact, I've discovered you did me a favor."

"What's that supposed to mean?"

"We weren't meant to be."

"That's not true."

"It is true, or you wouldn't have done what you did."

"I regret that. I freaked out. I handled it badly."

"Yes, you did, and now you can either pay the venue or pay me. One way or the other, you're going to keep that promise to me even if you broke every other one. Now please go." I step aside so he can walk by me. Only after he's past me do I realize I'm holding my breath. I've never been afraid of him before, and I'm not now, but I'm also not entirely sure I shouldn't be.

"I'm not paying the venue or you."

My heart sinks. "Then I guess I'll see you in court."

"You have no case," he says with a mean edge to his voice.

"I have the promises you made and the text messages to prove it. My lawyer is very confident we'll win." I'm so thankful for Elena and Milo in that moment that I could nearly weep. "It'd be cheaper for you to deal with this now than to let it drag through court."

He stares at me for a long intense moment. "You really won't consider giving us another chance?"

"I really won't." I'm amazed that none of this is the slightest bit upsetting to me when I was devastated after he canceled the wedding.

"I thought I knew you, Gianna."

"Likewise, Jared. I guess we're both disappointed."

I'm so proud of myself for how I've handled this encounter. I walk away from him without looking back, and once I'm inside the house, I lean back against the locked door and release a deep breath. Then I laugh. It's amazing to realize I felt absolutely nothing for the man I should be married to.

What a relief to know that relationship is so over as to be dead and buried. I pull my phone from my pocket and walk to the sofa as I type a message to Elena, updating her on the encounter with Jared.

Two seconds after I send the message, she calls me. "Are you all right, honey?"

God, I already love this woman and the way she mothers everyone. After four years of fiercely missing my own mother, she's like a burst of sunshine in my life. "I'm fine, thanks."

"I can't believe he had the nerve to come to your home. I'll speak to his attorney about that."

"I think I took care of it."

"Do you feel up to telling me what he said?"

"He's not going to pay the venue, and he asked if I'd consider giving him another chance. He said we could reschedule the wedding and not lose the money. It was very satisfying to tell him thank you, but no, thank you."

"I'll bet," she says with a laugh.

"Nothing says romance like 'hey, honey, let's tie the knot after all so we don't lose all that money.'"

Elena laughs again. "No kidding. I'll reach out to his attorney and ask him to advise his client to stay away from you or we'll request a restraining order."

"God," I say on a sigh. "I can't believe it's come to that. I thought we'd be leaving on our honeymoon next week."

"Did you cancel the trip?"

"It's nonrefundable."

"Did you pay for that?"

"I did."

"I can amend the suit to cover the cost of the trip."

"That's all right. I'm trying to decide if I want to go on my honeymoon alone."

"I'm so sorry this has happened to you, Gianna. Milo told me you lost your parents, too. That's a lot."

"I'm starting to fear I'm living under a dark cloud."

"That's not true. With all you give to others through your work, I believe you'll eventually come out on top."

"Any time now," I say with a laugh.

"One thing I've learned in my life is that there'll always be highs and lows, but usually, there're more highs overall."

"That's good to know. I'm deeply grateful for your help."

"I'm happy to do it. Try not to worry. We'll get this resolved so you can move on."

"That'd be nice."

"If he shows up again, call the police. He's got no business at your home. Not anymore."

I walk into the kitchen and take a wineglass from the cabinet. "No, he doesn't."

"Be safe, Gianna."

"I will."

"I'll be in touch."

After we end the call, my phone rings again with a call from Milo.

"Hi there," I say to him as I pour a glass of Chardonnay from the bottle I've got going in the fridge.

"I was with my mom when she called you. Are you all right?"

"I'm fine."

"Gianna…"

"I'm okay, Milo. I promise. I held my own and got off a few good retorts that made me feel good about myself, especially after he suggested we reschedule the wedding so we won't lose the money."

"He *actually said that?*"

"Yep."

"Wow. That takes some balls."

"Like I said to your mom, nothing says romance like that, huh?"

"You deserve so much better," he says softly but intensely. "*So* much better."

"You're right. I do." An idea comes to me in a rush of adrenaline and emotion that nearly takes my breath away. Before I take even a second to think about whether I should, I share the thought with him. "Milo…"

"Yes, Gianna?"

"How would you feel about recuperating on a cruise ship rather than at home with your family?"

"Would you be on that cruise ship with me?"

"I would."

"Then I'd feel very good about that. In fact, I'd feel great about it. You'd be saving me from full-on family suffocation."

"And you'd be saving me from going on my honeymoon alone."

"When do we leave?"

In the background, I hear his mother ask, "To go where?"

"Hang on, Mom. I'll be right there. Sorry, Gianna. I'm back."

"We'd leave on Sunday morning and go to Fort Lauderdale. The ship leaves Sunday afternoon and comes back next Saturday. We have stops in the Bahamas, the Cayman Islands, St. Martin and Montego Bay, Jamaica."

"That sounds amazing."

Suddenly, I'm excited about the trip again, knowing he'll be coming with me.

"Do you think the doctors will freak about me doing something like that right out of rehab?"

"You'll be with a highly qualified nurse."

"That's true."

"Why don't you mention it to Dr. Northrup the next time you see him? If you could maybe just say you'd be going with a friend who has medical training, that'd be good."

"I'll do that."

Another thought occurs to me. "You have a passport, right?"

"Yep. My parents took us to Italy for Christmas a couple of years ago."

"Was it amazing? I'd love to go there."

"It was. Best trip ever, but I have a feeling my next trip will top it by a mile."

"Not sure about that."

"You'll be there, right?"

"Yes..."

"Then it's already the best trip I've ever gone on."

MILO

"You're doing *what?*"

For a second, I worry my mom might pass out when I tell her I'm going on Gianna's honeymoon with her. "You heard me."

"You're in the *hospital,* Milo. You can't go from the hospital to a cruise ship."

"Who says? I'm in *rehab,* not the hospital, and Jason says I'm doing great. Besides, I'll be with a nurse."

"What can she do in the middle of the Caribbean, or wherever you'll be, if something goes wrong?"

"Nothing will go wrong, Mom. I'm fine."

"I don't like this."

"So noted."

She's stopped by with breakfast on her way to a check-in with her oncologist.

Just as she's about to say something else, Jason walks in with his team of residents in tow.

"How's my number one patient doing today?" he asks. "Oh, hey, Elena."

"Morning, Jason. I need you to talk some sense into your number one patient."

"Why's that?"

"He thinks it would be a good idea to go on a cruise two days after he leaves rehab."

Jason's brows furrow, and my heart sinks. If he says I shouldn't go, that'll be that. "A cruise, huh?"

"A friend, who's a nurse, invited me on an already-paid-for trip after her travel companion backed out. I thought I could relax and recuperate there as easily as I could at home."

"It won't be as easy as being at home," Mom says. "Tell him, Jason. He's not ready to travel like that."

"He's cleared to go home from a medical standpoint, so I can't tell him not to go." To me, he adds, "Again, I'll remind you that you'd be risking a setback if you tried to do too much too soon."

"I'll take it as easy as I would at home. Nothing but rest and relaxation, and I'll keep doing all the PT exercises every day. I promise."

"And you'll continue to wear the brace."

"I'll continue to wear the brace. I'll prove it with tan lines above and below it."

To Mom, Jason says, "He's young and strong, and he's bounced back quickly. I'm okay with his plans if he takes it easy."

"I will. I promise."

"I don't like this," Mom says.

"I'll be fine, Mom. I promise. I really want to go." I hope I don't have to remind her I'm almost twenty-seven and can do whatever I want. Not that I'd ever say that to her after what I've put her and the rest of my family through over the last few weeks.

"You're long past the point where I can tell you what to do," she says, sounding defeated. "I just think it's a lot so soon after what you've been through."

Jason removes the brace to check my incision and does the same basic neuro exam he's performed every day since the surgery. "You're doing great, Milo. You're still my star patient."

"Hear that, Mom?"

"I heard it."

"I'll process the discharge paperwork for tomorrow morning," Jason says.

A resident hands me a business card that has a date and time written on it for my follow-up appointment with Jason in three weeks.

"Hey, Jay," I say as he prepares to follow the residents from the room.

"What's up?"

"Thank you for everything. For saving my life and my mobility and taking such good care of my parents while you were taking good care of me."

"You're welcome. I'm glad I was in the right place at the right time."

"We'll be thankful for that—and for you—for the rest of our lives," Mom tells him.

"You guys have a good day, and don't fight after I leave," Jason says with a grin.

We laugh as he exits the room.

"Imagine being able to operate on someone's neck and spine and know what the hell you're doing," I say to Mom when we're alone.

"I can't. He's brilliant."

"Yes, he is."

She checks her watch. "I'd better get going."

"Don't leave mad with me—or Gianna."

"I noticed you didn't tell Jason you're going with her."

"She works with him. She asked me not to say too much about who I was going with. And don't be mad with her for asking me."

"Of course I'm not mad with her. It's very nice of her to invite you. I'm annoyed with *you* for giving me something new to worry about."

I hold out my hand to her.

She comes over to take hold of it.

"Don't worry. I promise I'm fine. I'm going to be fine. And I'm very, *very* excited to be going on a trip with her."

"You haven't even been on a date with her, and you're going on a cruise together. You young people today do everything ass-backwards. Are you laughing at me?"

"Sorta?"

"Stop that." She leans in to kiss my cheek. "I'll be back later."

"I'll see you then. Don't be mad with me."

"Oh, Milo," she says with the starting of tears, "don't you see? I'm so thankful you lived that I could never be mad with you again."

Amused, I raise my brows and give her a salty look. "That's good to know."

"Don't become unmanageable now. You've always been my easy one."

"I'll do my best to keep my golden child title."

"You do that. And please… don't think I'm not happy about you and Gianna, because I am. She's a lovely girl, but she's been through a lot."

"I'm fully aware."

"Take care of your big, beautiful heart in all this, you got me?"

"Yes, ma'am."

"All right, then. I'll see you later."

"Love you, Mom."

"Love you, too, sweetheart."

After she leaves, Derek, the therapist I've secretly nicknamed Satan, comes to get me for my first round of PT for the day, but even that can't dampen my good mood. I'm on top of the world knowing I'll be taking off with Gianna in three days for a week of fun in the sun.

CHAPTER 10

GIANNA

Asking Milo to go on my honeymoon with me counts as the craziest thing I've ever done. I start to panic during my shift about people at work finding out I invited a former patient to go on the trip with me.

In my nearly three years at Miami-Dade, I've worked so hard to cultivate a stellar professional reputation. It would kill me to do anything to mess with that after busting my ass to make a name for myself at the hospital. Doctors often ask for me when they bring patients to our ward because they know they can count on me. I'd hate for it to get out that I'm taking a trip with a former patient, but knowing how things work in this place, it'll be tough to keep a lid on news like that.

And if it gets out? Will I mind being the source of workplace gossip?

Not if it means I get to spend more time with Milo.

That kind of recklessness is *so* not like me, but after what I've been through the last few years, I just don't care. And that, too, is not like me. I always care more than I should about everything, which makes me a great nurse. But sometimes it causes me to give too much of myself to people who don't deserve it.

Like Jared.

I gave that relationship my all for the two years we were together. I put up with his passive-aggressive mother, his borderline-creepy father, his whiny sister, her bratty kids and his obnoxious fraternity brothers because I wanted to make him happy. Look at where that got me. I'm tired of bending over backward to make everyone else happy, like I did for my brothers after our parents died.

I left college at the University of Florida where, other than the tragic and traumatic disappearance of a suitemate my freshman year, I'd been enjoying being a Gator. I moved home to Miami so my brothers could finish high school without being uprooted. I finished college as a commuter to Florida International University, which is a very good school, but it's not the University of Florida.

What I got in return were two boys who wanted nothing to do with me as their guardian and years of arguments, battles of will and many sleepless nights while I juggled school, housework, laundry, grocery shopping, taxi service and anything else they needed. I went to every one of their games, had their friends over, took them anywhere they needed to go and did what I could to fill the horrible void in all our lives by sticking to our family traditions.

For all they could've cared.

But hey, they got to finish high school with their friends. Someday maybe they'll get a clue about what I gave up to be there for them, but that hasn't happened yet, and I'm not sitting around holding my breath waiting for them to realize it. I don't resent them. I swear I don't. I did the right thing coming home to live with them, and I'd do it again in a heartbeat.

However, I'm ready to be a bit selfish. Being around Milo

makes me happy. It's that simple. Whether anything will come of it remains to be seen, but I like him. I like the way he makes me feel special and *seen* and a little off balance, but in a good way. The best kind of way. Hindsight has painted a picture of my relationship with Jared that I don't particularly care for, and now that the heartbreak has faded, I'm relieved we didn't get married.

I would've put my heart and soul into making that marriage work, but he wouldn't have. I can see that now in a way I couldn't in those first shocking days after he told me the wedding wasn't going to happen. Embarrassment was my primary emotion then. Having to tell a church full of people was the worst. But being married to him would've been far worse. I've had nothing but time to pick through the remnants of that relationship, the way a homeowner would look for what was left after a tornado leveled their house. In the bits and pieces, I haven't liked what I've realized about how I bent myself into a pretzel trying to fit into his life, while he made no concessions at all toward me.

My brothers could see that, and they tried to tell me he was an arrogant jerk, but I didn't want to hear it. I'd invested so much of myself into the relationship by then that I needed it to work.

Ridiculous.

I can see that now, but then? I couldn't see the proverbial forest for the trees. I was in love, don't you know?

Ugh.

I get so mad when I think about what I allowed to happen to my own life. Despite that, I know I should cut myself a break after everything I went through, all while finishing nursing school and launching my career. It was no wonder that Jared found me more than pliable when it came to accommodating his life. I didn't have the time or the energy then to fight for what I wanted for myself.

Now I do, and right in this moment, what I want is more time with Milo.

Beyond that, who knows?

Annie and I end up in the break room around two after a frantic few hours dealing with six new patients and three others going home.

"I'm starving," Annie says as she downs half a sandwich and chases it with a Diet Raspberry Snapple.

"Same."

"Are you still taking next week off?"

"Yep."

"Did you ever sell the cruise to someone?"

"Nope. I'm going on it."

Annie's eyes lift over the glasses she wears when her eyes can't handle contacts. "By yourself?"

"Nope."

"Are you going to make me pull this out of you?"

"If I tell you, you have to promise you won't tell anyone else."

Her eyes bug, giving her the appearance of a spooked owl. "Oh. My. *God.* You invited that sexy Milo Giordino, didn't you?"

"You won't say anything?"

"Of course I won't, Gi. If you can't trust me by now, who can you trust?"

That's true. She's been my ride-or-die friend since the day I started on 5 East. "I invited him to come, and he accepted."

"That is *awesome*. I love this so much."

"I do, too. He's fun, funny, sweet…"

"Sexy as fuck."

"Is he? I hadn't noticed." In fact, I haven't stopped thinking about shirtless, sweaty Milo since I happened upon that delicious scene a couple of weeks ago.

"Sure you haven't," she says with a snort of laughter. "I can't believe you're taking that hot guy on your honeymoon. The ultimate revenge on asshole Jared."

"He came by my house last night."

"*What?* Holy shit! What'd he want?"

She's visibly fuming by the time I finish filling her in.

"I can't freaking believe he hasn't paid the tab by now. And that you got *sued*! Fucking hell, Gi. He has some nerve coming back around with his tail between his legs because he doesn't want to fork over the money for the wedding that wasn't."

"Right?"

"Good for you for telling him where to go."

"It was rather satisfying."

"I'm sure it was!"

"The whole time he was there, I kept looking at him and wondering how I ever thought I loved him."

"Any feelings you had for him died when he told you he couldn't go through with the wedding."

"Yes, they sure did."

"He wasn't worthy of you."

"Did you always think that or just since the implosion?"

"Kinda always, but who wants to hear that when they're planning a wedding?"

"If you ever see me in that situation again, tell me, will you?"

"I will. I promise. It was hard to watch sometimes. You were so, so good to him, and I just wanted to ask what he'd done for you lately."

"I've been thinking a lot about why I tried so hard to make that relationship work when I knew deep inside it wasn't."

"You lost your family. It's only natural to want to create a new one for yourself."

"A therapist would have a field day with me and all my issues."

"There's nothing wrong with you," Annie says fiercely. "*He* was the problem. Not you. And the reason he came back to you wasn't just about the money. By now, he can probably see that he lost a treasure in you. It's no mystery to me why he'd want you back."

"Well, he can't have me."

"That's the spirit. So you and Milo are going on your honeymoon."

"Yep."

"That ought to move things along."

"Or show us we're only meant to be friends."

"I don't think that's going to happen. I saw the way he looked at you when he was a patient here."

"How did he look at me?" I ask, feeling a wave of heat overtake me. Is it hot in here, or is it me?

"Like he wants to have you for dinner."

"Oh my God, Annie. Stop it. He does not."

"He does, too. That's my story, and I'm sticking to it." She lets out a low hum as she smiles at me. "That small cabin, one bed, nothing but time to hang out. You'll find out what's what with him."

I didn't, until right this second, think about the sleeping arrangements. Duh. It's a honeymoon cabin. Of course there's only one bed. I swallow hard at the thought of sharing a bed with sexy Milo.

"Girl, you're lit up like fireworks on the Fourth of July," Annie says with a laugh.

"I like him."

"I know you do, and that's a *good* thing, Gi. He's a great guy, and if anyone deserves a great guy, it's you."

"We all do."

"You first."

"Thanks for letting me talk endlessly about myself since everything happened. I appreciate you more than you'll ever know."

"I'm just glad to see you rejoining the land of the living after all the bullshit with *him*."

"It's nice to be back."

MILO

Almost seven weeks after getting shot, I'm transported home by Nico late on a Friday afternoon. I take in the familiar sights on the way with a greedy exuberance for the outside world and the palm trees I love so much. I'll never again take routine things for granted, such as going to work, cutting grass, cleaning the pool, hanging out with family and friends, driving my truck. I've missed my life more than I knew until I'm back out among the places that make up my daily routine.

"Mom and Dad are bringing dinner over," Nico tells me. "Everyone will probably end up at our place at some point tonight."

"That's fine."

"We're all so freaking glad to have you coming home."

"It's good to be out and about again."

At a stoplight, he glances over at me. "In case I haven't said it lately, I'm so sorry you lost such a big chunk of your life to this insanity."

"Knock that shit off, or I'll go live with Mom."

"You're not living anywhere but with me."

"Eventually, I need to get my own place, especially now that you have a family of your own."

"You're my family, and you're not going anywhere. That's the end of that."

"Listen to me," I tell him. "I know you love me, that you always have, and you always will. I can't begin to know what this has been like for you and Sofia. If the roles were reversed, I'd be just as crazy as you've been. I'm sorry we all had to go through it because her ex-husband couldn't handle her moving on from him. But you and I… And Sofia and I… We need to find a way past it, so it doesn't continue to hang over us forever. I don't want that for any of us."

"I hear you," Nico says, sounding weary. "Sofia and I have been talking about that, too. We're working on moving past it, but we're not quite there yet. You've got to be patient with us when we want to wait on you hand and foot at home for a while."

"You've only got me for two days before I'm getting away for a week."

"Away to where?" he asks, sounding shocked.

I can't believe Mom didn't tell him. "Gianna invited me to go on a cruise with her."

"What? When did that happen?"

"Two days ago. I can't believe you haven't heard this already."

"I've been working nonstop. She just came right out and asked you to take a cruise with her? And what did Jason say about it?"

"The cruise was supposed to have been her honeymoon, and Jason said it's fine with him as long as I do nothing but rest and relax."

"Wow. Good for you, bro. I know you like her a lot."

"I really do, and I can't wait to spend a whole week with her."

"A honeymoon is one hell of a first date."

Laughing, I say, "Right?"

"She's cool. I like her for you."

"Well, that's all that matters."

"Haha. Very funny."

"You have no idea, do you?"

"About what?" he asks, sending me a confused look.

"How much your opinion has always meant to me. If you didn't approve, it wouldn't be nearly as much fun for me."

"I approve," he says gruffly.

When I shift my gaze toward him as much as I can within

the constraints of the neck brace, I'm shocked to see tears in his eyes.

"Sorry," he says. "It's just gonna take some time."

"Take all the time you need. I'm not going anywhere."

"Except on Gianna's honeymoon."

"Yeah, except for that," I say with a grin. "But what I meant is I didn't die, and I'm not gonna, so quit your worrying."

"Working on it, bro."

"I know you are. I'm just glad this didn't come between you and Sofia."

"That's taken some effort, too."

"Things are okay with you guys, though, right?"

"Yeah, we're good. But it's been rough for us to have you in the hospital. We're glad to have you coming home."

"Me, too."

"You should invite Gianna over tonight for your welcome-home party."

"Yeah, I will." My phone is buried in my backpack, and I can't get to it from where I'm sitting in the truck. "I'll text her when I get home."

A short time later, Nico pulls up to the guard shack in our gated neighborhood, and I'm stunned to see a WELCOME HOME, MILO! banner attached to the small building. "What the heck?"

"The neighbors love you. The Millers did that."

"That's really nice."

Doug, the lead security guard for our neighborhood, leans out of the shack to greet me. "Welcome home, Milo. It's so good to see you back where you belong."

"Good to be here. Thanks."

He lifts the arm on the gate and waves us through.

As Nico drives the winding road to home, I see WELCOME HOME, MILO! signs on every lawn in the development.

"Wow." I'm truly moved by the outpouring from the neighbors.

"That's what you get for being Miss Congeniality around here."

That comment is much more in keeping with the way Nico normally talks to me than all his mopey sadness has been lately. "Haha, you know it."

"They all brought more food over, too."

"It's very nice of them."

"As Dad would say, you get what you give in this world, and you give a lot. I'm glad to see you getting it back."

"Even though I wouldn't want to be shot again any time soon, it's been nice to feel so much love from everyone."

"The one benefit of nearly dying is finding out how lucky you are."

"Yeah, for sure. Not to mention meeting a hot nurse and getting sponge baths."

"No need to gloat."

It's nice to laugh with him again after weeks of incredible tension. I've felt almost as sorry for him as I did for myself in all this.

My dad's car is parked in front of the house when we pull up. Both my parents come rushing out of the house, along with Sofia and Mateo, to welcome me home.

"Don't crowd him," Nico says.

"Hugging is not crowding," Mom says, teary-eyed as she greets me. "Welcome home, love."

"Thanks, Mom." I hug Dad, Sofia and Mateo, ruffling his hair and making him giggle. I've missed the little guy, even though he's been in for visits.

Before we know it, we're swarmed by neighbors wanting to say hello and welcome home and drop off more food. Nico invites them in, and before long, we've got a full-on party going that only grows as my sisters arrive with Austin, Everly and Wyatt in tow.

When I realize I never texted Gianna to invite her to join us,

I signal to my mom, who's the closest to me. "Can you grab my phone out of my backpack? I want to text Gianna."

"I talked to her earlier and told her to come by."

"Oh, great. Did she say she was going to?"

"Yep."

"Did you tell her what to do at the gate?"

"Yes, sir."

"Thank you."

"No problem."

"Was there news in her case?"

"That needs to come from her. I can't talk about that with you, which you know after being raised by an attorney."

"Yes, I do know that," I respond, smiling at her. "I hope you can make it all go away. She's so stressed about it."

"I know she is, and of course I'll make it go away. Have you met me?"

"I'm very thankful for my Doberman mother, especially when she's going to bat for my friends."

"Glad to do it. That guy she was going to marry is a piece of work. I think she dodged a bullet with him." She no sooner says that than she winces. "Too soon for bullet references."

"It's fine," I say with a wave of my hand.

"No, it's not." She seems to try to shake off disturbing thoughts related to guns and bullets. "Are you hungry?"

"Starving."

"I'll fix you a plate."

"Thanks."

While I wait for her to return, I compose a text to Gianna. *Heard you were invited to my welcome home party. Hope you can make it.*

She writes back a few minutes later. *Yes! I'm on the way. See you soon.*

Hearing that she's coming makes me so fucking happy. Happier than I've ever been, if I'm being honest. I have no complaints about my life. I've been inordinately blessed with a wonderful family and childhood, great friends, a job I love and plenty of everything. It's only been in love and romance that things have been lacking.

Until recently, that is.

It's just so funny to me that getting shot might turn out to be the best thing that ever happened, because I met her. Ridiculous, right? Nico is eating himself up with guilt about me taking a bullet that was meant for him, but that bullet may end up being the luckiest break of my life. Not that I'd say that out loud to him or any other member of my family, especially not after what they went through waiting to hear if I would survive.

But I'm amused by the hand of fate in this situation.

My mom returns with a plate of delicious Italian and Cuban food and a tall icy Coke that tastes particularly good to me, probably because she serves it to me in my favorite Miami Marlins glass. It's very nice to be home.

Everly comes over to give me a shy smile. "How's your boo-boo?" she asks.

"Much better."

"That's good. Did they stick you with lots of needles? I hate needles." She suffered from leukemia, and my sister saved her life by donating bone marrow. That's how Maria and Austin met.

"They did, and I hate them, too."

"Do you want a brownie? Rie and I made them." We love the nickname she gave Maria almost as soon as they met.

"I'd love one."

"Be right back."

"Is she bugging you, Milo?" Austin asks.

I still can't believe my sister is married to one of the best pitchers in Major League Baseball. That he's an awesome guy, too, is a bonus. "Not at all. She's adorable. She's getting me a brownie."

Everly returns with three brownies balanced on a napkin that she hands to me. "Elena said you need to be fattened up, so I brought you three."

"Elena said that, did she?"

Everly nods, her serious expression making her cuter than she already is.

"You want to come up here and sit with me?"

She nods again.

Austin intervenes before she can leap onto my lap by lifting her and settling her between my legs.

"Help me eat all these brownies you got me."

"She's already had three," Austin says.

"What's a couple more?" I ask him.

Everly giggles as I hand her half a brownie. She pops it into her mouth before Austin can object.

"Your uncle is spoiling you, baby girl," Austin says, smiling at us.

"That's what uncles are for, right, Ev?"

"That's right!"

"I'm the funcle."

"What does that mean?" she asks, looking up at me with big eyes.

"It means fun uncle."

"Funcle. I like that."

I have a feeling she's going to call me that for the rest of our lives, which is fine with me.

She's still snuggled on my lap sharing brownies and other treats my mother brings to "fatten me up" when Gianna arrives.

The energy around me changes when she comes into the room. Everything feels electrified. I wonder if she feels it, too. I hope so, because over the last few weeks, she's become the most important person in my life.

CHAPTER 11

GIANNA

Seeing him cozied up to Everly makes my ovaries stand up to take notice of what a good father he'll be someday. They're so cute as they whisper and giggle and feed each other bites of brownie. And when he looks up and sees me there, his warm smile is the best thing I've seen all day. He always looks so happy to see me. A girl could quickly become addicted to a man who makes her feel like she's the sun that lights up his world.

Jared never made me feel a fraction of what Milo does just by smiling at me.

That thought fills me with a certain amount of despair at realizing I could've married him without knowing something so much better was possible.

"What can I get you to drink, honey?" Elena asks, rousing me out of my thoughts.

"Is white wine an option?"

"Sure is. I've got Chardonnay, Pinot Grigio and Sauvignon Blanc."

"I'll do the Chardonnay, please."

"Coming right up." She pats me on the arm. "Go say hi to Milo. He was so happy to hear you were coming."

"I will. Thanks."

The Giordinos are always so nice and welcoming toward me. I've spent so much time in their presence at the hospital that it was no big deal to come to Milo's house to see him, knowing the whole family would be there to welcome him home.

"Hey, Gianna," Maria says from her post on the sofa. She has her feet up on an ottoman and her hand on her expanding abdomen.

"How're you feeling?" I ask her.

"Fat and uncomfortable. My ankles swelled up today at work —and yes, they tested my blood pressure before I left. All good."

"That's a relief."

"I know."

"Quit hogging her, Maria," Milo says. "She came to see me."

"My baby brother is getting impatient to see you," Maria says, rolling her eyes. "Don't let me keep you."

I love this family and the way they spar with affection. In my family, the sparring is rarely affectionate. I hope we'll get there as my brothers get older and stop resenting me for being the legal adult who kept them out of foster care after our parents died. And yes, I've reminded them of that. They were unmoved.

Milo extends a hand to me. "There you are."

I take hold of his hand as if that's the most natural thing in the world, as if I've been holding hands with him for years rather than occasionally over the last few weeks.

"Is she your *girlfriend,* Funcle Milo?" Everly asks in a singsong voice.

"I'd really like her to be."

"She's pretty."

"Isn't she?"

"I can hear you guys talking about me," I tell them, smiling.

Everly giggles.

Nico appears with a chair for me that he places next to the chaise where Milo is holding court.

"Thank you."

"Welcome."

He's gone as quickly as he appeared.

"Don't mind him," Milo says as I take a seat. "He's still a mess."

"I like your house."

"It's his house. I'm just the tenant."

Sofia comes over with a plate of appetizers, cheese and crackers for us. "You're much more than a tenant to him —and me."

"Thanks," he says, smiling at her. "You can quit looking so traumatized. I'm home, and everything is fine."

"Keep telling me, okay?" she asks in accented English.

"As often as you need to hear it."

"Thank you for not dying. It would've ruined your brother's life—and mine."

"I'm glad to still be here for many reasons, but mostly because I want you two to be happy together. Don't worry about me. I'm fine."

She leans in to kiss his cheek. "I'm so glad," she says tearfully as she leaves to tend to other guests.

Mateo comes to fetch his pal Everly.

"See you later, Funcle Milo," she calls over her shoulder as she takes off with Mateo.

"Story of my life," he says to me. "All the pretty girls leave me for other guys."

"They do? Are they crazy?"

"Most of the time, they do. They want someone who's going to treat them shitty, and that's never going to be me."

"I know girls like that. I went to high school with them. I never understood that mindset."

"I never have either, but it's been an issue for me. Nice guys finish last, or so they say."

When he hands me the plate, I realize I'm still holding his hand and release it to take the plate from him. I'm trying to process what he said about being a nice guy and finishing last. How is that possible? He's all the things anyone could want in a man.

Or I should say all the things *I want* in a man.

"Do you think less of me after hearing that?"

"Of course I don't. I just can't believe you don't have a line of women out the door who want to nurse you back to health."

"There's only one woman I want to nurse me back to health."

He's so cute and sincere that I wish we were alone. If we were, I might lean over to kiss him. But since I can't do that, I just smile at him. "Since you're my favorite patient ever, I'd be glad to nurse you back to health."

"I may have a lot of needs."

"Like what?" I ask, playing along.

"I miss the sponge baths."

I sputter with laughter. "Those are over, mister."

"Aw, come on. You got me addicted, and then you took them away from me."

"Because you're perfectly able to shower on your own again."

"What fun is that?"

I roll my eyes at him. "I can see you're going to milk this nursing thing for all it's worth."

"Duh." He pops a cheese and cracker into his mouth and chases it with a swig from his Marlins glass. "What's the plan for this trip you're taking me on?"

"I have to deliver food to the hospital at nine a.m. on Sunday, and then I can pick you up, if that works for you."

"It does. What's with the food for the hospital?"

"The nurses cook for the PICU families, and this is my week."

"What does PICU stand for?"

"Pediatric ICU."

"Ah, I see. It's nice that you cook for them."

"The nurses at Miami-Dade have been doing it for years. There're so many of us that we only do it once or twice a year. My date just happened to fall this week, and since the ship doesn't leave Fort Lauderdale until three, I didn't bother to switch with someone."

"What time do you want me to be ready?"

"Is ten okay?"

"Sure. And what's the dress code?"

"The dinners are dressy, but everything else is casual."

"Got it."

"I, um, there's one other thing..."

"What's that?"

I look around to make sure no one will overhear us. "It's just that we'll have to share a bed, and I'm not sure if you'll mind..."

His gaze collides with mine, and I feel my face heat from a rush of emotions. "I don't mind."

"This is the craziest thing I've ever done, in case you were wondering."

"What is? Taking an ex-patient on your honeymoon when we haven't even been on a date yet?"

"Yeah. That."

He reaches for my hand again and kisses the back of it. "I can't wait to go with you on your honeymoon. It'll be the best first date in history."

ELENA

I keep half an eye on Milo and Gianna as I prepare dinner for the family in Nico's kitchen. If I'd gotten my way, I'd be making this meal at my house, but the boys insisted on Milo coming home to Nico's, so here I am trying to figure out where I went wrong with my eldest son. How can he have only a plastic colander?

"I know I bought you a stainless steel one when you moved into your first apartment in college."

"I think it got crushed when one of my roommates sat on it," Nico says.

"Who *sits* on a colander?"

Nico gives me the look that's made women fall at his feet since he was twelve. "Do you honestly want the answer to that question?"

"No, I don't. Give me the plastic one if that's my only option."

"I'm sorry you have to work under these conditions."

"I'll cope somehow." I glance at Milo and see him kiss the back of Gianna's hand. "Your brother is smitten."

"I see that."

"Did he tell you about the cruise?"

"He did."

"I don't like him being out to sea while he's still recovering."

"Jason signed off on it."

"Still..."

"Let him go, Ma. He's crazy about her, and he deserves to get away from it all after what he's been through."

"What if something happens when he's far away from medical care?"

"They have medical facilities on the ship, and he's going with a nurse. She'll know what to do if anything comes up."

"It makes me anxious to think of him so far from us when he's still so fragile."

"He's not fragile. He's fine."

"What are we talking about?" Dee asks when she joins us.

"Gianna invited Milo to go on a cruise with her next week," Nico says, "and he's going. Mom thinks it's too soon for him to travel."

"Hmm," Dee replies. "What did Jason say?"

"That it's fine as long as he takes it easy," Nico says. "Not to mention, he's going with a nurse."

"She can't help him if he has an emergency in the middle of the ocean," I remind them.

"If he was going to have an emergency, wouldn't he have had it by now?" Dee asks.

"I suppose. It's just..."

"Mom, he's fine," Nico says. "And he's crazy about Gianna. Let him go have a great time. Does anyone deserve that more than he does?"

Someday they'll understand, when their injured child wants to do something slightly crazy before they probably should. I hope they'll look back at this moment and understand how I felt. Until you're a parent yourself, you can't possibly understand the many ways a parent worries.

Dee hugs me. "He's in good hands with Gianna, Mommy."

"I know."

"And I've never seen him look at anyone the way he looks at her," Dee adds.

"I know that, too." I can't deny the unmistakable spark between the two of them, and I'd love to see Milo happily settled with a lovely woman like Gianna.

"It'll be okay," my younger daughter assures me. "I promise."

I watch as Nico cozies up to Sofia and Dee rejoins Wyatt, who puts an arm around her as he smiles warmly at her. Austin is tending to Maria on the sofa while Everly says something that makes them both laugh.

And Milo... He's clearly enchanted by Gianna, which makes my mama heart happy for them.

My kids grew up way too fast. I feel like I blinked, and they were all adults, running their own lives and falling in love. The shooting was a stark reminder of how quickly everything can change. I suppose it's going to take some time before I can stand down from the heightened state of alert I've been in since that traumatic night.

Lorenzo comes over to check in with me. "What's wrong?"

"Nothing."

"Don't lie to your husband."

"Just worrying about Milo going on the cruise."

"You won't be able to talk him out of it no matter what you say, so you might as well let that one go."

I sigh as I lean into him, knowing he's right as usual. "I miss when they had to do what I told them to."

Lo laughs. "Right? Those were the days."

"Indeed they were, even if they drove us crazy then."

"Did they ever. Remember when we threatened to move out if they didn't clean up their crap?"

"I remember so many things, mostly the chaos and the joyful noise of having them all at home."

"The good news is, we still see them almost every day, but we don't have to put up with the chaos. How lucky are we? Four great kids, two new grandchildren thanks to Everly and Mateo, two amazing sons-in-law, soon to be a lovely new daughter-in-law and now maybe another wonderful daughter-in-law coming along to love."

"We're very lucky, indeed."

"It's all gonna be fine," Lorenzo assures me.

Since he's usually right, I decide to try to relax about the cruise and wish my sweet Milo bon voyage.

CHAPTER 12

MILO

Saturday night, Nico gets my suitcase out of the attic and insists on handling most of the packing for me. I hope that by the time I get home from the cruise, he will have chilled the eff out, and things can get back to normal around here. Since that's not going to happen today, I direct him to my dresser and closet for the clothes I need for the trip while I sit on my bed, propped up by a pile of pillows.

He's hardly let me do a thing for myself since I got home last night.

"Don't you have to work tonight?" I ask him.

"Not until later."

Sofia is working at the restaurant, and Mateo is having a sleepover with his paternal grandmother—you know, the mother of the man who tried to kill me. Nico isn't one bit happy about that.

"Why do you look like you're going to kill someone?"

He stops what he's doing and turns to me. "Do I?"

"Yeah, you're super spun up."

"I don't like that Mateo is with Joaquín's mother. What if one of his criminal friends tries to take off with him or something?"

"I can't believe Sofia would let him go there if that was remotely possible."

"She says he's perfectly safe there, but I'm on edge."

"Which is understandable in light of all that's happened."

"Yeah. Which bathing suit do you want?"

"I guess I'll take them all."

He folds everything and places each item into the suitcase until we're both satisfied I have everything I need. My navy blue sport jacket goes on top, folded neatly in half.

"Thanks for the help."

"No problem. Do you need condoms?"

"Uh, wouldn't it be presumptuous to bring them?"

"Wouldn't it be worse to need them and not have them?"

"I guess so."

He goes to his room and comes back with an unopened box of the kind we both like. He's the one who bought me my first box. "I don't need these anymore. They're all yours."

"Thanks."

"You're welcome." He checks his watch. "I'd better get going."

"Before you do, come here." I point to the edge of the bed. "Sit."

When he's seated, he gives me a strange look. "What's up?"

"I want you to do something for me while I'm gone."

"Sure. Anything you need."

"I want you to chill the fuck out before you have a stroke or something equally unpleasant."

"I'm fine. I'm not—"

"Nico. Shut up and listen to me. Ever since this happened," I say, gesturing toward my neck, "you've been wound tighter than a drum. And I get why. Of course I do. But you have to find a way to move past this and get back to normal."

He stares at the floor.

"I know this has been rough on you."

When he looks up at me, I'm shocked to see tears in his eyes again when I hardly ever saw that before the shooting. "Do you? Do you have any idea what this has been like for me?"

"I can only imagine how awful it's been."

He shakes his head. "You have no clue what you mean to me, probably because I never thought it was necessary to say the words."

"I *do* know, Nico. How could I not know when you've been right there for me my whole life? You don't have to say the words. Neither of us does. You and me… It just *is*. You're my best friend in the whole world, and I'm yours, and that's just how it's always gonna be. No matter what."

"I have nightmares about it," he says softly. "About you getting shot and dying and me being left to go on without you, knowing it was my fault you got shot in the first place. All I can think about is how I spent more time busting your balls than I did being nice to you before this happened, and if you'd died, you might not have known…" His voice breaks on that last word.

"It wasn't your fault, and I've always known. *Always*, Nico. Just like you can't bear that I got shot, I can't bear to see you like this. I'm really worried about you, and I'm not just saying that. We're all worried."

"I'm trying to get past it. I swear I am."

"This week, I want you to take some time to decompress and try to relax before you do something stupid like drop dead. Where would that leave me? Unprotected in this terrible world without my big brother to look out for me."

"I hate that I wasn't there when it mattered most."

"Nico… Please, you've got to stop this. It's not healthy to put yourself through this any longer."

"I know," he says with a deep sigh. "Sofia says the same thing."

"She's right, and so am I. The people you love the most are all safe. Joaquín and his cousin are in jail, probably for decades. You can let down your guard now."

"I'm working on that."

"When I get home, it's back to normal. Ball busting, insults and no more waiting on me like I'm feeble. You got me?"

He offers a small smile. "Yeah, I got you."

"Thank you for taking such good care of me since this happened."

"Least I could do."

"But we're done with all that now."

"After I carry your suitcase downstairs, you mean."

"Yeah, after that."

We share a laugh, and for the first time since disaster struck, I feel like we're on our way back to normal. At least I hope so. "Go to work and leave me alone."

"I'm going. Call me if you need anything. I can be home in a minute."

"I won't need you, and I'm not calling. I can take care of myself."

"Fine. Be that way."

"Have a good night at the office, dear."

He walks out on a huff of laughter that pleases me. I really hope this week apart can help get us back to normal, or whatever counts for normal after something like this happens.

After I hear Nico leave, I realize I'm alone for the first time since the shooting. My mother must not realize that, or she would've organized a team of family members to keep me company. With a fridge full of food delivered by family and friends and hours to myself, I'm happy for the peace and quiet, which has been hard to come by lately.

The first thing I do is text Gianna. *Look at me! I'm home alone!*

Awww, did they leave little Milo to his own devices?

They did! I'm waiting for them to figure out I'm home alone, and then there'll be an invasion. Shhhh, don't tell anyone.

Your secret is safe with me!

How's the cooking going?

Good! I'm almost done. I made four pounds of pork tenderloin with a huge pan of potatoes, vegetables and homemade applesauce.

Yum. I'm gonna need you to make that for me someday.

I will!

Something to look forward to.

What if you can't stand me after a week together?

That's not going to happen.

How do you know?

Because I can't wait to spend this week with you and next week and the week after and all the weeks.

How can you already know that for certain?

I just do. Is that okay?

It is, as long as you know... I'm not sure I'm ready for this... Even though I invited you on my honeymoon. LOL

That's kind of a mixed signal... haha.

I know!

Listen, I get it. You're coming off a terrible breakup, and all the legal stuff has been awful. But meeting you has been the best thing to happen to me in, well... ever. I'm prepared to be patient and wait for you to be ready for whatever this turns out to be...

As soon as I send that, I worry that I've once again given her too much too soon. I'm not sure what it is about her that makes me want to lay all my cards on the table so there can be no doubt in her mind about where I'm coming from.

When she doesn't reply for a few minutes, I text her again. *Did I freak you out?*

Haha, no, I was getting stuff out of the oven.

Oh, phew. I was picturing you running for your life from the crazy ex-patient who's coming on way too strong.

Nah, you're fine. I appreciate the honesty. It's actually rather refreshing.

Blame it on the near-death experience. That changes everything.

I'm sure. How has it changed everything for you?

Well... One minute you're going along, living your life, minding your own business, and in the next, it's nearly taken from you in a single second of madness that has nothing to do with you. It makes you think about what's important.

What's important to you now?

The same stuff that was before—my family and friends and my job —and now you're important to me, too.

Just like that?

Just like that.

You're important to me, too.

Have I ever read five better words than that? Nope. Not ever.

It's just that the timing is kind of weird for me.

I get it. I promise I won't push you for more than you're ready for, even while we're on your honeymoon.

She responds with laughing emojis. *Weirdest first date ever?*

What a story we'll have to tell the grandchildren someday.

So much for not getting ahead of ourselves...

Whoops. I add laughter emojis.

Are you packed?

Yep. Nico, my personal assistant, did it for me before he went to work.

That's good! I need to finish packing and get to bed. I'll see you around ten?

I'll be ready. Can't wait.

Me, too. Thanks for coming.

Thanks for inviting me. Sleep well.

You, too.

I put down the phone and close my eyes, smiling as I anticipate seven days alone with her. Maybe that will be enough time to prove to her that I can back up my words with actions. I heard her when she said she isn't ready to start something new. But hopefully, she'll turn to me when the time is right for her.

However long it takes, I'll be waiting.

GIANNA

I'm so excited for a week off from work and the chance to get to know Milo away from the hospital and his big family and all the other distractions of life. When I get up the next morning, I text my brothers to remind them that I'll be away this coming week.

I'll check in when I have Wi-Fi, but try not to have any emergencies for the next seven days.

Since it's only six a.m. out West, I don't expect to hear back from them until much later, if at all. It doesn't surprise me anymore when they don't respond to my texts. An older woman I work with tells me this is normal for young men in their late teens and early twenties, who are the world's worst communicators, according to her.

All I can do is try. I keep hoping that eventually, the distance between us will lessen as they move into adulthood and away from their reliance on me as much more than an older sister. I'm their first call when something goes sideways, but I often wonder if they ever give me a thought except for when they need something.

Probably not.

Before I leave to deliver the food to the hospital and then pick up Milo, I take the time to dust my mother's beloved curio cabinet, which is full of her treasures. She collected Lladrós, porcelain objects made in Spain, that were her prized possessions. Personally, I don't see the big deal, but out of respect to her, I keep them dusted the way my mother did. Every Sunday morning after church, she took each object out of the cabinet to dust it, and then she cleaned the glass shelves.

I've rarely missed a Sunday with the Lladrós since she died. As I return them to their places, I hope that wherever she is, she can see me caring for the things she loved, including the sons who brought her so much joy.

After I finish the cleaning, I shower and change into one of the pretty summer dresses I bought for the trip when I thought I'd be going with my new husband. Sometimes I can't believe everything that's happened since I booked the cruise he wanted to take. I hate crowds, so I'm certain that being on a cruise ship with thousands of other people isn't going to be my thing.

I load up my car with the food, my suitcase and a beach bag and take the familiar roads to work. I pull up to the hospital's staff entrance just after nine o'clock and haul the huge tote I bought just for this purpose to the PICU on the sixth floor. There's a family room with a refrigerator that we fill each Sunday to give the parents of children fighting serious illnesses one less thing to worry about during the coming week. It's one of the traditions I love best at Miami-Dade, which is a huge, sprawling medical complex that at first seemed like a cold and sterile place.

However, I've found it to be anything but. I've made some great friends here, and I love contributing to the community within the hospital by cooking for the PICU families, volunteering to visit elderly patients who have no family and participating in holiday toy drives and food drives and all sorts of other things throughout the year.

I'm on my way out of the PICU with the tote tucked under my arm when I run into Jason Northrup and his residents.

"They've got you working on a Sunday, huh?" I ask him.

"No rest for the wicked. I've got three patients on this floor and two on yours to check on before I can head to brunch with the family. I thought you were on vacation?"

"I'm leaving today on a cruise."

His eyes briefly widen before he schools his expression.

I fear I just spilled the beans to him, since he probably knows Milo is going on a cruise, too. I keep forgetting Jason is married to Milo's cousin.

"Well, have a great time. We'll miss you this week."

"Thanks. I'll see you when I get back."

"Bon voyage."

As I walk away, I'm worried about how unprofessional that might've appeared to him. Crap. I hope he doesn't think less of me for inviting a former patient on a trip. The slightly nauseated feeling stays with me as I drive to Milo's house and give my name at the security hut. Milo must've told them he was expecting me, because the arm lifts immediately to let me in.

I pull into the driveway and see Milo standing in the doorway watching for me. He's wearing a navy polo shirt and khaki shorts. All thoughts of professional nausea are forgotten as my heart does a little happy dance at the sight of him. That can't be good for someone who's not ready to have her heart dancing at the sight of anyone. My heart isn't getting the message that it's not ready for whatever this might turn out to be with Milo.

"Wait, let me do that," I tell him when he starts to bring his suitcase out of the house.

"Nothing makes me feel less like a man than having a woman carry my suitcase for me."

"Oh stop. It's temporary."

"Still… Thank you for doing that."

I lift the suitcase into the trunk next to mine. "No problem. Don't forget your glasses."

"I'm back to contacts now that I'm out of the halo."

"Oh, okay. But they were kind of cute."

Smiling, he says, "I've got them with me. Let me just grab my backpack. I'll be right out."

"Should you be carrying the backpack?"

"It's not that heavy."

He steps out of the house a few minutes later with the backpack slung over his shoulder. After he locks the door, he comes toward me, smiling. "Let's get this show on the road."

"I figured your whole family would be here to see you off."

"They're at brunch at the restaurant, or they probably would be. I'll take you to brunch when we get back. It's something we do every Sunday."

"I love that your family is close like that. It's so nice."

"Most of the time, it is. Other times, it can be a little suffocating, such as when one of us gets shot and nearly dies. This trip is a great chance to push reset on all that, so thank you for inviting me."

"Thanks for coming."

"Is it hard for you? To be taking this trip with someone else?"

"Not like it would've been before the lawsuits and stuff. I'm just so over him, it's not even funny, especially since he asked me to go through with the wedding so he wouldn't have to pay all that money for nothing."

"Yeah, that's what every girl dreams of hearing from the man she loves."

"Right?" I ask with a huff of laughter. "I keep replaying that encounter in my mind and wondering if he honestly thought I'd agree to reschedule the wedding after what he did."

"He's a fool."

"Yes, he is."

"He's probably realizing what a huge mistake he made letting you go."

"Who knows what he's thinking? I just don't care anymore, which is a relief."

"I'm sure it is. I'm sorry you had to go through such an ordeal with him, and that it's still not entirely over."

"It's over in all the ways that matter, and your mom is taking care of the rest, thank goodness."

"I hope you can take a deep breath and just relax this week. You deserve a break from it all."

"We both do."

I take the exit for Interstate 95 North for the forty-five-minute ride to Port Everglades in Fort Lauderdale. There were cruises we could've taken from Miami, but the excursions were better on the one from Fort Lauderdale. I turn the radio to Big 105.9. "I hope classic rock works for you."

"Is there anything else?" he asks.

I keep waiting to find something about him I don't like, but so far, I'm coming up short. Jared loves country music. That was a problem for me. I put up with it to make him happy, but I don't enjoy it, and he never wanted to listen to my music. He said it gave him a headache.

That's just another on a long list of ways I capitulated to him. I ate the food he liked at the restaurants he preferred, attended the sporting events he enjoyed and hung out mostly with his friends. I'll never do that again. I don't care how great a guy seems. If he can't meet me in the middle, I'm out.

"What're you thinking about over there?" Milo asks, breaking a long silence.

"About how I let Jared make all the decisions in our relationship, including the music, and wondering why I allowed that."

"Why do you suppose you did?"

"I've felt so alone since everything happened. I have lots of great friends and a job I love, but I was lonely. A friend set me up with Jared, thinking we'd hit it off, and for a while, we did. It's only in hindsight that I can see that I was jumping through hoops to make him happy with little concern for what made *me* happy." I look over at Milo, who's turned in his seat so he can see me while wearing the neck brace. "That's probably too much information. Sorry."

"It's not too much. I like to hear about your life."

"And I like to hear about yours. Have you ever tried so hard to make someone else happy that you lost yourself in the process?"

"All the time. I'm famous for going out of my way in relationships and ending up alone at the end."

"Why do we do that to ourselves?" I ask.

"I have no idea, but I'm trying to break the habit and not doing a very good job of it."

"Why do you say that?"

"Because I already know I'd do just about anything to see you smile."

CHAPTER 13

MILO

I love being with her. I love the way her scent surrounds me like a cloud of the sweetest fragrance I've ever experienced. I love the red-and-purple floral dress she's wearing and how it leaves her shoulders bare. I was never particularly attracted to shoulders before I saw hers.

I love the way she speaks so freely about her ex and their relationship with me, but I despise the haunted look in her eyes when she talks about how it went so wrong. I love that we have a whole week together to get to know each other and to hopefully set the foundation for so much more.

I've never felt quite like this about any woman, but I know I must tread carefully with her. Still, the fact that she asked me—of all the people she knows—to come on this trip with her is a sign that she's at least interested in spending more time with me.

Alone time.

Or as alone as we can be on a ship with thousands of other people.

"Have you been on a cruise before?" I ask her.

"Nope. You?"

"Nope."

She hesitates before she says, "I'm going to be honest…"

"I wouldn't want you to be any other way with me."

"I have a phobia about being stuck on a ship with so many strangers."

"Me, too. That's why I've never been on one."

"Same."

"So if you have this phobia, why'd you plan a cruise for your honeymoon?"

She glances over at me with a weary look that says it all. "It's what he wanted."

"Yep."

"Gianna…"

"Yeah, so, I was a doormat with him, and here I am stuck with a trip he wanted that I agreed to pay for since he was paying for the wedding."

"We'll get even by having the best time ever, and I'll protect you from the crowds."

"That'd be good. If I can be honest again, I kinda hate people in large quantities."

I snort with laughter. "Right there with you, sweetheart."

Gianna shivers. "I'm so freaked out about this trip that I almost canceled it. If you couldn't have gone, I would've canceled."

"It'll be fine. We'll keep to ourselves. After all, we are on your honeymoon."

"That's right. I emailed my travel coordinator to swap you out for Jared, but she said it was too late to change the accommodations from the honeymoon package. I apologize in advance for whatever level of shitshow this turns out to be."

"No worries," I say, chuckling. "I'm just here for the all-you-can-eat buffets."

"I read that the food is pretty good, and we got the booze package, too."

"Even better. We'll have a blast."

When we arrive at Port Everglades, we join a long line of cars being directed toward the long-term parking lot. Gianna has a parking pass that she puts on the dash.

"Parking is included in the honeymoon package," she tells me.

"Can't wait to see what else is included."

"I'm terrified."

We share a laugh that breaks any remaining tension that might've been left as we embark on this adventure together. It's amazing how comfortable I feel with her after knowing her only a short time, during which I couldn't do a damned thing to move things along other than talk. We did a lot of talking, more than I've done with any woman at this point in a relationship, and that's one of many reasons why I feel so good about spending a whole week with her.

We haven't run out of stuff to talk about yet. Not even close.

As we approach the terminal, pulling suitcases behind us, Gianna stops short.

"No. *Way.*"

"What?"

She uses her chin to nod toward a man standing off to the side of the crowd heading into the terminal. "That's Jared."

"What's he doing here?"

"That's what I'd like to know, too."

Gianna storms over to him, and I follow, not sure what else I should do.

"What the hell are you doing here?" she asks him.

"Going on the trip we planned together."

"You're not going anywhere."

"Don't be ridiculous, Gianna. Isn't it bad enough that we're going to lose all that money on the wedding? And besides, you didn't even want to go on a cruise."

"You're damned right I didn't, but like everything else, I went along with what you wanted and paid for a trip I had zero interest in taking."

"Exactly." All at once, he seems to notice me. "Who's that?"

I'm not sure what possesses me… "I'm Milo Giordino, Gianna's boyfriend. And you are?"

I'll never forget the stunned expression that overtakes Jared's face or the way he looks at her with utter surprise. "What the hell, Gi?"

"You dumped me, Jared. The day of our wedding, the same wedding you pushed me to have and then left me holding the tab. I've moved on. I'd suggest you do the same. Come on, Milo. We don't want to miss a minute of our trip."

I happily take hold of the hand she extends to me. "Later," I say to him as I follow her inside while he watches us go, seeming speechless.

"Thank you *so much* for that," she whispers the minute we're far enough from him that he can't hear her.

"It was entirely my pleasure." I tighten my grip on her hand ever so slightly, just enough to let her know I have no plans to let go.

"I can't believe he had the nerve to show up here like I'd be fine with going on a trip with him after everything he's done."

"I'm extremely aroused by the way you told him off."

"Stop it," she says, laughing. "You are not."

"Am, too. That was hot." I fan my face with my free hand as we wait in a very long line to check in. I fear it's the first of many lines we'll be in this week.

I see a woman holding a sign over her head that says MR. AND MRS. JARED AND GIANNA ALLEN.

"Uh, Gianna, is that for you by any chance?"

"Oh my God! I told her the wedding didn't happen. What the

hell?" She takes hold of my arm so we won't get separated as we make our way toward the woman with the sign. "I'm Gianna. Please tell me you got my email about the change of plans?"

"I did," the woman says, "but I already had the signs made, and there wasn't time to get new ones. Handwritten signs are against company policy. I'm Diana." She shakes hands with both of us. "If you follow me, I'll expedite your boarding process. Do you have your passports?"

I hand mine to her as Gianna does the same.

"Right this way."

In less than thirty minutes, we're welcomed on board the *Fun in the Sun* and brought to our cabin on the concierge deck. I have no idea what that means, but I find out soon enough that it comes with complimentary rum punch as a welcome beverage and a charcuterie board waiting in our surprisingly spacious cabin, where there's a heart on the bed made of rose petals.

"Wow," I say to Gianna as Diana throws open the curtains to reveal a balcony. "This is awesome."

"Nothing but the best for you, hubby," she says with a grin.

I'm glad that she seems happier now that we're on the ship and in our very nice room.

"I'll be back to check on you when we're underway," Diana says. "Is a seven thirty dinner seating all right with you?"

Gianna glances at me.

"Works for me."

"That'll be great," Gianna says. "Thanks, Diana."

"Wonderful. I'll meet you back here after we've left port and take you on a tour."

"Sounds good." The minute Diana leaves the room, Gianna scoops up the rose petals and drops them into a trash can. "Sorry about that."

"Don't be. It's no big deal to me."

"I'm also sorry we had to deal with Jared. I just can't believe he had the nerve to come here thinking he was going on this trip."

"In a way, I feel sort of sorry for him."

She gives me an incredulous look. "*Why?*"

"He had you, and he screwed it up. That's got to be eating him up inside, especially now that he knows you've moved on with me."

I'm nearly shocked speechless when she comes over to me, goes up on tiptoes and kisses me square on the lips. "You're a very nice man, and I'm so glad you're here with me."

Never one to look a gift kiss in the mouth, I hook an arm around her to keep her from getting away. "I'm very glad to be here, and if you wanted to do that again, I'd be all for it."

"Do what?" she asks with a grin. "This?" She kisses me again, and this time, she lingers a bit, just enough to give her no doubt what her sweet kisses are doing to me.

"Hmm, that. More of that." The stupid neck brace is impeding my ability to kiss her the way I want to, so I reach up to release the Velcro straps holding it in place. It falls to the floor behind me. When she starts to protest the removal of the brace, I stop her with a tongue-twisting kiss that she responds to with the same level of enthusiasm I've given her.

"This is the best honeymoon ever," I whisper against her lips, which curve into a smile.

Her eyes are closed, her cheeks are flushed, and she's the most beautiful woman I've ever seen, which I decide to tell her.

"You don't have to say that."

"I never say anything I don't mean." I tuck a strand of hair behind her ear and run the tip of my index finger over her cheek. "From the first second I saw you, I thought you were stunning."

"You were high on pain meds then."

"And still I saw *you*, Gianna, and was dazzled by you."

She leans her forehead against my chest, but she keeps her

arms around my waist. "I told you I wasn't ready for any of this, and then..."

"And then you kissed me, and it was the best kiss of my whole life."

"Mine, too," she says softly.

That's the best news I've ever heard.

GIANNA

I can't believe I just kissed him like that, or that he kissed me back like he'd been dying to. As our first day on the ship unfolds with delicious food, potent cocktails and breathtaking scenery, I feel myself begin to relax in a way that I haven't in years. Milo is great company, as I knew he would be when I invited him to come with me.

After our kisses in the cabin, there's a low hum of tension between us that only adds to the enjoyment of our first day at sea. I'm so happy to be away from work and home and Jared and the mess of our breakup that I don't even mind being surrounded by strangers on the deck where we settle to get some late-afternoon sun.

Milo is wearing red swim trunks that sit low on narrow hips.

Other women are checking out his chiseled chest and arms as well as his six-pack abs. They give him hungry looks that he doesn't notice. Or if he does, he doesn't let on to me that he notices the attention. I'm wearing a white bikini I bought for the trip. I thought it was somewhat conservative until I saw Milo's wide-eyed reaction to it.

I'm acutely aware of him on the next lounge chair. A low hum of desire has settled between my legs and is keeping my nipples at full alert, which makes me feel even more exposed. It's my own fault. What was I thinking when I suddenly kissed him? I wasn't thinking. Strangely enough, I have no regrets. Kissing him was the nicest thing that's happened since the Jared disaster upended my entire life.

Although, I'm starting to think that Jared dumping me wasn't a disaster at all. In fact, it could turn out to be the best thing to ever happen to me, as preposterous as that would've seemed at the time.

I look over at Milo, whose handsome face is tipped up toward the sun. With sunglasses hiding his eyes, I can't tell if he's awake or dozing. He's got a towel rolled up behind him to prop his head at a comfortable angle since I made him put the brace back on before we toured the ship with Diana.

I'm such a mess. How many times did I tell him I'm not ready to start something new, and then I kiss him like that? I run my fingers over my lips, which are still tingling from the sexiest kisses of my entire life. Yes, you heard that right. Kissing Jared was nothing like kissing Milo. Sex with Jared was pleasant, but I never felt electrified like I did just from kissing Milo.

What would it be like to—

No. Stop it. You invited him on this trip because he needs rest and relaxation after his ordeal. Not to be objectified.

Sometimes my inner voice is a real buzzkill.

"What're you wound up about?" Milo asks in a gruff, sexy tone.

"I'm not wound up."

"You're not going to start lying to me on our honeymoon, are you?"

He's cute, amusing, sexy and sweet. He's the real deal and the full package. *Ha. Full package.* He's definitely that, too, judging by the erection I felt pressed against me while we were kissing.

"I'm a jumbled mess."

"No, you're not. You've been through a lot, but you're doing great."

"How do you know that?"

"Because you came on this trip despite the disappointment. You invited a new friend to come with you. And you cooked for the PICU parents before you left. That doesn't sound like a mess to me. That sounds like an amazing, strong woman who's ready to move on to the next stage of her life."

"Damn, I look good to you."

"You have *no idea* how good you look to me, especially in that bikini. You're so beautiful, you nearly stopped my heart."

"It wouldn't take much for a girl like me to get addicted to the way she feels when you say things like that."

"Feel free to get addicted. I'm already there, especially since you kissed me."

"Yeah, about that..."

"No regrets, Gianna. I've wanted to kiss you since the second I first saw you."

"We've already established you were whacked out on pain meds then."

He turns onto his side and raises his sunglasses, revealing gorgeous brown eyes. "And still I wanted to kiss you and hold you and *know* you. I've never felt that kind of immediate attraction to anyone before."

I bite my lip as I study his handsome face. "If I'm being honest..."

"I always want you to be honest with me."

"I experienced the same buzz of attraction, and then I felt guilty about thinking my new patient was hot."

Oh, that smile... It's lethal and devastating and all the other things, and when he directs it at me, I can't for the life of me remember why it was that I thought I wasn't ready for this or for him. I'm *so* ready. Whether I still will be once we return to dry land and reality is anyone's guess.

He extends his hand to me.

I reach out to link my fingers with his as he gazes into my eyes.

"I know the timing stinks for you, with this being your honeymoon and everything, but I'm crazy about you, Gianna, and I'm so happy to be here with you."

"I'm glad you're here, too, and I'm starting to think the timing might be perfect after all."

MILO

Something has changed since we kissed earlier. She seems lighter, less burdened and maybe a little bit uninhibited, which is fine with me. I want her to relax and enjoy her vacation in every possible way. She's had so much weight on her shoulders, and she's carried it admirably. I can only imagine how difficult it was for her to step up for her younger brothers, sacrificing her own plans to care for them after their parents died.

It makes me crazy to think how that bastard Jared treated her, especially knowing what she'd already endured.

"What're you thinking?" she asks. "You look awfully fierce all of a sudden."

"I'm thinking about how I wished I'd met Jared for the first time when I was capable of punching his lights out for how he treated you."

"I bet you could've done it, even with your neck in a brace, but I'm glad you held back."

"It wasn't easy."

"I still can't believe he showed up expecting me to take him on this trip after he canceled our wedding and got me sued by the venue."

"He's got some nerve, that's for sure."

"I loved the way you stepped right up and floored him by saying you were my boyfriend."

"That might've been my finest moment."

"Thank you again for thinking fast."

"My pleasure. You know he didn't deserve you, right?"

"I do now, but enough about him. I want to talk about us."

"Are we an us? I'd like us to be. Would you?"

"I think maybe I would."

"And you feel ready for that?"

She thinks about that for a few seconds before she replies. "I wouldn't have thought so as recently as a few days ago. It's been a year tomorrow since everything blew up with Jared, but the minute he told me he couldn't go through with the wedding, it was like everything between us was gone. Even though I was devastated, I didn't love him anymore."

"I can understand that."

"It was so strange, though. The day before, I expected to love him for the rest of my life, and the next day, it was just... gone."

"He hurt you and disappointed you. Of course you didn't love him anymore."

"And he embarrassed me. Having to face everyone after he called off the wedding was the worst thing ever. Thank God for my friends, who stepped up that day to handle the details, because I was too shocked to function."

She takes a deep breath and releases it slowly. "And then when he refused to settle up with the venue, and they were threatening me... That's when I started to actively hate him, which is terrible, too. I've never hated anyone in my whole life. Well, except for the person who took my college friend Skylar from us, but that's a whole other story."

"I want to hear about Skylar."

"I'll tell you sometime," she says sadly. "Not here, though. It's too heavy for a vacation that's supposed to be fun."

"Another time, then. And Jared gave you good reason to hate him."

"I know I've already said it, but I really am over him. Everything but the anger, anyway."

"You certainly have a right to the anger."

Her gaze connects with mine, and it's all I can do not to gasp from the punch of desire.

"I really liked kissing you," I tell her.

"I liked kissing you."

"We should do more of that."

"Do you think so?"

"Uh-huh. What're you doing right now?"

"As in right this minute?" she asks with a smile pulling at her sexy lips.

"As in right this minute."

"Hanging with my new guy."

Hearing her call me that does it for me like nothing else ever has. "I could use a nap. What about you?"

"A nap sounds good to me."

I sit up as quicky as I'm able to and give her hand a gentle tug. We gather our belongings and head back to our cabin two decks below the pool. In the elevator, we don't say a word to each other, but I curl my hand around hers to keep her close. My heart is beating so fast, I worry I might pass out or something equally embarrassing.

CHAPTER 14

MILO

She uses the keycard to get us into the cabin, where we both drop our stuff right inside the door and reach for each other.

Once again, I rip the stupid brace off my neck so I can kiss her properly.

Since she never bothered to put her coverup back on, I have unfettered access to the softest skin I've ever felt, and I take full advantage of the long-awaited opportunity to touch her. "God, Gianna. You're so fucking sexy, you take my breath away."

She runs her hands over my chest and up to link her fingers behind my neck. "So are you. When I saw you lifting weights in your room that night…"

"What?" I ask in a gruff tone.

"I couldn't stop staring."

I kiss her again, and as her mouth opens to my tongue, my knees go weak under me. That's never happened before. Nothing like this has ever happened. Not to me, anyway. As her tongue rubs against mine, I'm aware of my life changing forever, and I'm totally fine with that if it means my life will include her.

We land on the bed in a graceful move without missing a beat in the best kiss of my entire life. I keep waiting for my neck to protest the movements, but the only ache I feel is coming from an erection that wants in on this party right now. Being wrapped up in Gianna is as amazing as I thought it would be. In fact, it's even more amazing than I could've imagined, especially when I feel her hands sliding down my back and over my ass to pull me closer to her.

That puts my hard cock in direct proximity to the heat between her legs, and the moan that escapes from me surprises us both.

"Did that hurt your neck?"

"It's not my neck that hurts."

I love her smile and the way it lights up her soft brown eyes. As I rock against her, those gorgeous eyes seem to roll back in her head.

"Is this too much too soon?" I ask, only because I want to be sure she's as into this as I am.

"No, it's not too much."

"Would this be too much too soon?" I ask as I tug on the tie to her bikini top.

"No," she whispers as she licks her lips.

The movement of her tongue sliding over her lips makes me harder than I already was as I untie the knot behind her neck and draw the top down to reveal her breasts. For a second, all I can do is stare. She's beautiful everywhere. In a matter of seconds, I already know I could spend days, weeks, *years* worshiping her full breasts and the pretty pink nipples that go tight against my tongue.

She buries one hand in my hair as she grips my shoulder with her other hand. When she tightens the hand in my hair, the tingle travels straight down my spine.

"Tell me to stop," I whisper against the slope of her breast.

"Don't you dare stop."

I raise my head to meet her gaze. "Are you sure?"

She nods. "I'm very sure, as long as you aren't overdoing anything."

"I'd love to overdo it with you." I can't believe this is happening on our first day at sea. When she invited me to come on the trip, I had no idea what to expect. Suffice to say, I didn't expect this. Not that I'm complaining. Hell no. No complaints. As I kiss my way down to her flat abdomen and run my tongue over the line above her bikini bottom, I'm thankful to Nico for packing the condoms.

She's writhing under me, sending the signal that she wants more.

I go up on my knees to untie the bows at her hips and draw the fabric away, revealing more of her loveliness and discovering she's completely bare between her legs. How did I ever get so lucky to be here with her? Oh right, I got shot. As bad as that was, it was worth it since it led me to her and this surreal moment.

"Milo… Your neck."

"I'm fine."

"Please be careful."

"Don't worry about me." I kiss the inside of her right thigh. "I want you to relax and think only of yourself."

"I'm not so good at that."

"Try."

I prop her legs on my shoulders and set out to give her so much pleasure that she can't think of anything or anyone but herself for a few minutes. The scents of sunscreen and hot woman fill my senses as I seek to bring her the ultimate pleasure with my fingers and tongue.

She's so responsive that I worry I'm going to come before she does.

"Ung, Milo… Oh my *God…*"

Her hips lift off the bed as she tries to get closer to me.

I move carefully so I won't disturb my healing neck right when things are getting interesting. She's so hot, wet and tight. She's everything I've ever wanted and so much more than I dreamed possible for myself. And she's right here, spread out before me, allowing me to pleasure her to a screaming orgasm.

I'm operating from pure instinct when I free my cock from my swim trunks and push into her, riding the waves of her orgasm and nearly coming the second my flesh connects with her slick heat. This must be what heaven feels like.

She clings to me, her fingers digging into my back, making me crazy as I move in her.

As I look down at her, she looks up at me, our gazes colliding in a moment of pure, sweet perfection.

"Crap. Condom." I start to withdraw from her, but she stops me.

"I'm on long-term birth control, and I was tested after Jared dumped me."

"I had a physical right before I was shot and was also tested."

"Then we're all set."

I push back into her and hold still. "I can't believe this is really happening."

"Me either, but I'm glad it is."

"I'm so glad. This is the best honeymoon I've ever been on."

Her laughter fills me with the strangest feeling of rightness. I'm falling hard for her and falling has never felt better.

GIANNA

He's amazing in bed, but I suspected he would be. He's all about me and my pleasure in a way that no one else has ever been.

Other guys I've been with were all about themselves, and if I managed to get off, too, that was a bonus.

Not Milo.

His only goal is to make me happy, and what a refreshing change of pace that is for someone who's used to so much less.

Speaking of more... He's also the biggest lover I've ever had. In the past, I would've said size doesn't matter, but he's proving otherwise as he finds places inside me I didn't know were there until he showed me.

A year ago, I wouldn't have been able to imagine a time when I'd be thankful to Jared for calling off our wedding. But now, as Milo takes me on a wild, sensual ride that leads to the most powerful orgasm I've ever had, I'm nearly weak with relief that I didn't marry Jared.

"Damn," Milo whispers as he comes down on top of me, his lips moving over my neck as he holds me close. "That was... I have no words."

"Same." I gently knead his shoulder muscles. "Is your neck okay?"

"Every part of me is better than it's ever been."

Since he's still inside me, I'm immediately aware when he gets hard again.

"Sorry," he says, starting to pull back from me.

"Don't go." I wrap my arms and legs around him to keep him with me.

We rock together in small movements that have me right back on the edge of release in a matter of minutes. This is crazy. I've never let go this way before, and my inability to come on command was a source of tension with Jared.

Maybe that was because I was with the wrong guy.

That realization is so overwhelming, it takes my breath away as Milo picks up the pace and takes us both to the peak of pleasure once again.

Afterward, he withdraws from me and moves to the side, keeping his arms around me.

I snuggle up to him, my leg between his and my head on his chest. I'm so relaxed and sated, I can barely keep my eyes open.

The next time I open them, it's considerably darker in our room.

Since I need to use the bathroom, I try to disentangle from Milo without waking him.

His eyes pop open. "Wow. We totally crashed."

"Yep."

"Did we miss dinner?"

"No, we've got some time." Despite having sex with him—twice—I feel self-conscious about walking around naked, even if it's almost dark in our room. I grab the coverup from my bag and put it on before I duck into the small bathroom. I'm surprised by the image that greets me in the mirror. My hair is a mess, my lips are swollen, and my cheek bears signs of razor burn. But my eyes are clear and focused, and I can't help but notice I look happy for the first time in a long while.

After I take care of business, I brush my hair and teeth and then study myself in the mirror again, looking this time for signs of regret.

I see nothing that looks like regret.

I give myself a victorious little smile and leave the bathroom to find Milo sitting on the edge of the bed in all his naked glory.

He gestures for me to come to him.

I step between his legs, and he wraps his arms around me, his head pressed to my abdomen. "This has been the best day of my life, and it's not over yet."

I loop my arms around his neck and kiss the top of his head. "Mine, too."

"How will we ever top this honeymoon with the real one?"

I go perfectly still as the impact of his statement hits me.

"I know. That was *way* too much too soon, but it's fun to imagine where this might be heading."

That's when I realize I've done it again. I've fallen head over heels for yet another man and given him the power to crush me. While I suspect this one might be different, I've felt that way before. I was so sure Jared was different, but he was the worst one yet.

"Don't get all jammed up," Milo says, looking up at me. "I'm not asking you for anything other than exactly what you're capable of giving."

I appreciate that he understands me in a way that few people ever have. In that way, he's very different. "I'm sorry. I don't mean to be so weird."

"You're not. You've had a rough go of it, and I get that it's a big deal to be starting something new when you're maybe not as ready as you'd like to be."

"I want to be ready. More than anything, I don't want to make another mistake."

"This doesn't feel like a mistake to me. If we decided not to give this a chance to play out, that would be the mistake."

"I don't want either of us to get hurt."

"I will never hurt you. Not on purpose, anyway. Tell me you believe me."

"I want to."

"You can. I swear to you on everything I hold dear that you can trust me with your heart." His hands drop to my legs and slide up the back of them to grasp my ass. "You're everything I've ever wanted and then some. I'll be as patient as you need me to be until you get to a place where you feel comfortable."

I press against him suggestively. "I'm feeling rather *un*comfortable at the moment."

"I can help with that."

"I don't want to overdo it. You'll be hurting later."

"I'm totally fine."

He guides me down, and as I straddle him and take him in once again, I let my head fall back in surrender to the incredible thrill of being with him this way. When he bites my nipple through the coverup, I gasp from the impact that hits me in all the most important places. This man... This beautiful, sweet, sincere, sexy man...

He might be the one to restore my faith.

MILO

We get dressed up for dinner, and she slays in a clingy black dress that leaves enough skin bare to have me counting the minutes until we get back to our room. Even after having had her three times, I want more. So much more. But I have to slow my roll so I don't overwhelm her. It's just hard to restrain such powerful emotions.

After today, I already know I want forever with her. Hell, I knew that the day I first saw her. It's funny how you can see a certain person and feel for them what you've never felt for anyone else. There're plenty of beautiful women on this ship, all of them dressed to the nines for dinner, but they may as well be trolls.

There's only her. She's all I see, all I want, all I need.

While we're at dinner, a member of the crew comes by to tell us they're expecting some rough seas overnight on the way to Nassau. He asks us to be careful walking around the ship.

"Do you get seasick?" I ask her. I'm wearing the blazer over a dress shirt and khaki pants. Gianna insisted I put the brace back on, so I did what I was told by my favorite nurse.

"I don't think so, but I've never been in rough seas before, so I'm not entirely sure. How about you?"

"I do a lot of offshore fishing with my family. I never get sick. Nico does, though. It pisses him off."

She laughs. "I'll bet it does."

"He hates to show any sign of weakness, except for lately. I'm hoping this break will get us back to normal because he's driving me crazy."

"I feel for him—and Sofia. They can't help but feel responsible for what happened to you."

"I get that. I really do, but it's over and done with."

"Not for them. You can see that, right?"

"I can. Of course I can, but they can't keep this up forever."

"They might try."

"I'll have to move out if they keep that up."

"They'll never let you leave."

"I'm a fully grown adult. I can do what I want."

"You'd break Nico's heart if you moved out."

"He can't possibly expect me to stay forever, especially now that he and Sofia are getting married and starting their own family."

"Of course, I don't know him the way you do, but I bet he'd protest you going anywhere. At least for a while."

Groaning, I say, "I worked hard to overcome the baby-brother label with all my siblings. I'm not about to go backwards."

"Aw, they love you."

"A little too much sometimes. Especially lately."

"You scared them, Milo. Your situation was grave at first. I saw your mom crying in the hallway once. Dr. Northrup was trying to comfort her, but she was inconsolable, and your sisters were, too."

"I feel bad that I put them through that."

"It wasn't your fault, but you need to expect them to be extra protective for a while."

"I guess there are worse problems I could have."

"For sure. It's cool that you're all so close. Have you always been?"

"God, no. The stories of us fighting as kids are epic. My parents used to say that they feared we wouldn't speak to each other as adults."

"That's funny. My brothers were so much younger than me that they fought with each other. After... When I was their guardian, that's when we did the most fighting."

"That was rough, huh?"

"The worst. They wanted nothing to do with me bossing them around, and honestly, I went easy on them. But any rule was one rule too many. They fought me on everything. I heard one or the other say, 'You're not my mother,' a thousand times. I couldn't wait for the younger one to leave for college, and then I felt guilty that I was so relieved they were gone."

"No one could blame you for that, Gianna."

"Still... I felt guilty."

"What're their names?"

"Greg and Leo. Greg is a junior at UCLA, and Leo is a sophomore at UC Irvine."

"What're they majoring in?"

"Greg is pre-law and Leo is in business for now. He's not sold on it, though. He may switch to finance."

"They're as smart as their sister."

"They're smarter. I had to work like a dog for every good grade I ever got. It comes much easier to them. Everything does."

"My siblings would say the same about me. The baby of the family has it made—or so they always said. Although, I will admit some things were easier for me."

"Like what?"

"My parents were less stringent about things like curfews with me than they were with Nico, but then again, they needed to be tougher with him. He was always up to something. I never was."

"Aw, you were such a good boy."

"I tried to be, not that I didn't get into my share of trouble with my friends. But it was all pretty innocent compared to Nico getting arrested in high school for drag racing on Calle Ocho."

"Whoops."

"I know. I thought my dad's head was going to explode over that one. I like to think I learned what *not* to do from Nico. He was always in trouble for something. It's a wonder my parents had more kids after him."

"That's funny. He seems so settled now with Sofia and Mateo. The ultimate family man."

"That's a recent development. Prior to that, he was a total player. I used to joke that he changed women more often than I changed my underwear. He would fire back and say no wonder my underwear is so crusty. Or something like that."

She laughs so hard that tears fill her eyes. "That's hilarious."

"Comments like that are much more in keeping with my usual groove with Nico. That's why the solicitousness is driving me crazy. I don't know what to do with this new version of him."

"Hopefully, you guys can get back to normal now that you're out of the hospital and doing so much better."

"I really hope so."

"You two are very cute together."

I scowl at that. "We are not."

"Yes, you are. My brothers used to fight like angry cats, so it's nice to see brothers as close as you and Nico are."

"From the day my parents brought me home from the hospital, he's been my best friend. Always there for me, even with six years between us. There was this one time when a kid was picking on me at school, calling me chubster and four eyes after I started wearing glasses and other awful names. I told Nico about it, and he asked me where we might find him. I said he works at McDonald's. So one Saturday, the two of us grabbed lunch there, and Nico stared at him the entire time. I don't think he blinked once in the entire hour we were there."

"That is awesome. Did it work?"

"Oh yeah. That kid never hassled me again—and neither did anyone else."

"I love that so much."

"He's a great big brother. He always has been. That's why it's so hard to see him suffering."

"He must've been devastated when he realized that bullet was meant for him."

"I can't even begin to know what that must've been like for him. I'm just glad it didn't tear him and Sofia apart. She's so perfect for him. I've never seen him as calm and settled as he is with her. At least until this happened."

"They'll get back there again. If they've made it this far, they're solid."

"I really hope so. I'd hate to have anything to do with messing things up for them, even indirectly."

"It's sweet how much you care about both of them."

"I really do. Sofia is great, and so is Mateo. They endured a nightmare with her ex and then with Mateo having cancer. They deserve some peace in their lives."

"Everyone does. Why is that so overrated? Why do people love drama so much? I hate that. I had friends in high school and college who were constantly stirring up shit and then complaining about why their lives were so chaotic. I never understood why they did that."

"People are weird. I think social media makes it even worse, which is why I've never joined any of the platforms."

"Me either! I hate how everyone shares everything these days. It's so weird to me."

"Yet another thing we have in common."

We share a warm smile that fills me with an incredible

feeling of euphoria. I've never experienced anything like it, not with a woman, anyway.

"When my parents died, one of my cousins posted about it before we'd told everyone who needed to know. I was so angry with her about that."

"Wow, that's crazy. Why would someone post that without checking with you first?"

"That's what we wanted to know. Leo told her to take it down, but the damage was already done. We got shocked calls from two of my father's childhood friends who heard about it on Facebook."

"I'm sorry. That must've made a horrible time that much worse."

"It did. Our cousin felt terrible about it. She apologized profusely, and of course, we forgave her, but like you said, it was the last thing we needed right then."

"What were they like? Your parents, that is."

"Your parents remind me a little of them. They were very devoted to each other, like yours are."

"They've definitely set the gold standard for marriage goals."

"Mine were like that, too. If there is any blessing in what happened, it was that they went together. We couldn't conceive of one without the other."

"I know what you mean. When my mom had breast cancer, I was almost more worried about my dad than I was about her."

"That must've been rough."

"It was, but she's doing great now, thank goodness. Her latest tests were good."

"I'm so glad about that for all of you—and me. She's been such a huge support to me with all the craziness with Jared. I feel a little guilty because she makes me feel like I have a mother again." She releases a nervous laugh. "I know that's weird."

"It's not weird. She has that effect on people. So many of our friends have 'adopted' our parents over the years. They always have a warm meal and a shoulder to cry on for anyone who needs them."

"They're lovely people."

"They really are. I appreciate them more all the time. But we were talking about your lovely parents, not mine. You were going to tell me more about them."

"Ah, right. Well, my mom was a dental hygienist. While we were growing up, she worked 'school hours' so she could be home with us in the afternoon and run us around to practices and stuff."

"What did you play?"

"Field hockey and lacrosse, all the way through high school."

"Wow, that's awesome. I never have been able to wrap my head around how to play lacrosse."

"It's a wild game that requires incredible stamina. I was always wiped out after a game."

"I'm very impressed—and a little turned on, to be honest."

Her laughter is the best thing ever, as is the flush that colors her cheeks. "Stop."

Grinning, I say, "I don't want to stop. Anyway, back to your parents…"

"My dad was a construction supervisor. He had a big job overseeing as many as twenty different projects at a time."

"Wow, that's cool. He must've been busy."

"He was. That's what made their deaths while on a well-deserved vacation that much worse."

"Oh no. That's terrible."

"They were killed in a car accident in Jamaica, which was super complicated. The State Department was involved in getting them home."

"I can't imagine what a nightmare that must've been."

"It was so shocking and devastating. For a couple of weeks afterward, it felt like a bad dream. I kept thinking they'd come strolling through the door and say it was a terrible misunderstanding or something."

I reach across the table to take her hand. "I'm sorry that happened to you and your family. Saying I'm sorry sounds so insignificant."

"It's not. Thank you. We were surrounded by incredible support for those first few weeks. My parents had great friends who've propped us up ever since. And my dad's company was incredible. They paid his full salary for a year, and his life insurance made it so my brothers could go to college, although we still incur travel and living expenses. We were lucky, though. Thanks to my parents' frugality, their house was paid for, and that made it so we didn't have to move on top of everything else."

"Where were you when this happened?"

"At the University of Florida in Gainesville. I was a second-semester junior. I transferred to FIU to finish so I could be at home with my brothers, who wished I was anywhere else but with them."

"Damn, Gianna. That must've been so rough."

"It was pretty awful for a while, but we've pushed through it, and our goal is to keep making them proud."

"They'd be so proud of you. I have no doubt."

"I hope so."

"How could they not be?"

"Thank you. They were thrilled about me becoming a nurse."

"I wish they could've seen how amazing you are with your patients."

"I like to think they're watching."

I give her hand a squeeze. "I'm so amazed by you. In every possible way."

"Can I tell you something?"

"Anything."

"Not once in the two years we were together did Jared ever

ask me to tell him about my parents. Of course he said he was sad they died, but he never asked me to tell him *about* them."

"He didn't deserve you."

"No, he really didn't, and I was in such a fog that I didn't even realize that until after it was over."

"Don't be too hard on yourself, Gianna. You went through a terrible thing that left you raw and unprotected in the aftermath. Your defenses were low, and he took full advantage." I lean in a little closer. "I wish I'd punched him when I had the chance."

CHAPTER 15

GIANNA

I'm falling so hard for him. I was before today, but after today… it's just gotten worse in the best possible way. He's so attentive, and he *listens*. He asked to see pictures of my parents and brothers and truly cares about what I have to say rather than always talking about himself, which is what I'm used to. It was never about me with Jared. Not ever.

And why was I okay with that?

The only thing I can think of is that I was still so numb from losing my parents that I got swept up in something that became too big too soon. And yes, that's exactly what's happening with Milo, and yet, I'm strangely calm when I shouldn't be.

I keep thinking about how Annie told me to go for it with Milo, that I deserved to be with a nice, sweet, sexy guy. And he's all those things as he holds me close on the dance floor after dinner. Our bodies fit together like two pieces of a puzzle, and he holds me like I'm the most precious thing in his life. Maybe I am, and wouldn't that be something?

I haven't felt like the most precious thing in anyone's life since I lost the people who always loved me more than anyone else.

"How's it going down there?" Milo asks as we sway to dreamy music from a live band.

"Best honeymoon I've ever been on."

His silent laughter rocks his body and makes me smile. "Me, too." After another minute, he says, "You want to keep dancing, or you want to go explore a bit?"

"I'm up for whatever you want to do."

He pulls back to look down at me. "I'm up for anything, too." To prove his point, he presses his hard cock against me. "But that'll keep if you want to hit the slots or something."

"I'd love to. I probably ought to confess my secret obsession with slot machines."

"Uh-oh. I knew you were too good to be true."

"There's still time to abandon ship now that you know this."

Milo keeps an arm around me as he guides me from the dance floor. "I'm not going anywhere but to the casino."

He no sooner says that than the floor under us seems to suddenly disappear. Only his arm around me keeps me from stumbling.

"We must've hit those rough seas they mentioned," he says.

I'm immediately queasy, but I keep that info to myself as we make our way up two decks to the casino as the ship pitches and rolls. "I'm wishing I never saw *Titanic*."

He cracks up. "Don't worry. There're no icebergs here."

"Thank goodness for that."

The second I see the bright lights of the casino, I feel a charge of excitement. "I used to play the slots with my mom. We'd go to the Hard Rock in Hollywood on many a Sunday afternoon. I haven't played since."

"Are you sure you feel up to it?"

"Yeah," I say with a sigh as I look around at the activity in the casino. "She'd want me to continue doing the things we loved to do together." I make my way toward a familiar-looking penny machine and take a seat. "Do you want to play?"

Milo sits at the machine next to mine. "I'd rather watch you."

A waitress comes by to take our drink order. Milo asks for a beer, while I order wine.

The casino is most definitely not included in the cruise package, so I insert a credit card to buy tokens and start pressing the buttons as I feel the rolling of the ship despite my fervent desire to ignore it. Despite my excitement to be playing slots for the first time since I lost my mom, the queasiness is getting worse, and the wine doesn't help.

"Are you okay?" Milo asks.

"I feel a little sick."

"Do you want to go back to the cabin?"

"Not yet." I force a smile for him even as my stomach roils. "I'm feeling lucky."

"Me, too," he says with a warm smile. "I've never felt as lucky as I have today, in fact."

"Today has been a very good day."

"I'm glad you've enjoyed it. You deserve to be happy."

"So do you."

"I'm extremely happy any time you're around."

I stare at him for so long, I nearly forget about the slot machine until an attendant comes by to ask if I'm done with the machine.

"Oh, sorry. No, not yet." I tear my gaze off my handsome companion and go back to pushing the buttons and watching the results, waiting for the right combination to come together to make this day completely perfect. After buying fifty dollars' worth of tokens, I'm nearly tapped out when a row of sevens gives me a thousand credits. The clanging of the machine brings back so many sweet memories with my mom that my eyes fill with tears.

I decide to cash out for now and use the new credits another time.

"Are you all right?"

"Yeah, sorry. Brings back a lot of memories. My mom won all the time."

"You didn't?"

"Once in a while, but not like she did."

I take the receipt for the tokens from the machine and take hold of the hand Milo offers me. "It was fun to do this again. Thanks for indulging me."

"My pleasure."

As we leave the casino, the floor rolls under us again, and I grasp Milo's jacket to keep from toppling over. My head is buzzing with a weird sensation that's new to me, and my stomach is so upset, I fear I might puke in the hallway.

"Let's go back to our room and get some air on the balcony," he says. "That might help."

I'm not so sure, but I take his word for it and let him lead the way back to our room. "I never thought to bring meds for seasickness. I didn't think I'd need them."

"I'll run to the ship's store and see what they have."

I'm so thankful for his calming presence as I feel worse by the second. It's so strange because the ship is barely moving, or so it seems, but you can't tell me that by the way my body is reacting.

In our room, Milo leads me straight to the balcony and throws open the doors to fresh, cool air that's an immediate relief. I take deep, greedy breaths, hoping the air will soothe me.

"Better?" he asks.

"A little. Thanks."

"I'm going to the store. I'll be right back."

"I'll be here."

While he's gone, I close my eyes and focus on breathing as I feel the ship moving through the choppy seas. Why didn't I think to bring something for seasickness, just in case? Isn't the Caribbean supposed to be calm? Are we even in the Caribbean yet? I have no clue, but I sure as hell wasn't expecting to feel so sick.

Thank goodness I'm with Milo, who's caring and considerate, whereas Jared would've been annoyed to have to tend to me when there was booze to drink and poker to play. Once again, I'm left stunned by the hindsight that keeps appearing where he's concerned. Why in the hell did I ever agree to marry a man like him?

In the year since he abruptly ended our relationship, I've come back around to one thought time and again—if my parents hadn't died, I never would've given Jared the time of day, let alone pledged to spend my life with him. There it is. The ugly truth. I was so screwed up after losing them and giving years of my life to my ungrateful brothers that I nearly made a very big mistake while trying to fill the void.

I shudder with revulsion, as much from my thoughts of him as from the seasickness. I hate to think that it took meeting Milo and experiencing his kind of sweetness to realize that Jared was so wrong for me, it's laughable. I would've been miserable married to him. How could I not have seen that? I'm still struggling with that question as much as I am with the nausea that's getting worse despite the fresh air.

Ugh, am I actually going to vomit?

I no sooner have that thought than my stomach surges and answers the question definitively. I'm up and running for the bathroom before I even decide I need to move quickly. I'm leaning over the toilet, expelling everything I've consumed all day, when Milo returns. It takes all the strength I have to close the bathroom door.

"Are you all right?" he asks from outside.

"Nope."

"Let me in. I want to help you."

"There's nothing sexier than seeing someone puke."

"You'll always be sexy to me, no matter what."

"Milo..."

He opens the door just in time to pull my hair back as another round of vomiting has me moaning from the embarrassment as much as the discomfort.

"You'll never want to have sex with me again after this," I whisper.

"I'll always want to have sex with you, so cut that out." He wipes a cold washcloth over my face and mouth that feels heavenly. "Do you think it's over?"

"For now, maybe."

He helps me up and puts toothpaste on my toothbrush, standing behind me in case I get wobbly. Then he helps me change into a T-shirt and boxers before helping me into bed.

"I'm sorry I ruined our first night at sea—and our first date."

Sitting on the side of the bed, he smooths the hair back from my face. "You haven't ruined anything. This is the best first date I've ever been on, and I hope..."

"What? What do you hope?"

He leans in to kiss my cheek. "That maybe this was my last first date."

MILO

She's sick all night. Nothing seems to help, even the seasickness medicine I got for her at the ship's store. I'm starting to worry it's more than seasickness when she finally falls asleep around five a.m. I snuggle up to her and close my eyes, exhausted from seeing her through such violent illness.

I'm so accustomed to strong, capable Gianna that it's distressing to see her so sick. But I'm glad I could care for her the way she cared for me when I was in the hospital.

With an arm around her so I'll know if she gets up again, I close my eyes and fall into a deep sleep. I awaken hours later to sun streaming in through the balcony door we left open overnight.

Gianna is lying on her back, looking up at the ceiling.

"How're you feeling?"

"Better."

"I'm so glad to hear that."

She looks over at me. "You were a trouper last night. Thank you for taking such good care of me."

"I was glad to return the favor, but I never want you to be sick like that again."

"This might be our first and last cruise."

"Fine by me."

"What time is it?" she asks.

"Twelve thirty."

"We missed the excursion to Nassau."

"Oh well. You wouldn't have felt up to that anyway. How do you feel about room service and movies today?"

"I feel very good about that." She takes my hand and cradles it between both of hers. "I also feel very good about you and this."

"I do, too. I feel very, very, *very* good about us."

"This is crazy, right? I mean, what are we even doing on a cruise ship together?"

GIANNA

His smile is a thing of beauty. "It's the best story ever, and if you ask me, we're both exactly where we belong with the person we were meant to be with."

While I tend to agree with him, not that long ago I thought Jared was that person for me.

Milo presses his finger on the spot between my brows. "Why the confused look?"

"I'm having the hardest time understanding what the hell I was doing with Jared. Everything you say and do is the opposite of what he would've said or done. He would've been so annoyed by me getting sick and ruining his good time. Why did I put up with that?"

"My Nona likes to say that people come into our lives for a reason, but they're not always meant to stay forever. Maybe he came along to show you what you don't want."

"That's possible, but how do you explain the fact that I was going to marry him? I'm really wrestling with that question. If he hadn't canceled the wedding, he'd be here instead of you, and that just feels so wrong."

"Do you believe that almost everything happens for a reason?"

"I used to until my parents died suddenly, and I couldn't find any good reason for that. I've had a crisis of faith ever since that. I used to go to church every week with my parents, but I haven't stepped foot in church since their funeral."

"That's understandable."

"I'm mad with God after He took them from us," I whisper, as I'm afraid to say it loud enough for God to hear me.

"I don't blame you. I'd be mad if I were you, too."

"You don't think I'm awful for being mad with Him?"

"Not at all." He caresses my cheek and slides his fingers through my hair. "I think you're amazing for holding up so well during such a tragedy and stepping up for your brothers."

"I did what anyone would do for their family, even if it sucked."

"Someday, when they're much older than they are now, they'll appreciate what you did for them and the sacrifices you made."

"You really think so?"

"I do. They're too young now to understand what you saved them from in foster care."

"I never could've let that happen to them. I didn't even know, until after my parents died, that they'd appointed me the boys' guardian if anything happened to them. I mean, why would they tell me that? They didn't expect anything to happen."

"It was good that they took care of that, though."

"It made everything easier after they died. We didn't have to go to court or anything."

"They were looking out for you, even from beyond."

"I guess. You want to hear something truly awful about me?"

"How can there be anything awful about you?"

"This is bad."

"Okay, lay it on me."

"I'm angry with them, too, for leaving us and for leaving me to deal with my brothers, who were so *awful* to me."

"No one could blame you for that, Gianna. Your whole life was turned upside down, and so much responsibility was put on your shoulders. Anyone would be angry about that."

"But to be angry with my dead parents, who did everything for me when they were here? I hate feeling that way, but I can't help it."

"I'm the youngest in my family, so I never would have had to care for a younger sibling if the worst thing had happened to us. I'm twenty-six, almost twenty-seven, and I can't *imagine* life without my parents. Not for one day, let alone forever. You have the right to feel any way you want to about what happened to them."

"It wasn't their fault. It's not like they wanted to die."

"Of course they didn't. I never knew them, but I know the wonderful daughter they raised, and I bet they'd totally understand you being angry with them for leaving you to manage your brothers. While they were in Jamaica, I bet they were enjoying being away from two teenage boys who were probably driving them crazy, too."

"They were. My mother used to talk to me about how they could've come from the same parents as I did. I never gave them any trouble."

"My parents say that about Nico and me," he says with a grin. "We're total opposites. They say he's lucky he had siblings, let alone three of them."

"That's funny."

"My siblings call me the 'golden child' because I was always well behaved and did what I was told."

"Aw, you're such a sweet boy."

"For all the good that's done me. Like I told you, women always want the bad boy. They were crazy about Nico."

"Not all women want the bad boy, Milo. Some of us just want peace and comfort and happily ever after."

He leans over to kiss me, and I recoil, imagining that my breath must stink after puking all night.

"Let me brush my teeth."

"Go for it. I'll be right here."

"Be right back."

When I stand, I'm hit by a wave of dizziness that has me sitting on the bed until the room stops spinning.

"Are you okay?"

"Just a little dizzy."

"We need to get some food into you. What do you feel like?"

"If there's French toast or pancakes, that would be good."

"I'll see what I can do."

While he gets up to find the room service menu, I head for the bathroom and nearly scream at the vision that greets me in the mirror. My hair is a beehive of mess, I have dark purple circles under my eyes, and my face is ghostly pale. Dear Lord. It's a wonder he didn't run screaming from the room at the sight of me this morning.

I do what I can to fix myself up, brush my teeth and wash my face. But I still look like hell, and I hate that when I'm having such a nice time with Milo. If I told him that, he'd say to knock it off, that I've seen him at his worst, too.

I love being with him, sharing confidences with him, kissing him and everything else with him. He feels like home to me, which is something I haven't had since the accident that took my parents. Our home was a war zone for years after we lost them, and I'm still decompressing from those years, even with my brothers out of the house now.

Home has been a complicated proposition for me lately. I thought I'd be making a new home with Jared, and the loss of that dream was the most difficult part of him ending our relationship. I know now that he couldn't give me what I needed, but Milo could, and he comes with a beautiful, welcoming, loving family that makes me want to glom on to them and the sweet comfort they offer so effortlessly.

I run a brush through my hair and pinch some color into my cheeks before leaving the bathroom to rejoin Milo in bed. I love his suggestion to snuggle and watch movies all day. I couldn't care less about an excursion when I'm exhausted and depleted after a rough night. Spending a day hunkered down with him sounds like perfection to me.

"Are you bummed to miss seeing Nassau?" Milo asks when I'm back in bed.

"I was just thinking how relieved I am to have nothing to do today. I'm sorry that you didn't get to go, though."

"I'd much rather be here with you."

"Once again, I'm forced to acknowledge that Jared wouldn't have been so gracious. He'd have been annoyed to miss something we'd paid for, even if it was because I was sick. He was always so impatient to go and do and hurry up and get where we were going. It drove me nuts trying to keep up with him."

"It's good that you're able to see these things with the benefit of hindsight."

"I'm still stuck on wondering why I didn't see it at the time, and I'm sorry to keep bringing that up, but being with you is making me see what was missing with him."

"Which is a lovely compliment, so thank you."

"Thank *you* for being so awesome."

"I hated seeing you feeling so lousy."

"Nothing says sexy honeymoon action like a good dose of seasickness."

Milo laughs. "Lesson learned. This'll be our first and last cruise. Our next vacation will be an all-inclusive resort with no sea time."

"You really think we'll have another vacation?"

"Baby, if I have my way, we're going to have everything."

CHAPTER 16

MILO

I can't believe I just put that right out there, but I have no regrets. I'm falling in love with her, and I want her to know how I feel, even if it's probably too soon for her after the Jared disaster. I liked hearing that being with me is helping her to see what was lacking in her relationship with him. I'm fine with being compared to him, since I keep coming out on top—and I plan to make sure I always do.

He didn't deserve her, and I want to always be worthy of her. I'll do whatever it takes to make her happier than she's ever been and to fill the gaping void her parents' deaths left in her. I know there's no replacing people who are irreplaceable, but my family and I will do what we can to make her feel loved and cared for again. That's one thing the Giordinos excel at doing.

My parents and siblings already loved her for taking such good care of me in the hospital, and that was before they got to know her better. Now I can tell they think she's perfect for me, and that works out well. I could never love someone they didn't like. And I'm starting to think I love Gianna, if the need to be with her all the time, to make her happy and to care for her through all of life's ups and downs is any indication.

"I ordered French toast and fruit for you," I tell her when she returns to the bed, where I'm sitting waiting for her.

"Thank you."

I hand her a glass of ice water. "Drink this. You don't want to get dehydrated."

"I probably already am."

"Do you think you should go to the clinic?"

"Nah, I'll be okay if I take it easy today."

My phone chimes with a text from Nico. I pick it up off the bedside table where it's been since we left port. I've barely looked at it with someone so much more important to focus on.

You won't believe it... Dom eloped with someone named Stacey that he went to HS with. They reconnected when he came back to Miami for the holidays. They took off to Vegas for a long weekend, and now they're married. WTF?!?

"Holy shit," I tell Gianna. "My cousin Domenic eloped over the weekend with someone none of us know. Her name is Stacey."

Nico sends me a picture of the newlyweds. *He says he's never been happier and wants everyone to be happy for him.*

I share the follow-up text with Gianna. "Wow."

I write back to Nico. *Holy crap! Bombshell. Did he tell his parents?*

I asked him that but haven't heard back. How's the trip?

Great, except Gianna was seasick last night. She's better today, but it was rough.

Aw, too bad. That sucks. Glad she's better. Are you guys... having fun?

Yes, Nico, we're having fun. Butt out.

Hahahaha. That'll be the day. I like her for you, bro. We're all hoping you guys have a great time and that this is the start of something awesome for you.

I think it will be. I'm crazy about her.

Love it. Keep me posted. And don't go eloping. You'll break Mom's heart. And mine. I'm ready to be your best man—but only if you'll be mine. You will, right?

Hell yes. You got it. Have you guys set a date?

We're looking at the fall when it's not so crazy hot.

Let me know when and where, and I'll be there—after I throw you one hell of a bachelor party.

I'm not afraid of what you'll do for me, but you should be VERY afraid of what I'll do for you. He adds a devil emoji for effect.

Hahaha. I'm very afraid.

You should be. The minute you're engaged, I'm booking the Ball & Chain.

That makes me laugh. *Go away and leave me alone. I'm very busy.*

Have the best time, bro.

Will do. Say hi to everyone.

He responds with a thumbs-up.

"He just asked me to be his best man when he marries Sofia."

"Aw, that's so sweet."

"I'm so glad he's marrying Sofia."

"Do you like Austin and Wyatt, too?"

"Oh, I love them both. Despite all his success, Austin is so normal and down-to-earth. Lots of fun to be with. And Wyatt… You'd never know he's basically living on borrowed time."

"What do you mean?"

"He had a heart transplant at seventeen."

"Oh my God. How old is he now?"

"Thirty-four."

"Damn."

"The life expectancy is around eleven years."

"I know."

"He's in perfect health, though, and Dee is determined to

enjoy every second she gets with him and to hell with what 'might' happen."

"That makes her very brave."

"I know. I was unnerved by it when I heard he was already something like seven years past his so-called expiration date, but she doesn't want to talk about that. They're even planning to have kids."

"Good for them. What else can you do but live your life, right?"

"I suppose. I just worry about what'll become of her if she loses him."

"She'll survive because she always knew it was a risk, so it won't be like some sort of big surprise that comes out of nowhere. When I was in school, we learned about a thing called anticipatory grief, which is what you go through when you know you're going to lose someone. They wanted us to be aware of that with patient families. Dee is probably working through some of that now, which will prepare her for whatever challenges they might encounter."

"I'm really amazed by her strength. It never occurred to her to say, 'Nope, I can't do this.' She was all in with him, and that was that. Even when he tried to talk her out of being all in, she wasn't hearing it."

"Your family is very inspiring in so many ways."

"They're pretty awesome."

"Is it okay to say that I like being with them almost as much as I like being with you?"

"That's more than okay, since I could never be with someone who doesn't gel with them. I dated this one woman, Natalia. Carmen and my sisters couldn't stand her. They said she was snotty and pretentious."

"Was she?"

"Maybe a little. But I was mad that they never gave her a chance, which sort of ruined it for me."

"Their opinions matter that much to you?"

"Unfortunately, yes. The three of them and Nico have always been larger than life to me. I guess that's the burden of being the youngest. But there were pluses, too. I always had a ride anywhere I wanted to go and could hit them up for money and advice and anything else I needed."

"You really milked the baby brother thing, huh?"

"Maybe just a little," I say with a grin.

"It's obvious they all adore you."

"Never more so since I was nearly killed."

"Ugh, I can't even think about that without wanting to cry."

"Don't cry, sweetheart. I'm right here, and I'm going to stay right here for as long as you'll have me." I reach for her hand and link our fingers.

"That's apt to be a while."

"That'd be more than fine with me."

"I can't believe this. I can't believe *you*. A year ago, I was in a heap of heartbreak thinking my life was destroyed, and now..."

"Now what?" I ask, holding my breath as I wait to hear what she'll say.

"Now it's like Jared never happened, and all I want is to be with you."

Now *those* are the best words I've ever heard.

GIANNA

Today is right out of a dream, even though we've done nothing but eat room service and watch movies. I picked the first one —*Notting Hill*—and he chose the second, one of the Fast and Furious movies. I dozed off during that one, but he didn't mind. He held me and rubbed my back while I slept, and when I wake up, I feel almost back to normal and more relaxed than I've been in longer than I can remember.

He's so easy to be with. It's effortless between us, and the voice inside me is saying things like "this is the way it's supposed to be," and "thank God you didn't marry Jared."

The thought of being married to Jared is preposterous after spending two days with Milo. I'm not saying this thing with him will last forever, but I'm so glad I've gotten to be with him and to experience this adventure with him. Lost inside the bubble of my honeymoon that wasn't, it's easy to get caught up in the magic of it all with him. But will that magic follow us back to reality, to jobs and family and other challenges?

That remains to be seen. For now, I intend to enjoy every minute of the magic bubble while it lasts. "I'm going to grab a shower. If you feel like going out tonight, we can."

"I'm up for whatever you want to do. If you want to be lazy for a while longer, I'm down with that."

"Let me see how I feel after the shower."

"I'll be awaiting your update."

I go up on my knees and surprise him with a kiss. "Today has been so fun."

He twirls a length of my hair around his finger. "For me, too."

"Even though we didn't do a damned thing?"

"I was with you. That's all I need to have fun."

"You're so certain about me."

"Does that scare you?"

"Not like it should."

"I don't ever want you to be afraid of me or anything to do with me." He places his hand on my chest, over my heart. "I know you've suffered a lot, and I hate that for you. All I want is to make you happy, which is all it will take to make me happy."

"I hate to feel lucky because you got shot and nearly killed."

He laughs. "Trust me, I feel lucky about that, too, even if it sucked in so many ways. To think I might never have met you if I hadn't been shot… Life is crazy sometimes."

"It sure is, and for once, it's been crazy in a good way lately."

"I'm glad to be your good crazy."

"Will you understand if at some point I freak out because this is happening too fast for me?"

"I'll be right here to remind you that sometimes fast is good."

"Thank you for being so understanding. You make it easy to be a neurotic mess."

"You're anything but a mess. You've been through a lot, and you're still dealing with fallout. I get that. But guess what?"

"What?"

"Life marches on regardless of what's happening in our worlds, and sometimes all we can do is hang on and enjoy the ride."

"I'm really enjoying the ride."

"I'm glad to hear that. You need to give yourself permission to chalk up the Jared thing to something that wasn't meant to be and fully enjoy the present. Take a page from Dee's book. Let's live like we're dying."

"Nobody is dying on my watch."

"You're very sexy in nurse mode, except when you're coming for my catheter. Then? Not so much."

I laugh so hard, I have tears in my eyes. "You were very stoic."

"It hurt like a motherfucker."

"I'm very sorry."

"Sure, you are, Nurse Ratched."

"You were very brave."

"I was quaking on the inside."

"You boys and your penises. You're so delicate."

"On behalf of mine and all the others in the world, I resent that."

I kiss his pouty lips. "I have a feeling you'll get over it the minute I give him a little attention."

"I'm already over it if you're considering some attention."

"Let me shower first."

"My penis and I will be right here thinking of the many ways you can give him attention."

I roll my eyes and leave him to his thinking while I shower away the sickness. The hot water feels like heaven, loosening the knots in my shoulders and the ache in my abdomen. I hate vomiting. It's the worst thing, especially in front of my new boyfriend, or whatever Milo is to me. But he rolled with it like it was no big deal and earned major points for being so sweet and understanding. As I rinse conditioner out of my hair, I think about how my mom used to tell us if something—or someone—seems too good to be true, they probably are.

In Milo's case, that just doesn't ring true. I haven't seen an ounce of insincerity or anything to set off alarms, and trust me, I'm looking after missing so many red flags with Jared. But from everything I've seen, Milo is exactly what he seems. And even though I'm still a bit hesitant, I just want to wallow in the comfort of being with him.

If he breaks my heart, I'll lose faith in all men.

It's that simple—and that complicated.

After I dry my hair, I smooth scented lotion over my body and don a robe provided by the ship, tying it around my waist when I go out to rejoin him. The first thing I notice is that he's removed his neck brace. His eyes are closed as he moves his head back and forth, stretching his muscles.

"Let me help."

His eyes open and then widen when he looks at me, as if he can't believe I'm real. I love the way he looks at me and could easily get addicted to the sort of attention and affection he gives so effortlessly.

I nudge him to scoot forward on the bed and get behind him to massage his neck and shoulders, being careful to avoid the healing scar.

His head drops forward, and he moans. "Feels so good."

"Is the scar still itchy?"

"Not like it was."

"It's looking a little red. Does it hurt?"

"It's more of an ache than a hurt."

"Has it been that way all along?"

"A little more so today than yesterday."

"We need to keep an eye on it. It could be infected."

"No way."

"Yes way."

"What do we do if it is?"

"Get you to the clinic for IV antibiotics."

"Yikes. Let's hope it doesn't come to that."

"I'll be watching it."

"I'm very lucky to have my own personal nurse to tend to my every need. I have a few other aches and pains you might be interested in checking."

"Is that right? Anything serious?"

"A few that might be."

"Show me."

He reaches up to take my hand and drags it down his muscular chest to encircle his erection, which is long and thick.

I love the deep moan that comes from him as he uses my hand to stroke himself.

"God, that's hot, Gi."

I move from behind him and settle between his legs. "Sit back and relax."

"Right. You want me to relax when you're doing *that*?"

"Yeah, I do."

He leans back against the pillows, but every muscle in his body is on full alert as he waits to see what I'll do.

I lean over him, letting my hair drag over his abdomen.

He gasps and tightens his hold on my hand around his cock. "Gianna..."

"Yes, Milo?"

"I, um... Oh *God*."

He says that after I take him into my mouth.

"You're supposed to be relaxing," I remind him.

"Sure. Like that's going to happen."

He makes me laugh even when I'm trying to be serious. I add that to the growing list of things I like about him as I take him in again, thankful that he doesn't try to give me more of him than I can handle, the way Jared did—once. After that, I refused to do this with him. But I'm not going to think about him, not when Milo is hot and hard in my mouth and squirming under me as his hands tangle in my hair.

He's breathing fast, and his abs are quivering as I lick and stroke him.

"Gi... Gianna..."

I hear the note of warning, but I keep going until he cries out as he comes.

"Damn," he says on a deep exhale. "That was... Holy shit." He holds out his arms to me, and I crawl on top of him.

"Does it hurt your neck to have me on top of you?"

"God, no. Nothing hurts. You're beautiful and sexy, and I'm falling so hard for you. No wait, that's not true. I've already fallen for you, and I'm just hoping you feel a fraction of what I do, because that would make my whole life perfect."

"I do feel it, Milo. How could I not? You're the best."

He tightens his arms around me, and I feel him come back to life under me. "Sorry. That's gonna happen any time I'm holding you."

"That's okay."

"You should take it as a compliment. I look at you, and I want you. I hold you, and I want you. I kiss you, and I want you. I talk to you, and I want you. You're in the room? I want you. You're not in the room? I want you."

"That's a whole lot of want."

"Along with a big bunch of need."

"This is getting serious."

"What did you think would happen when you took me on your honeymoon?"

Right when I start to feel a bit panicked, he makes me laugh again, and I forget why I was worried when he smoothly rolls us over so he's on top of me. He gazes at me with warm brown eyes that convey nothing but affection and desire. "I hope you know..."

He stops himself when he seems to think better of whatever he was going to say.

"That I know what?"

"I realize the timing is tough for you, that you feel like it's too soon after... well, you know. But everything about this feels so right and so perfect to me. I've never been happier to lounge in bed all day with anyone the way we have today. And, well, I just wanted you to know that."

I place my hand on his face and feel the sting of his whiskers against my palm. "And I want you to know that it's been a while since I've felt as cared for as you made me feel when I was sick. I'm always taking care of other people."

"You deserve to have someone who thinks only of you."

"And you want to be that person?"

"More than I've ever wanted anything in my entire life."

CHAPTER 17

MILO

It's all so perfect that I worry it can't possibly last. Even though we hate a lot of things about the cruise, we still manage to have a great time. On the excursion to Grand Cayman, we meet another couple on their honeymoon. Jamie and Breck are from Chicago and are super fun to hang out with. Initially, we told them we were on our honeymoon, too, but on the beach in St. Martin, we come clean with them about the true story.

"So, wait," Jamie says. She's blonde and curvy and has a native Texan twang that cracks us up. "Y'all met when you got shot and she was your nurse after her wedding was canceled?"

"Just like that," I reply, smiling at Gianna.

"I would never have guessed that you weren't legit," Breck says. He's got dark hair and muscles on top of muscles. The two of them are clearly mad for each other.

"Our first date was this cruise," Gianna adds.

"That's so cool," Jamie says. "What a story you'll have to tell if you stay together. Do you think you will?"

"If I have anything to say about it," I respond, gazing at Gianna.

"We're sure going to try," she adds, which is the best thing she could've said. "We're having fun."

Other than Gianna's growing concern over the redness surrounding my incision, everything is great. I promised her I'd go to the clinic when we get back to the ship later today. I don't want to mess up her day by mentioning that I feel like I might have a fever, which is a strange sensation when you're lying in the sun.

"So how did you guys meet?" Gianna asks the other couple.

"We met on spring break in Cancun when we were in college. I was at the University of Texas, and Breck was at Loyola in Chicago. We somehow made it work long distance for a year, and after he got a great job in finance in Chicago, I moved to live with him. Now I'm the office manager at his firm."

"How long were you together before you got married?" Gianna asks.

"Four years."

"That's amazing. Congratulations."

"Thanks. We're happy to have the wedding behind us so we can get back to normal, right, honey boo?"

"That's right," Breck says. "Our mothers drove us crazy planning the extravaganza. It got way out of hand."

"But it was a magical day," Jamie says. "I loved every second of it. Did your mom drive you crazy, too?"

"I wish," Gianna says. "She and my dad died in an accident more than four years ago."

Breck gasped. "Oh God. I'm so sorry I said that about our mothers."

"Don't worry about it. You couldn't have known."

"I'm so sorry, Gianna," Jamie says. "That must've been awful."

"It was."

"She was in college when it happened and moved home to care for her two younger brothers until they graduated from high school."

"Wow," Jamie says. "That's incredible. Are you super close to them?"

"God, no," she says on a laugh as she sips a piña colada. "They can't stand me because they had to do what I told them to when I was the last person they wanted as their guardian. Sadly for them, it was me or foster care. I think they would've preferred foster care."

"They'll appreciate it someday," Breck says. "My parents got divorced when I was in eighth grade. It was ugly, and my older sister stepped up for me, taking me to her place for weekends and stuff. At the time, I didn't really think much of her either, but with hindsight, I can see that she saved me from a lot of crap. They'll see it, too."

"Maybe. But even if that never happens, I'd still do it again, for my parents."

"They'd be proud of you, sweetie," Jamie says. "Heck, I barely know you, and I'm proud of you."

I squeeze Gianna's hand. I love to hear people acknowledging the sacrifices she's made for her family.

Breck clears his throat. "If I can also say... What's with your ex calling off the wedding? He's a fool."

"I know, right?" I smile at Gianna, who's hot as fuck in a black bikini. "His loss is my gain."

"It's funny how things happen, isn't it?" Gianna poses the question to all of us. "Jared calls off our wedding because he 'just doesn't feel ready for that kind of commitment,' and then Milo takes a bullet that was meant for his brother, and here we are, sitting on a beach in St. Martin, making new friends together."

"Life is crazy," Breck says. "I was five minutes away from different plans on the day I met Jamie. I think all the time about how I wouldn't have even known what I missed out on if I'd gone on that snorkeling trip instead of hanging on the beach that day."

"Aw, honey boo-boo. You're the sweetest."

Breck kisses the back of her hand. "I wouldn't have wanted to miss meeting you. That would've been tragic."

"That's really sweet, Breck," Gianna says. "It makes me wonder what we've all missed by doing one thing instead of another."

"My Nona believes we're all on the path we're meant to be on," I say. "She says nothing happens by accident."

"Your Nona is very wise," Jamie says, and then she laughs. "Aren't we a philosophical bunch today? I don't know about y'all, but I need another cocktail."

"I'll come with you," Breck says. "Can we get you another round?"

"Sure," I say for both of us. "Thanks."

"Nice people," Gianna says after they walk away.

"Very nice, but please don't ever call me honey boo-boo, okay?"

"No problem," she says with a snort of laughter. "Do you believe the same thing your Nona does, that nothing happens by accident?"

"I think maybe I do."

"So it's possible that I had to go through what I did with Jared and you had to be shot so the universe could bring us together?"

I turn on my side to face her, all worries about a fever forgotten. "What other explanation could there be for our immediate connection after the universe was kind enough to put us in the same place at the same time?"

She reaches over from her chair to mine, placing her hand on my face, her eyes soft with affection until they change suddenly. "Milo. You're burning up."

"From being in the sun."

"No." She sits up and reaches for the dress she wore over her bikini. "We need to get back to the ship."

"Not for a few more hours."

"Right now."

Jamie and Breck return, carrying two drinks each.

"I'm sorry to say we have to leave," Gianna tells them. "Milo has a fever, and I want him to get checked on the ship as soon as possible."

I'm all set to object again, but as I stand to put on my shirt, the whole beach seems to tilt like I'm on an amusement park ride. What the hell is that about?

Gianna grabs my arm. "Milo!"

"We'll come with you," Breck says.

The next hour is sort of vague as the three of them escort me back to the ship and straight to the clinic. I doze off for a while and come to with only Gianna there, watching over me with a worried expression.

"What happened?"

"You've been totally out of it."

"For how long?"

"About twelve hours now. We were this close to having you airlifted back to the States."

"Seriously?"

"Very." Her eyes fill with tears. "You scared me."

"I'm sorry." I start to raise my arm to take her hand, but my arm feels like it weighs a ton.

She covers my hand with hers. "Don't try to do anything yet. Your fever only broke an hour ago."

I blink her into focus and see that she's wearing the same dress she wore to the beach. "Have you been here all this time?"

"Where else would I be?"

"Gianna..."

"Yes, Milo?"

"I don't want you to worry about me."

She smooths the hair back from my forehead. "Too late."

"Sorry to ruin our good time."

"As long as you're going to be okay, nothing is ruined."

"You didn't tell my family about this, did you?"

She shakes her head. "I was going to have to if we airlifted you. Thankfully, it didn't come to that. They had good IV antibiotics on board. The clinic is much more impressive than expected."

"Have you been riding roughshod over them?"

She raises an eyebrow that makes her look sassy even if I can see she's exhausted. "What do you think?"

"I think I got very lucky the day you became my nurse, and I keep getting luckier all the time."

GIANNA

After Milo is released from the clinic with oral antibiotics, we sleep for twelve hours. I wake several times and check to make sure his fever hasn't returned. I was scared for a while there, especially since the infection came on so suddenly. It's rare for a wound to become infected so long after surgery, but it can happen. We got lucky that he responded so quickly to the antibiotics, but the incident weakened him.

I'm not letting him do anything but lie in the sun on the ship for the last two days on board.

He turns on his side and puts his arm around me. "Are you fretting?"

"A little."

"I'm okay."

"You are now, but it was scary for a few hours."

"I'm sorry to put you through that."

"It's been an eventful trip."

"You know how the wedding vows talk about sickness and health?"

"Uh-huh."

"We've already proven ourselves to each other during sickness on our honeymoon."

"That's true."

"When we get home, we'll focus on enjoying some good health."

"I'd be all for that."

"We're just getting started. Tell me you know that."

"I do. I'm looking forward to what comes next."

"Me, too."

~

Two days later, we dock in Fort Lauderdale and follow the crowds off the ship. I'm relieved to be back on land, especially since he's not bouncing back from his setback as quickly as I'd like him to. He says he's fine, but he's weak and moving slowly. Thankfully, the incision looks much better.

"Am I taking you back to your place?" I ask when we're in the car.

"What're my options?"

"You could come home with me, if you wanted to."

"I want to as long as I won't be in your way."

"Not at all, but I do have to go to the grocery store and do some laundry before I go back to work."

"That's fine by me."

"All right, then."

Milo takes my hand and rests his head against the seat. "I hate feeling so wiped out." He shifts his gaze toward me. "Thank you for being such a trouper the last couple of days."

"It was no problem."

We skipped the excursion in Montego Bay to stay on the ship the last two days, which he said he felt bad about.

"I'll make it up to you with a trip to an all-inclusive resort as soon as we can get away again."

"Don't worry about that. I couldn't care less about the excursions."

"It's depressing to think our next vacation could be quite some time from now, since I've already missed so much work. But I'm sure we'll find a way to entertain ourselves here until we can go on vacation again."

I smile at him. "I have no doubt about that."

MILO

I text my family to let them know we're back in Miami and that I'll be at Gianna's.

Nico responds first. *I guess that means the trip went well.*

The trip went well.

When will we see you? Mom asks a few minutes later.

In the next couple of days. Will check in tomorrow. I don't want them to see me until I'm feeling back to where I was when I left on the trip. My mom and Maria, the nurse, will take one look at me and see the setback. I don't feel like dealing with their concern, especially when Gianna is offering the opportunity for more time together.

She lives in her parents' home in Silver Bluff Estates, about thirty minutes south of Little Havana.

"I played baseball with brothers who lived out this way."

"It was a nice place to grow up."

As we pull up to the two-story tan stucco house, we notice a car parked at the curb.

"Who's that?" Gianna asks.

If she has to ask, at least it isn't Jared.

We get out of the car while a woman alights from the car at the curb.

"Julia? Is that you?"

"It's me."

Gianna meets her in the driveway and gives her a hug.

"I knew you were due back today, so I decided to come by rather than texting."

"Why? What's going on?"

"Can we talk inside for a minute?"

"Sure. Um, this is Milo. Milo, Julia, my friend from college."

"Nice to meet you," she says.

"You, too."

We leave the bags in the car and go inside.

Gianna disengages the alarm and offers Julia a glass of water. "That's about all I have."

"I'm fine, and I'm sorry to drop by like this, but I wanted to tell you in person that Scott's been arrested."

Only because I'm watching her so closely do I see all the color leach from Gianna's expression.

"*What?*" she asks on a whisper.

I have so many questions, but I keep my mouth shut because this news has clearly flattened her. She sits next to Julia on a barstool in the kitchen.

"We're all shocked," Julia says tearfully.

Feeling like I'm intruding, I lean against the counter, hoping one of them will say something that clues me in to what's going on.

"When did this happen?"

"Two days ago. I heard it on the news this morning. The report only said he was arrested in connection to the disappearance of his college girlfriend, Skylar Jones, who's been missing for seven years."

Oh shit.

"I… I can't believe it. He's done so much to try to find her. All this time, we've stood by him…"

I can't help myself. I go to her and rest my hands on her shoulders, wanting to offer comfort since she's clearly in distress. I'm shocked when her muscles go rigid under my hands, as if a stranger just touched her. I immediately back away.

"I spoke with Allison this morning," Julia says. "We agree that it must be a mistake. If he did it…"

"Then none of us can trust our judgment when it comes to men."

I want to wail in objection and remind her that she can trust me, even if she can't trust anyone else.

"I'm so sorry to do this to you when you're just back from your trip and after everything else that's happened."

"No, you were right to tell me. Of course I want to know, and I'd much rather hear it from you than on the news."

Julia leans in to hug her.

They hold each other for a long time, and when they finally pull back, they're both in tears.

"Brings it all back, doesn't it?" Julia asks her softly.

"Yeah." Gianna wipes away tears.

"I need to get going," Julia says. "Call me later?"

"I will. Let me know if you hear anything."

"For sure."

"Nice to meet you, Milo."

"You, too."

Gianna walks her out and comes back with tears on her cheeks.

"What can I do for you?"

"I… um… I don't know. I just… I don't know."

Everything about her is different than it was before she saw Julia. It's like she's someone else.

"Do you want to talk about it?"

The look she directs my way is so full of pain and agony that it nearly takes my breath away.

"Gianna…" I step toward her.

"I can't, Milo."

I stop in my tracks. "What can't you do?"

"Any of this. I just can't."

"Wait. What?" I keep my voice calm when I'm anything but. "I understand the news Julia delivered was devastating, even if I don't know the details. But please don't push me away because of something that has nothing to do with me or us."

I ache for her when she breaks down into sobs. I need to comfort her, so I move carefully to put my arms around her. When she leans her head against my chest, I release a sigh of relief. Even though I'm exhausted and my legs are still a bit wobbly beneath me, I'm glad to be the one helping her through this latest crisis.

I'm not sure how long we stand there like that, but I'm thankful she's allowing me to comfort her. "Please don't push me away, sweetheart. I want to help."

CHAPTER 18

MILO

After a long while, she steps back from me and then leads the way to the living room. We sit on the tan sofa in the tastefully decorated room, which is probably just as her mother left it. I look forward to the opportunity to take a closer look at the photos of little Gianna on the walls.

"I was a freshman in college," she says softy, "when one of my suitemates disappeared. Her boyfriend, Scott, lived downstairs and was so distraught that we all supported him through the investigation, the accusations, the never-ending nightmare. They'd been together since high school, and our hearts were broken for him. For all the years since, we've stood by him even as the cloud of suspicion never lifted from him. He was the last to see her alive, but he insisted he had nothing to do with it."

"That must've been so difficult."

"It was. Julia was much closer to Skylar than I was, but it was the worst thing I ever went through until my parents' accident. And now... after all these years... that Scott has been arrested.

It's just... I'm so shaken. He's been like a brother to me. That he could've been lying to us all this time..."

I have no idea what to say, so I just keep an arm around her and listen.

"They were so in love. We were all envious of her, that she'd found 'the one' so early in her life and that they were making it work in college. He was a great boyfriend. Super supportive of her and nice to us and her other friends. Some of the guys would get upset if we wanted to do a girls' night, but Scott would offer to drive us and pick us up after."

She drops her face into her hands as she begins to cry again. "After my parents died, he stayed here for a week. He did everything for me. He even went with me to pick out the caskets and plan the funeral. For a time, before I met Jared, I considered taking him up on his offer to go to dinner sometime. If he killed her... I don't know what I'll do."

"I know this is shocking news, but you should wait to hear more before you think the worst."

"They wouldn't have arrested him and made that public if they didn't have evidence of some kind."

"Probably not, but I still say you should wait until you know more."

"I trusted him, Milo. We all did. Our group of friends from the freshman dorm are still very close because of what we went through. Julia and Ali were supposed to be in my wedding. He slept in this house with me and my brothers. What if he did kill her and I let him stay here with us?"

"You let a trusted friend stay with you. Anyone would've done what you did, based on what you knew at the time."

"God, I feel sick. Heartsick and every other kind of sick."

"I'm sorry, Gianna. I hate this for you."

She takes a deep breath and makes a visible effort to rally. "I need to grocery shop and do the laundry..."

"We'll use Instacart." I call up the app on my phone. "Do your order and type in the address. I'll get the suitcases and do the laundry."

"You don't have to do that."

"I want to. Let me help."

"Thank you, but you're not lifting the suitcases. I'll do that."

"Fine, but I'm doing the laundry."

For the first time in an hour, the right side of her face lifts ever so slightly into a smile. "I'm sorry to mess up our good time."

"You didn't." I kiss her forehead and then her lips. "And I can only imagine how you must be feeling, that if you can't trust your friend of so many years, how can you ever trust anyone, especially a man, but please don't do that. I promise you can trust me with your life and in your life, and I'll never do anything but love and protect you and care for you with everything I have to give."

She starts to cry again, and I hold her close while her sobs break my heart. I'm relieved that she's leaning on me rather than pushing me away, but I'm still worried that the news about her friend is going to cause a rift between us. How could it not, coming so soon after Jared broke her heart? I'm determined to remain steadily by her side until she believes that she can count on me.

I start by overseeing her order on Instacart while she sits listlessly on the sofa, reciting the groceries she needs. I add a couple of extra things so I can make dinner for us and place the order. Next, I go out to her car and retrieve the suitcases, which happens before she can register an objection to me carrying them. I still feel shitty, but I power through because she feels worse than I do, and I want to be there for her.

I find the laundry room right off the garage entrance to the house and toss in clothes from both our suitcases and start the wash.

Gianna takes a call from her friend Ali, and I hear her

commiserating about how devastating the news about Scott is to them. "What do we do?" she asks at one point.

I wish I could hear Ali's answer.

"Yes, I know," Gianna says. "Keep me posted? Okay, talk soon. Love you, too."

I take a seat on the sofa next to her. "What did she have to say?"

"The same stuff as me and Julia—disbelief and despair over how we could've been supporting the guy who killed our friend for all these years. She said Skylar's parents are beside themselves. They've treated Scott like a son."

"Wow, I can't imagine how they must feel."

"It's just inconceivable to all of us that he might be responsible for years of heartache." She seems to try to shake off the despair. "I'd understand if you didn't feel like hanging out. This is a lot."

"I'm not going anywhere, unless you want me to leave."

"I don't."

"Then no more worries about me. We need to take care of you. What can I do for you?"

"I don't even know."

"How about a bubble bath and a glass of wine?"

"That actually sounds good."

"Where will I find a tub?"

GIANNA

I direct Milo to the main bedroom, which belonged to my parents. I haven't done anything with their room and rarely go in there, but there's a soaking tub in the attached bathroom, and a relaxing bath does sound good to me right now. I'm so incredibly shaken by the news about Scott that I can't imagine anything will calm my nerves, but I appreciate Milo's efforts.

"Leave it to me," he says, getting up to make it happen.

I should be tending to him after what he's been through in the last few days, but I can't seem to do anything other than sit in complete disbelief. I think about Scott running to me when my parents died, how he was such a huge help to me and my brothers as we walked through the unfathomable steps of planning a wake and funeral for them. He did everything he could to make it easier on us. I remember thinking at the time that he was the best person to help me, having been through something similar himself.

And to think now that he might've been responsible for Skylar's disappearance and presumed death...

I just can't believe it.

My brain refuses to process this information. It's simply inconceivable.

Milo returns and holds out a hand to help me up.

"You shouldn't be doing any of this."

"I'm fine."

"I'll be the judge of that."

"I love when you nurse me," he says, grinning.

I appreciate the moment of lightness in the cloud of darkness that's descended over the last hour. The last thing in the world I expected was anything like this waiting for me when I got home.

Milo helps me out of my clothes and holds my hand as I get into the tub, which is surrounded by lit candles that belonged to my mom.

"Feels good. Thank you."

"You're welcome. Be right back."

While I soak, he goes to find me a glass of wine that he delivers to me in the tub.

"A girl could get used to this level of service."

"That'd be fine with me."

He sits on the chaise lounge my father wrestled into the

bathroom after my mom bought it on a whim. The memory makes me smile. "That chair... My mom bought it without measuring anything, and my dad had to take the door off the hinges to get it in here. He wasn't happy, but she was thrilled."

"That's a sweet memory."

"They were funny together."

"My parents are, too. I want what they have."

"I've always wanted what my parents had."

"Maybe we can have that together."

"That'd be nice." I wish I could focus only on him, but the pit in my stomach is a reminder that I've suffered yet another serious shock. My cell phone rings.

"It's Leo," Milo says as he hands me the phone I left on the vanity.

"Hey," I say when I take the call.

"I'm at Greg's for the weekend. We heard the news about Scott, and we're in shock."

"Me, too."

"God, Gi... We can only imagine how you must feel." This is the first time my brothers have ever called to check on me, and the swell of emotion only adds to the turmoil swirling inside me.

"I'm devastated."

"Do you want us to come home?"

The offer brings tears to my eyes. "No, that's okay. My friends here are taking good care of me," I say with a meaningful look at Milo. "But it means a lot to me that you called."

"We wish there was something we could do," Greg says.

"This call was all I needed. Are you guys doing all right?"

They ask about the cruise, and we talk for a few more minutes about school and their jobs and when they might get home again.

"Keep us posted?" Leo asks.

"I will."

"Take care, Gianna," Greg says. "Let us know if you need anything."

"Thanks again for calling, guys."

I hand the phone to Milo. "Wow, that was a first. They sound really worried about me."

"It was nice of them to call."

"It was."

Milo sits back in the chair. "Tell me about Skylar."

As always, he surprises me in the best possible way by asking about my friend. "Oh, well... She was all lightness and joy, bubbly, funny, sweet. She had wildly curly blonde hair that she refused to straighten because, as she said, she didn't want to look like everyone else. The humidity in Gainesville made her hair *huge*, and she just laughed and referred to herself as the chia head."

"That's funny. She sounds like a great girl."

"She was, and she was madly in love with Scott. They'd been together since high school in the Tampa area. We used to call them Mom and Dad because they were like the parents of our group, always telling us to be safe and not drink too much and get some sleep and asking, 'Did you eat?' That kind of thing... The night she went missing, we looked for her everywhere we thought she might be. We called everyone, and then around five in the morning, we called the campus police."

"You must've been so scared."

"We were, and Scott... He was just inconsolable. From the first second she went missing, we were on Team Scott because we'd *seen* how much he loved her. The police questioned him a million times, or so it seemed, but his story never changed. He'd walked her to the library to study with a friend from her zoology class, and campus security had them kissing goodbye on video. She went into the library and was never seen again. No one recalls seeing her inside, the friend she was supposed to meet said she never showed up, and that was that. It was all so surreal.

"Like, how could a perfectly healthy young woman just disappear? And the kicker was that she'd left her phone in Scott's backpack by accident, so tracking her wasn't an option. We all attested to the police that she was always leaving her phone somewhere, so it wasn't unusual for her to have left it with him. Every one of us had been on searches for Skylar's lost phone at one time or another."

I swirl my fingers around in the bubbles, lost in the memories of another traumatic time in my life. "The worst was when her parents and siblings came to campus. They were just..." I shake my head. It's too much to even think about. "We searched for her for weeks. We missed classes. We were barely functioning. All our professors passed us, but that semester was a total wash. I thought about not going back for my sophomore year, but Julia, Ali and the rest of our friends... We all decided that Skylar wouldn't want us to leave. She'd want us to finish together, so that's what we planned to do. Over time, we started to get our groove back a bit, but there were always two important people missing. Scott never came back to school."

"I'm so sorry you've been through so much heartache in your life."

"It's been a lot, for sure. When Jared canceled the wedding, Julia reminded me that things happen in threes, and that was my third. She said I was good to go now." I glance at him, propped up on his arms as he sits by the tub. "I believed her."

"From everything you've told me about Scott, I find it hard to believe he could've had anything to do with it."

"I know. I feel like I really *know* him, and I can't for the life of me imagine him hurting her."

"Maybe you need to trust your gut where he's concerned. If you had something to fear from him, if any of you did, you'd know it."

"I'd like to think so, but they must have something on him if they arrested him after all this time."

"Let's wait and see. It might be a big misunderstanding."

"I'm not sure what to hope for—that it is a misunderstanding, or that Skylar's family and loved ones will finally have some answers." I put my hand on his arm. "Thank you for listening."

"Of course. No problem."

He means that, and I know it, and it's yet another reminder of how lucky I am to have met him. Jared would've had plans with his friends the minute we returned from our trip. There'd be football to watch or someone's birthday. It was always something. He'd have seen Julia waiting for me and taken off to let me visit with my friend, with no concern whatsoever for why she was waiting for us to get home.

I'd be dealing with this latest shock alone.

"I've made so many mistakes."

"What? No, you haven't."

"Yes, I have. Jared was a huge mistake, and honestly, it's taken being with you for me to see how much was lacking with him. It's a stark wake-up call that my judgment has been seriously lacking the last few years."

"I think you've been through a tremendous amount, more than some people endure in a lifetime, and you need to give yourself a break for anything that hasn't gone perfectly in that time."

"Like the fiancé who never should've been my boyfriend, let alone my fiancé?"

"Yep, especially that. It wasn't meant to be, but if you learned something from the relationship and from him, then it wasn't for nothing."

"I learned what I don't want."

"Which is good info to have going forward."

"Yes, it is." I give him a hesitant look. "I worry this is too perfect with you."

"It's not. We're going to have ups and downs like everyone does, but the one thing you can believe in is that I love you and I want the best for you always."

His words bring more tears to my eyes. "I love you, too. I can't believe how fast it happened, but it's true. I really love you."

Milo goes up on his knees to lean over the tub to kiss me. "As long as we have that, we can get through whatever comes our way."

I want so badly to believe that, but life has taught me to be wary of anything that seems too good to be true.

CHAPTER 19

MILO

Gianna tosses and turns all night long. At one point, I wake up to find her reading on her phone.

"Just looking at the updates about Scott. Sorry if I woke you."

"You didn't. What's being said?"

"The police aren't saying much of anything. His lawyer issued a statement that Scott vehemently denies having anything to do with Skylar's disappearance, that he loved her with all his heart and never could've harmed her in any way."

"What do you think?"

"I don't know what to think. I want so badly to believe him, but what's the new evidence?"

"I'm sure you'll find out eventually."

"I guess."

"Why don't you put it aside for a bit and try to get some rest?"

She places the phone on the bedside table.

"Come here." I hold out my arm to her, hoping she'll accept

the invitation to snuggle. We agreed I could take the brace off for bed, since I sleep much better without it.

As she curls up to me, I feel the turmoil inside me begin to settle a bit. No one ever told me that falling in love—truly in love for the first time—would be such a roller coaster ride. She's worth all the hills and valleys that we may encounter along the way. I already know that for certain. I have no regrets about telling her I love her. It seemed like she needed to hear it, and it felt right to say what I've felt for some time now.

It was a huge relief to hear it back from her, especially during more upheaval. My heart truly aches for everything she's endured, and I hope this latest chapter won't set her back too much.

"What are you thinking about?"

"You."

"What about me?"

"How amazing you are. Even with everything you've gone through, when you were my nurse, all I saw was a happy, cheerful, joyful person. I admire that you can project so much positivity when you're aching on the inside."

"It's not an act, if that's what you're thinking."

"Not at all. It came across as dedication more than anything."

"Work is a happy place for me, even though we're dealing with sick and injured and dying people. I love my job and my coworkers and most of my patients so much."

"I'm glad you have that outlet and that it makes you happy. You deserve that after working so hard to get through school while you finished raising your brothers."

"I did work hard and often went without sleep to get everything done, but it's worth it now. I have a great job that I love, my brothers are doing well, and occasionally, we even have fun together."

"You'll have more fun as the years go by. I'm sure of it."

"I hope so."

"My mom texted last night to remind me about brunch and to make sure you know you're invited if you'd like to go."

"That might be fun. I could use the distraction."

"The Giordinos are nothing if not an entertaining distraction."

She yawns and snuggles in closer. "Yes, they are."

"Get some rest, sweetheart."

"Thanks for being here, Milo. You've been so great since we came home to yet another disaster."

"I'm here for it all, good, bad and ugly."

"I've had enough of the ugly."

"Yes, you certainly have. I'm going to do whatever I can to make sure it's all good from now on."

"That'd be nice."

"It will be very nice. I promise."

"You shouldn't make promises like that to someone living with a black cloud over her head."

"There's no black cloud over your head, and if there is, I'll blow it up and make it go away. And I never make promises I can't keep." I rub soothing circles on her back. "Now close your eyes and shut down your busy mind so you can get some rest."

"I'm supposed to be taking care of you."

"We're taking care of each other. That's how this works."

"It's never been like that for me."

"Well, it is now, so you'd better start getting used to it."

"Is it safe to get used to it?"

"Very, very safe. I've never told anyone else that I love them, because I've never felt it like I do with you."

"What about Michele?"

"We never said that to each other, which I now see was something I should've paid closer attention to. I was very into her, but the word 'love' never burned the tip of my tongue wanting to be said to her like it has with you."

"That sounds serious. Should I attend to those burns?"

Chuckling softly, I say, "In the morning."

"Don't let me forget."

"I won't."

I'm awake for a long time after I feel her finally relax into sleep, thinking about how I can make this permanent with her as soon as humanly possible. After the shocking news about Scott and everything with Jared, I worry about something else happening that'll undercut her confidence in me and us, men in general and the possibility of happily ever after.

Who could blame her for that?

I'm determined to show her something so great that she'll never want to be without it or me. That's my only goal in life other than getting back to full strength and returning to work and the rest of my life as soon as possible. If I'm not working or sleeping, I'll be focused on Gianna and doing whatever I can to reassure her that I'm for real and I want her in my life forever.

The next thing I know, the sun is streaming in the windows.

Gianna is still asleep, so I stay still, hoping she'll sleep awhile longer since she had a rough night.

A short time later she stirs, her eyes popping open to find me watching her.

"Morning."

"Morning."

"I thought I was still on the cruise."

I'm aware of the exact moment when she recalls what happened yesterday when we got home from the trip. Her smile fades and her eyes close.

"I'd forgotten for a second about Scott."

"You needed the rest."

"Do you still want to go to brunch?" she asks.

"Only if you do."

"It might be fun to go. It'd be better than sitting here obsessing about things I can't fix."

"That's true."

"Let's go, then."

"Sounds good."

We take showers and head out about forty minutes later.

"I can't believe you did all that laundry and folded it. What was I doing while you were doing that?"

"I think you were talking to Julia and Ali."

"Thank you for taking care of it."

"No problem."

"I haven't even asked how you're feeling," she says when we're stopped at a light on the way to Little Havana.

"I'm fine. Almost back to where I was before the infection."

"You took the meds last night and this morning, right?"

"Yes, Nurse Gianna. I did."

"Good. No more setbacks allowed."

"Don't mention that to my family, okay?"

"I won't."

"Thanks for understanding. I just don't want my parents to worry any more than they already have about this situation—or for my mom to say, 'I told you so' about the risk of going on the trip."

"I get it. No sense firing them up when you're much better."

"Exactly." He looks over at me as much as he can with the neck brace back on. "You know there're a lot of us, right?"

"Yes, Milo. I met most of them while you were in the hospital."

"That was actually a fraction of the total."

"Wow."

"Yeah, so it's apt to be a bit crazy, especially with me bringing you after we just went on a cruise together. They'll ask questions that are none of their business, and that'll be the first five minutes."

It's so nice to hear her laugh after a tough day yesterday. "Will you stay by me?"

"The whole time."

"Then I'll be fine."

"Let me know if you aren't?"

"You'll be the first to know."

"I think it's Abuela's week to host brunch, so we'll be on the Cuban side. Do you like Cuban food?"

"I love it. Our next-door neighbors for years were Cuban and would make us food all the time. We sent Italian to them. They moved away about ten years ago but flew in from Santa Fe for my parents' funeral."

"That was nice of them."

"It was. We were so touched by how many people came from all over for them."

"And for you and your brothers."

"That, too."

"I'm glad you were so well supported."

"We really were. The outpouring was overwhelming and life affirming. They were very well liked."

"I wish I could've known them."

"I wish that, too. They would've liked you."

"I hope so."

"They would have. You remind me a little of my dad. He was always doing something sweet for my mom."

"That's a lovely compliment. Thank you."

"It's true. That's why I'm so sure they would've liked you."

"Maybe they arranged for us to meet under the craziest of circumstances."

"If they were responsible for you being shot, I'm not going to be happy with them."

I squeeze her hand. "But look at what I got from being shot. The best thing to ever happen to me."

"You really think that?"

"I really do."

"That makes me feel very lucky even when I've been very *un*lucky up to now."

"We're going to change your luck, remember? We're starting today with a whole new groove. All good things from now on."

"That'd be nice."

"It's going to be incredible. I know it."

GIANNA

He's so certain, and he's nearly succeeded in convincing me that something this great can be real. I want so badly to believe in him and in us and to commit fully to this new direction. If only the nagging doubts about my own judgment weren't taking some of the fun out of this for me. And yes, I know, that's on me, not him.

He's been nothing but straight up with me from the start, and I felt differently about him from the first time I met him. At first, I chalked it up to empathy for such a young man being struck down by a bullet meant for someone else. But as the days went by, I had to admit it was more than that.

It was him. It was his loving family. It was the way he looked at me and listened to me when we chatted and seemed interested in everything I had to say. I was immediately addicted to the heady feeling that comes with realizing you're receiving special attention from someone you genuinely like.

And then I saw him shirtless and sweaty.

That's when I had to admit to myself that this was turning into way more than a basic crush on a handsome patient.

After a week at sea and in close quarters with him, I like him even more than I did before, and he only cemented those feelings with the way he stepped up for me yesterday after Julia delivered the devastating news about Scott.

I can't imagine how much more difficult it would've been to be alone with that news, but Milo never left my side except to do something for me. Before I lost my parents, I would've turned to them at a time like that. After all, they lived through the horror of Skylar's disappearance when it happened and would've empathized with how I felt about Scott being arrested. They would've been as shocked as I was after having made him part of our family over the years.

"Are you okay over there?" Milo asks as I drive down Calle Ocho, the main road through Little Havana.

"I'm just thinking about how my parents would've been upset about Scott, too. They liked him a lot and were supportive of him after Skylar disappeared."

"I'm sure a lot of people are reeling from the news he's been arrested."

"I want to know what the cops have that ties him to it. He's never wavered in his story about where he was when she went missing or who he was with and has witnesses who could back up his alibi. What could have changed?"

"I guess you'll know soon enough."

"Julia wants to visit him in jail and find out what's going on."

"What do you think of that?"

"I sort of want to go with her. Do you think that's crazy?"

"Not at all. He's been your friend for a long time. You've traveled a difficult path together. Anyone would understand wanting to know why. But I want you to take care of you in all this. If it's too much for you, don't go."

"I'll think about it."

"I'll go with you if you want."

I glance at him out of the corner of my eye. "You'd do that?"

"Of course I would. I'd never want you to go through something so difficult alone if I could be with you."

"You're a very good boyfriend."

"This is what I've been trying to tell you and others for years."

"Their loss is my gain."

"Pull in right there. We can park in the back." After I pull into a spot, he adds, "You're sure you're ready for this? We'll be the main attraction."

"I'm ready, and it's fine. They're always so nice to me, and I'm eager to check in with your mom about the lawsuit."

"I'm sure she'll have an update."

CHAPTER 20

GIANNA

We get out of the car and enter the restaurant through the back door. A clatter of voices and a cloud of mouthwatering scents greet us. I've been here once before with friends from work for a going-away party for one of them and remember the food being incredible.

Milo reaches for my hand as we walk down a long hallway that leads to the main part of the restaurant, where family members have gathered around a huge table of pastries and other yummy-looking things. Suddenly, I'm very hungry for the first time since I got the news about Scott.

Like Milo predicted, the family swarms us, asking a million questions about the trip and Milo's health, and one of them even asks if we're an official couple now. I think that came from his sister Dee.

"Back off, locusts." Milo holds up a hand to keep them from completely overwhelming us. "Don't scare off Gianna on her first trip to brunch."

Elena pushes through the crowd to hug us both. "I'm so glad you're safely back where you belong, loves."

The oddest feeling comes over me, reminding me of returning to my own home after being away and how relieved my mother always was to see me after a time apart. I cling to Elena the way I would my own mother, and thankfully, she doesn't seem to mind. She's all soft comfort and sweet scent and endless love.

Lorenzo hugs us next, followed by Milo's Nona and his Abuela and various aunts, uncles, cousins and siblings.

"This is my friend Chris," Nona says, seeming embarrassed as she introduces us to the handsome man who has his arm around her. "This is my grandson Milo and his girlfriend, Gianna."

Chris shakes hands with us. "Nice to see you looking so well, Milo. You gave your grandmother and everyone else quite a scare."

"That's what I heard, and it's nice to finally meet you, too. I've heard a lot about you."

"Like what?" Chris asks.

"That's enough," Nona says, dragging him away from us.

"Was it something I said?" Milo asks, grinning.

"It's so good to have you back to brunch, sweet boy," his aunt Vivian says with tears sparkling in her eyes.

"It's good to be back," he tells her.

His cousin Carmen hugs him next. "You look so much better after some time in the sun, primo."

"I feel much better," he says with a side-eye glance at me, recognition of the secret we're keeping from them about his brief setback.

"How's my star patient?" Jason Northrup asks when he joins his wife and puts an arm around her.

"Doing great," Milo says. "The trip was just what I needed."

"You could probably lose the brace at this point."

Milo whips it off and tosses it on the floor.

"Alrighty, then," Jason says with a laugh.

"I hate that thing. Not as much as the halo, but it's a close second."

"Everyone hates them. Glad to see you doing so much better."

"I'm ready to get back to normal." We've agreed that he'll tell Jason about the infection when he sees him for the follow-up appointment in two weeks.

"I'm sure you are, but no heavy lifting or driving for another month. Doctor's orders. Oh and no charge for this office visit."

We share a laugh with them.

"You had a nice vacation?" Jason asks me.

"I did. Thank you." With Milo talking to Carmen, I quietly ask him, "Is this going to be weird between us?"

"What?"

"Me dating your wife's cousin after he was my patient?"

"Not for me. I'm happy for you guys."

"Oh, good. Thanks."

"You weren't worried about what I would think, were you?"

"Maybe a little."

"Don't be. You're one of the best nurses I've ever worked with, and you're never anything but super professional."

"Thank you for that, but dating an ex-patient is a strange scenario."

"Eh, it's fine. He wasn't your patient anymore when you started dating. It's no big deal. With the hours we work, it's not like there're a million different ways to meet people. I met Carmen on my first day at Miami-Dade."

"I didn't realize that."

"Yep, she was assigned to 'babysit' the new neurologist who'd arrived with a checkered record."

"*You* had a checkered record? Seriously?"

"Yep. I left quite a scandal behind at my last hospital in New York. Google me to read all the sordid details."

"I'll do that."

"Then you'll see why I'm the last person who'll ever judge anyone."

"Are you sharing your sordid past with Gianna, love?" Carmen asks him.

"Yep. I'm trying to make her feel better about dating an ex-patient."

"Ah, I see. Jason and I bonded over his sordid past."

"She helped me change my reputation by volunteering my services at Maria's free clinic. On the first day there, I met Sofia and Mateo and diagnosed his brain tumor."

"And saved his life by operating that same day," Carmen adds.

"I heard about that, but not the other stuff."

"I can't believe you haven't heard about the mess I left in New York," Jason says.

"No one at work talks about you as anything other than a superstar doctor."

"Well, that's nice to hear."

Dee's fiancé, Wyatt, another brilliant doctor at Miami-Dade, comes up to us and very quietly says, "Jason, I need you to get me to the ER. I woke up light-headed and short of breath, but I don't want to worry Dee. Can you make up a reason for us to leave?"

"Yep, I'm on it." Jason pulls his phone from his pocket. "Mass casualty incident at the hospital," he says to Carmen. "They're recalling everyone. You want to ride with me, Wyatt?"

"Sure, just let me tell Dee."

The two of them leave a few minutes later.

"What was that really about?" Carmen asks me, looking worried.

I'm not sure if I should tell her what I overheard Wyatt say to Jason.

"Is Wyatt okay?"

Since she'll find out soon enough, I tell her, "He said he was light-headed and short of breath. He didn't want to worry Dee."

"Oh my God."

"It could be a lot of things other than his heart."

Across the room, Dee is laughing and chatting with Maria, Nico, Sofia and their other cousin, Domenic. I just met him and his new wife, Stacey, who seems very nice. I say a silent prayer for Wyatt, a strong, handsome, incredibly talented man who's obviously madly in love with Milo's sister.

Elena waves me over to where she's sitting alone at a table set for ten.

I take a seat next to her.

"I was waiting to see you to update you on things with the venue. Jared has worked out a payment plan with them that they're satisfied with, and they'll be dropping the lawsuit against you this week."

"That's such a relief."

"I thought you might say that. Since he's acting in good faith to resolve the bill, I think it's probably safe to drop our counter-suit against him. But only if you agree."

"I do. I want to be done with all this."

"I'll take care of that tomorrow."

"Elena… Thank you so much for everything you did for me. I'll never be able to tell you what it means to me."

"I was happy to do it. I want to tell you something about me that I think you'll appreciate hearing. I lost my grandmother when I was twenty-three. She had an aneurism and was gone so quickly, she never knew what hit her."

"I'm so sorry. That must've been such a shock."

"Until Milo was shot, it was the worst thing that'd ever happened to me. Even worse than the breast cancer diagnosis.

Unlike my mother and I, she and I were very close. Much more like friends than grandmother and granddaughter. We talked about everything, even things no one talks to their grandmother about. Losing her left a hole inside of me so big that I thought nothing and no one could ever fill it. But then I met Lo and we had our family, and over time, the sadness faded a bit, even if I still miss her every day." She places her hand on top of mine. "I didn't lose both my parents at once, but I lost my most important person very suddenly, so I understand a little bit what you went through."

"That's very sad. I'm so sorry."

"Thank you, honey. The reason I'm telling you this is because I understand what a trauma it is to be a young woman who's lost the most important person or people in her life. For years after I lost my grandmother, I glommed on to my friends' mothers, my aunts, random women I met through work, trying to fill that terrible void. But it was a void that no one else could fill. I'm not suggesting I could begin to fill the void for you, but I want you to know I'm here for you, whether things work out between you and Milo or not. If you find yourself in need of mothering, you call me. You hear me?"

I'm about to bawl my head off. "Yes, I hear you, and I'm so deeply grateful for that. Even though I've started a successful career and taken care of my brothers, I've been kind of floundering for four years, like a boat that's come unmoored or something."

"That's it exactly. And I truly understand that feeling."

"Since I met you and your family, I've felt a little less alone."

"That's lovely to hear. We're always adopting new family members, and we're glad to have you join us. And I just have to say… I've never seen my Milo look at anyone the way he looks at you."

"He's…" I sigh. "There are no words."

She smiles. "He's the best of us. We all think so. It's been like that from almost the minute he was born. When we thought we might lose him…"

"I can only imagine."

"But no more sad thoughts today. Only happy things."

Milo comes over to join us. "Mom, what're you saying to her?"

"I'm telling her what a rotten, terrible, no-good, naughty boy you were and how she needs to watch out for you."

"Very funny. I was the only one who didn't give you gray hair."

"Until lately, that is. I've got thirty new ones with your name on them."

"Are you ladies ready to eat?" he asks.

"I am," Elena says. "Come on, Gianna, let's hit the buffet."

"Everything okay?" Milo asks me after his mother walks away.

"Everything is great," I reply, even though I'm still troubled by the situation with Scott and now worried about Wyatt, too. Fortified by my chat with Elena, I shake off those thoughts and take the hand Milo extends to me, determined to try to make this a good day.

MILO

The news about Wyatt arrives as we're sitting around four tables, stuffed to the point of explosion after devouring the Cuban buffet.

Dee lets out a sharp cry that gets everyone's attention. She jumps up. "Maria, Austin, drive me to the hospital. Right now."

"What's wrong?" Lorenzo asks.

"Wyatt's been admitted," Dee says tearfully. "They're not sure what's going on, but I need to get there. Please. Someone take me."

"Come on." Maria takes her sister's arm. "We've got you."

"We'll be right behind you," Elena tells her daughter. "Try not to think the worst, sweetheart."

"I'm trying."

Dee leaves with Maria and Austin. Everly is with his parents because she didn't feel like coming to brunch today.

"I can grab a ride with Nico if you want to go home," Milo says.

"I'm coming with you. I might be able to help get some answers."

"Thank you," he says, looking and sounding relieved.

We follow the rest of the family from the restaurant and head for the hospital, all of us praying that whatever is wrong with Wyatt is nothing serious.

DEE

This is my worst nightmare come true, and the thing is, before we left for brunch, I could tell something wasn't right with him. He assured me he was fine, but it bothers me that he was obviously lying to protect me from worrying.

Now I'm frantic after hearing he's been admitted. I try texting him, but he doesn't reply. Next I text Jason. And then I wait, hoping one of them might tell me what's going on.

Austin drives as fast as he dares to Miami-Dade.

Maria turns to me in the backseat of the G-Wagon he bought her for Christmas. "He's going to be fine. He's the picture of robust health."

I appreciate what Maria is trying to do, but he's still dealing with a heart that should've failed him years ago and still could at any time. As a nurse, she knows that better than I do. Traffic makes the ride even more interminable than it already is, and by the time we get to the Emergency entrance at Miami-Dade, my own heart is in danger of failing.

"You guys go ahead," Austin says. "I'll park and catch up to you."

I'm out of the car before he finishes speaking.

Maria is right behind me, but I don't wait for my sister, who's moving slowly due to pregnancy.

At the reception desk, I tell the woman on duty, "I'm here for Wyatt Blake. Dr. Wyatt Blake. I'm his fiancée."

"Dee, right?"

"Yes, that's me."

"He's been asking for you, and I have orders to bring you back as soon as you get here. Right this way."

If he's asking for me and giving orders, he must be okay. That's all that matters—that he's okay. If he is, I am. It's that simple. From the time he first explained his precarious health situation to me, I knew there would be difficult times ahead, but I never expected him to have any sort of medical emergency so soon after we agreed to spend the rest of our lives together.

I'm in no way ready to lose him. Not that I'll ever be ready for that. He could live another fifty years, and it wouldn't be enough for me.

I hear him before I see him, laughing at something Jason said inside the ER bay where he's in a hospital bed, attached to an IV pole and several monitors.

His expression softens when he sees me, and he extends his hand to me.

I'm in tears as I go to him, taking his hand and letting him draw me into his embrace. His familiar scent is immediately comforting.

"Shhh," he says. "I'm all right. I just now got the word that I have pneumonia. My heart is fine."

I'm a heap of sobbing woman, soaking up the love of the

man who means more to me than my own life. "How can you have pneumonia and not know it?"

"I've felt a little off the last couple of days," he says as he strokes my hair, "but it wasn't until today that I started to worry that something was wrong. I'm sorry I scared you. I tried to avoid that."

"Don't do that again. Tell me the truth about what's going on."

"I will, babe. I promise. Now stop crying. I can't bear to see you upset."

GIANNA

I feel like an intruder in an intensely private moment between Dee and her fiancé. I told Milo and his family I'd see if I could find out what was going on. "Sorry to interrupt," I say from the doorway. "The family is in the waiting room. Is there an update I can give them?"

"You can tell them I have pneumonia, and my heart is fine. I'm on IV antibiotics for at least the next twenty-four hours."

"Of course. I'll let them know."

"Thank you, Gianna," Dee says as she wipes away tears.

As I return to the waiting area, I wonder how anyone finds the courage to truly love someone else, knowing that any number of horrible things can happen to the most important person in your life. I've already seen how that can happen. Multiple times.

Wouldn't it be safer to be alone than to risk heartbreak again?

I've worked myself into a full-blown panic by the time I reach the waiting room, where Milo's family swarms me.

"He's okay. He has pneumonia, but his heart is fine."

"Oh, thank you, Jesus," Elena says.

Lorenzo puts his arm around his wife. "Thank you, Gianna. That's such a relief."

"How's Dee?" Maria asks.

"Better now that she knows it's not his heart."

"How bad is the pneumonia?" Nona asks.

"Wyatt seems stable. He was talking to and comforting Dee. He's on IV antibiotics for at least the next twenty-four hours. I think it's safe to head home. Dee is with him, and Jason is there, too."

"Holy shit."

Everyone turns to look at Carmen, who has an odd look on her face. "I just had the worst pain after feeling sick all morning."

She bends in half when the pain hits again.

I move quickly to lead her to the triage nurse.

"I'm pregnant," she whispers. "If I'm losing the baby…"

"Don't go there yet."

"I already lost one. No one knows."

"Let's get you checked and see what's going on."

"Will you stay with me?" she asks.

"Of course. As long as you need me."

They take her right back to an exam bay. I leave her only long enough to go get Jason and tell him Carmen needs him. I'll never forget the stricken look on his face when he realized something might be wrong with her.

Over the next two hours, I wait with her, Jason and her parents, who came running from the restaurant when they heard she was in the ER. She's in obvious pain and vomits twice while we wait for the doctors to determine what's going on.

"It's her appendix," the ER attending says when he returns after a long wait. "We need to get her upstairs for surgery."

Carmen's eyes fill with tears. "The baby…"

"Is fine," the doctor says. "We'll make sure he or she stays that way, okay?"

Carmen nods and holds tight to Jason's hand as an orderly wheels her bed from the ER toward the elevator. Milo, Maria and Austin, who stuck around to see what was going on, come to wish her well before they take her upstairs.

"You'll be just fine, Car," Maria says.

"That's right," Jason says even if he looks as freaked out as I've ever seen him.

It would be easier, so much easier, to stay single and avoid all the nonsense that comes with loving someone more than you love yourself. That gives them too much power. It gives them the ability to ruin your life in so many ways, it'd be impossible to count them all. If only the thought of never seeing Milo again wasn't truly devastating, I'd be so out of here the second after I help send Jason and his wife to the surgical floor.

I'd never do that to Milo, but the longer this goes on, the more I feel like true love and everything that goes with it isn't for me. It might've been, once upon a time, before the sudden deaths of my parents and everything with Jared, but now I know how fast things can change. I simply can't go through that again. What if I allow myself to fall irrevocably in love with Milo and he dies, too? Or decides he "can't do it," the way Jared did?

I've heard everything he's said, and I want so badly to believe in the happily ever after he's offering me. But even someone with the best of intentions can't keep terrible things from happening, things that ruin someone else's life because they had the courage to love you. I admit that the news about Scott, coupled with Wyatt's health crisis and now Carmen's surgery, has me spinning.

It's not fair to Milo to judge him and what he's offered based on the actions or crises that befall other people. But I want off the merry-go-round I've been on since the day I learned my parents were dead in Jamaica. I just want a nice, quiet, peaceful life, and if I have to stay single to do that, then so be it.

CHAPTER 21

MILO

Something is wrong. Since Gianna returned with a frantic and panicked Jason, she hasn't said a word to me or anyone.

Carmen's parents, Nona and Abuela went to the surgical waiting room. The rest of us were encouraged to go on with our day now that we know Wyatt will be okay and in anticipation of a few hours of surgery and recovery for Carmen.

As Gianna drives us back to her house after an eventful morning, I wish I knew what she was thinking. Or maybe I don't want to know. How could things have gone to shit in just a few hours? I want to ask her that, but I'm afraid of what she might say.

After the amazing week we spent together, how would I go back to life before her? I don't want to. She's changed everything for me, and all I want is more of her and what we have together.

By the time we get to her house, my nerves are shot. I have

no idea how to handle any of this. I've never been in a situation even close to what this is with her. Any chance for happiness in my life is directly tied to someone else, who may or may not want what I do.

She said she loves me.

I believed her.

Was that a big mistake?

I sure as hell hope not.

As we walk into her home, I can't take the silence anymore. "What's wrong?"

She stops short, her shoulders curving forward in a way that has me immediately going to her, wanting to offer comfort.

"Don't," she says softly.

"Don't what?" My heart is in my throat. I have no clue how to handle her pulling away from me.

"I just… I can't do this, Milo. I thought I could, but I can't. I'm not ready for any of it, and I know I'm being terribly unfair to you, but…"

I turn her toward me, and the despair I see on her face devastates me. "Why?" I ask, because it's the only word that comes to mind and the only thing I want to know.

"I… I'm not strong enough."

"Yes, you are. You're the strongest person I've ever known."

She shakes her head. "I'm not. I hear my friend has been arrested for possibly killing my other friend, and I turn to jelly on the inside. I witness Dee's grief over Wyatt's precarious health, and I can't imagine what it must be like… To love someone like she loves him and know she could lose him at any second." She looks up at me, her gorgeous brown eyes a sea of misery. "How does she bear it?"

"She loves him."

"*How* does she bear it?" she asks again, her tone soft but intense.

"I don't know, but she thinks the payoff is worth whatever suffering she has to endure to be with him."

"I can't do that. I'm not strong like she is."

"You are, Gianna. How can you not see it?"

"Maybe I was, once upon a time, but I'm not anymore. I'm raw. I'm not strong like Dee or Wyatt or Sofia or Nico or Jason or Carmen. I'm not fearless like Maria or able to overcome terrible illness the way Austin did with Everly. If that happened to someone I love, if they got sick or shot or died, I'd crumble."

"You wouldn't. You *didn't*. When you parents died, you came home and took care of your brothers, even though they didn't want you to. You did what was best for them at your own expense. How can you say you're not strong?"

"I'm not strong anymore. I'm different now. I have no defenses."

"You won't need defenses with me."

"Yes, I will! What if you get sick or hurt or... What if something happens to you, too?"

"I got shot and survived it. I think I've had my near miss. I'm probably good to go now."

"You can't know that for sure."

"None of us can, sweetheart. That's why we should live each day like it's our last and play hard and love hard and do all the things. I feel that way even more so since the near miss. I'm painfully aware of how close I came to losing everything. Now, I just want to live—and I want to live and love and do all the things with you."

Tears roll down her cheeks. "I can't."

She says it so softly, I almost don't hear her.

Almost.

I'm stunned, devastated, heartbroken and bereft all at the same time. I have no idea what to do or say to change her mind. She's completely shut down and closed me out just that quickly.

I quietly go upstairs to the room where we slept together last night and pack the few things I took out of my bag. While I'm up there, I text Nico and ask him to come get me at Gianna's and provide the address.

Hurry, will you?

What's wrong?

I'll tell you when I see you.

You're freaking me out.

Nothing like that.

Okay... I'm on the way.

Thx.

I sit on the bed and look around at Gianna's childhood bedroom, noting the cheerleading megaphone from her high school, her framed college degree from FIU and stuffed animals left over from childhood sitting in a hammock that stretches across the far corner of the room. She's updated the bedding, and the pictures on the wall are of her family and friends. If she had teenage crushes, those posters are long gone.

Wondering about who she crushed on as a teen is better thinking about what the hell I'm going to do now that she's called it off between us.

I understand the cumulative effect of one crisis after another better than she thinks. How could I not after Carmen's first husband being killed on the job as a cop, my mom having breast cancer, Dee falling for a man with a bad heart and me getting shot? I know what it's like to worry about someone you love to the point of making yourself sick over it. I know what it's like to care for someone deeply and have them not feel the same way about you.

I thought she was different.

I thought *we* were different.

I can't imagine a day without her in it, let alone the rest of my life, which now stretches before me as a barren wasteland. I sound dramatic, even to myself, but I'm so deeply in love with her that I already know I'll never stop thinking of her and wishing we could've made this work somehow.

She appears in the doorway.

I look up, and our gazes collide with such an impact, I'm surprised there isn't a sound, like a sonic boom or something.

"I'm sorry, Milo," she says tearfully. "If I were going to take a chance on anyone, I'd want it to be you."

"I'm right here, and I love you more than I've ever loved anyone. I'll love you forever whether I'm with you or not."

Her sobs kill me.

I get up and go to her. "Please don't do this. We're so good together. Surely you must feel that, too."

"I do, but I can't handle it, Milo. I just can't."

I have to let her go—for now, anyway—so she can work through whatever this is without me. As painful as it is, I want her to have what she needs even if it kills me to walk away.

My phone buzzes with a text that I assume is Nico telling me he's arrived. I reach for the handle of my suitcase. "I want you to remember that I love you, and if you change your mind or need me for anything, you know where I am. Doesn't matter when. Come find me. I'll always want to see you."

I kiss her cheek, which is wet with tears. Every step I take away from her feels like a knife to my chest. As I go down the stairs, I ache worse than I did after I was shot. I reach for the doorknob, and for a long moment, I don't move to leave. I keep waiting for her to call out my name, to tell me this was a huge mistake.

But she doesn't.

After I open the door, I step outside and carry my bag down the front stairs, feeling completely numb as well as blindsided. I never saw this coming, although I probably should have. She's still getting over what happened with Jared, and the news about her friend Scott reopened old wounds yesterday.

Nico jumps out of a black Lincoln MKX, one of the cars his company owns, and puts my bag in the trunk.

I get into the front and wince when my neck protests the move I make to reach for the seat belt.

"What's going on?" Nico asks.

"She ended it."

"*What?* Why?"

"Can we get out of here? Please?"

"Yeah, sure."

After Nico backs out of Gianna's driveway and heads for the road to home, I try to fill him in on what happened. "She said she loves me, but she's too raw and can't do it."

"She seemed fine this morning at brunch. Sofia said you guys looked really happy."

I ache over how only a few hours ago, I thought we were happy, too. "I think, maybe, she hasn't been fine all this time, even though she wanted to be."

"What does that even mean?"

"She's been through a lot with her parents dying, her fiancé calling off the wedding, a situation with a college friend who went missing and now that friend's boyfriend, who Gianna and her friends have stayed close with, has been arrested. She just found that out yesterday. Then we went to brunch, and she saw Dee melting down over Wyatt and then Carmen falling ill. She can't handle the pain of loving someone so much, or so she says."

"Damn. So what're you going to do?"

"What can I do?"

"You can fight for her."

"She doesn't want me to."

"I can't believe this."

"How do you think I feel?"

"Maybe she just needs a little time."

"Maybe." I'm not sure that all the time in the world will undo the damage life has done to her or allow her to open her heart to all the possibilities that come with love—the good, the bad, the hard, the wonderful, the terrible. I watch the familiar sights go by on the road to home, wishing with all my heart that I was still with her. I have a feeling that if I never see her again, I'll still be thinking of her in the second I take my last breath.

CHAPTER 22

MILO

I've never felt so low. Even the news that Carmen's surgery went perfectly, her baby is fine, and she'll be back on her feet in a couple of weeks can't rouse me from the deepest level of despair I've ever experienced. As soon as we got home, I came upstairs to my room, closed the door and took to my bed. I have no plans to ever come out again.

But of course in my family, no one will be left alone indefinitely.

Nico knocks on the door. "Let me in, bro."

"Go away."

"I'm not going anywhere."

Sighing with resignation, I tell him, "It's not locked." It will be from now on.

The door opens, and Nico comes in carrying a tray. The smell of whatever he's bringing makes my stomach growl loudly. "I thought you agreed to be done with all this nonsense."

He says nothing as he brings the tray to me.

I sit up because he's intent on feeding me.

After he puts the tray on my lap, I see that he's brought me minestrone soup, crusty bread and an icy Coke, which is one of my few vices. "Thank you."

He crosses his arms and gives me his sternest look. "Eat it."

"I will."

"Now."

"For fuck's sake, Nico. Knock it off."

"I want you to eat. You haven't had anything since brunch, and that was like eight hours ago."

"Are you keeping track?"

"Do I need to?"

"No."

"Have you heard from her?"

I shake my head. "I don't expect to."

"I just don't get what happened."

"I do. She wasn't ready for what this turned out to be. I hope that when she is, she'll call me."

"That could take months."

The statement hits me like a knife to the chest as I ponder months without Gianna's sweet face and delightful presence in my life. "If that's what it takes."

"What if she's never ready?"

"What can I do, Nico? I can't force her into something she doesn't want."

"She does want it. I saw that with my own eyes."

"Then she'll be back."

"And what're you supposed to do in the meantime?"

"Get back to work and live my life." I miss playing dominoes with the old men at the nursing home I visit and driving for Meals on Wheels on Saturdays. I hope all the seniors are still there when I get back to my usual routine.

Nico shakes his head. "You should ask Mom to talk to her. They've bonded."

"Absolutely not! And don't you dare do that. If she comes

back, I want it to be for the right reasons, not because Mom talked her into caring about me."

"No one has to talk her into caring about you, bro. She already does."

"Then we'll just have to see what happens."

"How can you be so chill about this?"

"I'm not chill. Not at all. I feel like absolute shit when I think about not seeing her for one day, let alone weeks or months. But this is what she needs right now, and I promised her I'd never let her down. I'm not going to start now."

"Do you love her?"

"So much."

"Does she love you?"

"She said she did."

"This is making me crazy for you."

"I appreciate that, but I have to let it play out, as hard as it is. She's been through so much. You can't believe how much. I suppose I should've expected her to pull back at some point." I look up at my brother. "I get that it's upsetting to you to see me upset, but I'm okay. I promise."

"She has to know you're like the best guy ever."

"And you're not at all biased?" I ask him with a smile.

"Hell no, I'm not. It's the truth, and everyone knows it."

"Thank you, Nico, but until she believes it, there's not much more I can do to convince her."

"Sure there is. Send her flowers and cards and let her know you're thinking of her every minute of every day."

"She wants to be left alone."

"No, Milo, she wants to be sure she can believe in you, so show her you're for real."

The idea sparks the first kernel of hope I've felt since Gianna sent me away. "I'll think about it."

"Do that, and in the meantime, eat."

"Yes, dear." I take the first spoonful of the soup, and the flavors explode on my tongue. "That's good. Who made it?"

"Sofia did, from Nona's recipe."

"Tell her I said it's amazing."

"I will. She's worried about you. Mateo is, too."

"Tell them I'm okay, and I'll see them in the morning, okay?"

"Yeah, but if you don't come out, I'm coming in after you."

"Thanks for the warning and the soup and everything else."

"You got it."

After he leaves the room, I eat the soup and the bread as well as the three chocolate-chip cookies that were wrapped in a napkin. Inside the napkin, I find a note from Sofia. *We love you, Milo, and she does, too. I know it. xoxo*

Sofia's kind words bring a smile. She's so lovely and perfect for my gruff, complicated older brother.

After I finish the meal, I put the tray on the floor and settle back against the pillows, thinking about Nico's suggestion that I remind her of who I am and what I have to offer her. Part of me thinks I should just leave it alone and hope for the best. But what if that's the worst thing I could do?

For the first time in hours, I power up my phone and scroll through the headlines, stopping on one about an update in the case of missing University of Florida student Skylar Jones and the arrest of her boyfriend. I devour the article that details the twists and turns of the case and the leads that led police to arrest the boyfriend who'd proclaimed his innocence from the start.

The article says that investigators arrested Scott Wallace on suspicion of his involvement in Skylar's disappearance, but nothing more about specific charges.

Reading about the case has me thinking of Gianna. I decide to send her a text. *I read about the latest with Scott, and I just wanted to say I'm sorry. I'm sure you're still upset. I wish there was something I could do for you. Thinking of you. Always.*

Before I can second-guess the shit out of every word, I send the text.

Everything I said is true.

That's what'll matter most to her.

GIANNA

I'm an emotional basket case, especially since I received the latest news that even though they haven't formally charged him yet, the police now seem to believe Scott was behind Skylar's disappearance. I'd been hoping it was something like he'd obstructed the investigation, but now I know it's worse than that.

I simply cannot believe it, even if the new information seems legit.

The group text with my college friends is on fire with commentary about what people are hearing from others as well as the publicly available updates.

Of course, Scott has been removed from the group.

I've lost all faith in humanity since he was arrested. Memories from years of close friendship run through my mind over and over as I look for signs of deceit that simply weren't there.

And then I receive Milo's sweet text, and I lose it all over again after going almost two hours without crying over the mess I made of things with him.

Thank you, I write back to him. *We're all shocked and sad and many other things. It's so hard to believe.*

I'm sure, he says in response. *I'm here if you need anything.*

From the second he left, I've felt sick to my soul at the thought of never seeing him again. But I still feel it was the right thing to do to hit pause for now. I'm a red-hot mess on the inside, and it's not fair to him to let our relationship continue when I can't make sense out of anything.

For the first time since I joined the team at Miami-Dade, I call out sick for the next two days because I simply cannot fathom taking care of anyone else when I'm in such a state.

We receive a text from Skylar's parents that has me in tears once again.

Hi guys. We're sure you're as upset and devastated as we are by the recent developments. From the start, we've wanted justice for Skylar, no matter where the investigation led. Needless to say, we never expected this. We've loved Scott and treated him like a member of our family from the start. That he could've been lying to us for years is simply unfathomable. Our plan now is to let the justice system do its thing while praying we might finally find our sweet Skylar and bring her home to rest in peace. Your support and love over the years has sustained us and will continue to as we enter the next phase of this nightmare. With much love from our entire family to each of you. Don, Tracy, Stefani and Sydney.

I sob as I think about Skylar's family and how devastated they must be to have spent so much time with the man who might've taken their daughter and sister from them. I cry for myself and all the other people who loved Skylar—and Scott. How could he have done this to us while pretending to care about us and Skylar and her family?

To realize I've been so close to a man who could be a psychopath is overwhelming, to say the least. He's slept in my house, with my brothers there, too. It makes me sick to think about the many ways I trusted him and even leaned on him after my parents died. I shudder with revulsion and so many emotions, it would be impossible to catalog them all.

The doorbell rings, and I get up to see who it is.

A man with an envelope is on the front stairs.

I open the door just wide enough to hear him.

"Delivery for Gianna Lombardi. If you could just sign here."

I reach my arm out to sign where indicated and take the envelope from him. "Thank you." I close and lock the door, taking the envelope from the law firm that sued me to the sofa to open it. Inside is a letter indicating the lawsuit against me has been dropped after financial reparations were made to the venue. They consider the matter resolved, and no further action will be taken.

Well, that's a relief.

I send a text to Elena with a photo of the letter.

It's such a relief to know it's resolved. I'll never have the words to properly thank you for your help with this.

There's so much more I want to say to her. I want to thank her for making me part of her amazing family and for raising such a wonderful son. But the minute I think of him, I'm a disastrous mess of tears again. I miss him so much. More than I ever missed Jared after we broke up, if I'm being honest.

That realization is another gut punch on top of so many in the last few days. I wish Milo was here to tell me everything will be okay, but if I've learned anything in the last four years, it's that I'm the only one who can fix things for myself. I have to get right in my own head before I can be with anyone, especially someone as special as Milo. He deserves only the best of everything, and I am so far from my best right now that I can't tell up from down.

It wouldn't be fair to drag him through my emotional battlefield as I work through my baggage. For the first time in two years, I reach out to the therapist who was so essential to me after my parents died and ask if she has any time for me.

She writes back. *I'm booked solid for the next few weeks, but I'm free right now. Give me a call if you are, too.*

I stare at the text for a full minute before I put through the call.

"Hi there," Chelsea says. "It's so nice to hear from you. I've been meaning to check in and see how things are going."

The sound of her voice brings back a million memories of the most difficult time in my life.

"Gianna? Are you all right?"

"No, I'm not. I'm a mess."

"What's going on?"

"The short story is Jared called off our wedding on the day of, I got sued by the wedding venue because they expected payment for the event that didn't happen, and as the one who signed the contract, I was on the hook for that. I fell for one of my patients and took him on my honeymoon cruise, where I discovered I'm in love with someone else not that long after I was supposed to marry Jared. That guy, Milo, he's amazing and wonderful and everything anyone could ever want. His mother, who's an attorney, helped me deal with the lawsuit, which has now been resolved by Jared paying the bill. Jared wants me back and thinks we should reschedule the wedding so we won't lose all that money, I told Milo I can't see him anymore, and now Scott, the boyfriend of my friend who went missing during my freshman year of college, has been charged in her kidnapping and murder after we supported him for all this time. Other than that..."

"Whoa, girl. Why'd you wait so long to reach out?"

"The Milo and Scott developments are new, and I'm just a mess over it all. Right when I think I can start this whole new relationship with a truly great guy, another guy who I've trusted and supported might be accused of murdering my friend. Add to that, everywhere I look I see people in love going through hell, and I just can't, for the life of me, go through any more hell, so I told Milo I couldn't do it, when all I want is to be with him."

"Take a breath, Gi."

I do as she asks.

"Now take another. Keep breathing."

I take a series of deep breaths and find that it helps calm my erratic heartbeat.

"Feel better?"

"A little."

"Let's take it a piece at a time. Why did Jared call off the wedding?"

"He said he wasn't ready after all, but since the lawsuit stuff, he's decided it would be better to go through with the wedding than lose the money."

"He sounds like an asshole who you're better off without."

I've always loved how Chelsea doesn't mince words. "I've come around to seeing that I was lucky he canceled the wedding. At the time, you couldn't tell me that, but I've seen sides of him since then that indicate our marriage would've been a short one. He actually showed up at the cruise terminal for the honeymoon that I'd paid for. Can you believe the nerve?"

"I hope you told him where to go."

"I did. I told him my new boyfriend and I were going to fully enjoy every minute of the trip."

"Good for you. And did you?"

"For the most part, except for when I got seasick, and he developed an infection. But we got through those things together."

"Look at you inviting a former patient on your honeymoon."

I moan. "That's just one of many things that have been way out of character for me lately."

"You must've really liked him to do that."

"I did. I mean, I *do*. I even love him." My voice catches on a sob. "I love him a lot."

"Let's come back to that. What happened with your college friend's boyfriend?"

I fill her in on the developments in Skylar's case, which she and I have talked about before.

"Oh God, Gi. I'm so sorry. That's got to be so shocking."

"It's beyond shocking. It's devastating. He was so good to me after my parents died."

"I remember you saying that."

"I let him stay in my house with my brothers here. It makes me sick to think of what could've happened."

"This is a lot on top of a lot for you. Anyone would be upset by one of these things, let alone all of them happening around the same time."

"I feel awful about what I did to Milo. He's never been anything but lovely to me."

"How did you leave it with him?"

"That I needed some time to get my head together, and I didn't think it was fair to drag him through that mess."

"What did he say?"

"That he would always want to hear from me, no matter how long it takes."

"He sounds like a great guy."

"He is," I whisper, wiping away more tears. "He's the best, or so it seems. How can you really know for sure?"

"That's a good question, and when I've encountered that myself, I've looked to the people in a man's life and what they think of him. Does he have people who love him and would do anything for him? Does he have a lot of friends and people who are important to him? Does he do what he says he's going to do? Is he there when things get crazy, or does he cut and run? Those are the sorts of things that matter to me. Everyone will have their own list of what's important."

"Your list is a good one, and the answer to all those questions is yes. When he was in the hospital, he was constantly surrounded by family and friends, so many we sometimes had to tell some of them to wait in the lounge. They brought food for him and for us. He's a Giordino. Like the restaurant."

"Oh, yum. That place is one of my favorites. They have the best Cuban in town."

"They have the best everything in town, including family members. They're all wonderful. I love them almost as much as I love him."

"So what's the problem?"

"I don't know. I want to go all in with Milo, but I was all in with Jared, and look at how that turned out. I don't want to make another mistake."

"Does Milo feel like a mistake?"

"No, he feels like forever, and that scares me. How could I think I was so in love with Jared a year ago and feel this way for Milo now? It makes no sense to me. And then Scott got arrested, and my faith in all men took a serious hit."

"I can understand how that would rattle you, but Scott has nothing to do with Milo."

"I know that. Of course I do. It's just that I don't trust myself to make good decisions anymore. I was so ready to marry Jared, and with hindsight, I can see that he wasn't right for me at all. Why didn't I see that at the time? Was I so desperate to fill the void left by losing my parents that I said yes to the first guy who proposed, thinking he'd solve all my problems? And how could I have put so much trust in Scott if he might be the one who killed Skylar?"

"Those are some big questions, for sure, and there's no doubt you've been through a lot in your life, things that would rock anyone's faith. But here's the thing, Gianna. Only you can know how you feel, and from what I'm hearing, your feelings for Milo are stronger than your feelings for Jared ever were."

"They are, and how is that possible? I've known Milo for such a short time. I dated Jared for two *years*."

"Sometimes you just know. My parents were engaged ten days after they met and married six months later. They've been married for thirty-five years, and I've never met two people more perfect for each other than they are."

"Wow."

"It's proof that when you know, you know."

"I guess so."

"How do you feel when you think about never seeing Milo again?"

"Devastated."

"Then maybe you should try to make it work with him, huh?"

"I want to… I really do. It's just that earlier, when I saw his sister freaking out because her fiancé, who's a heart transplant recipient, wasn't feeling well, it was a reminder that when you take a risk on love, there's always a chance you could lose the one you love the most. I just don't know if I could handle that if it happened to me."

"Which is fair, considering what's already happened in your life. But you probably thought you wouldn't survive Jared calling off the wedding and leaving you."

"I think there must be something wrong with me if I got over him so easily and moved on to someone else."

"There's nothing wrong with you. Since he canceled the wedding, you've seen parts of his character that he kept hidden from you before. Like how he reneged on paying for the wedding and got you sued by the venue. Among other things, such as suggesting you go forward with the wedding so the money wouldn't be wasted. Isn't that every girl's dream?"

For the first time in hours, I laugh. "No kidding, right?"

"He wasn't the guy for you, and thankfully you didn't have to find that out after you were married to him."

"For sure."

"People hide the less-than-perfect sides of themselves from others, but sometimes the less than perfect isn't so bad. Just because things didn't work out with Jared doesn't mean you can't trust your judgment about Milo."

"My judgment was off with Scott, too."

"Everyone's judgment was off with him, not just yours."

I hadn't thought of it that way before, but that's true. "Yes, I guess so."

"You shouldn't beat yourself up over that, Gianna. Like Jared, Scott showed you and everyone else what he wanted you to see. It's not your fault that you had faith in him. He never gave you reason not to, and it still may turn out that he had nothing to do with what happened to Skylar."

Hearing that, I feel some of the weight lift from my shoulders. She's right. I wasn't the only one who trusted Scott and supported him in the years since Skylar went missing. Her own parents did, too. And we still don't know much about why he was arrested.

"What are you thinking?" Chelsea asks.

"So many things. You're right about Scott. A lot of people trusted him."

"Cut yourself a break on that one, and on what happened with Jared. You dodged a future divorce when he canceled the wedding, as awful as that was. And there's absolutely nothing wrong with having feelings for Milo. It's not too soon or too fast or too anything. It just is."

"Thank you for this. You've really helped me."

"Are you going to be all right?"

"Yes, but I think I'm going to take some time to get my head together before I make any decisions about Milo or anything else."

"That's not a bad idea. Just don't take too long if he's the one you want."

"I hear you. Thank you again, Chelsea."

"Call me any time. I'm always here for you."

"You're the best."

We end the call with promises to check in soon. As the room grows darker, I remain on the sofa in the family room my mother decorated and let my mind wander over what Chelsea said. I keep coming back to the point she made about her parents. Engaged after ten days and still together thirty-five years later. So it is possible to fall in love as quickly as Milo and I did, and for it to last a lifetime.

I'm comforted by that, but I still feel unsettled.

Hopefully, with two more days off to get my head together, I can figure out what's next.

CHAPTER 23

MILO

Being without Gianna is utter misery. From the minute I wake up until the second I drop into restless sleep, I'm thinking about her, reliving our brief time together and fearing that's all we'll ever have. I dream about making love with her, about the way she looked at me as she took my cock into her mouth, about dancing with her on the cruise and how she looked in the various bikinis she wore on the trip. I recall every deep conversation about life and love and everything else we talked about.

I got a text yesterday from Jamie asking how I was feeling, and I wanted to write back and say I'm miserable because Gianna pulled back from me and us, but all I say is that I'm much better and thank her and Breck for helping when I fell ill. She responds with a hope that we'll get together again sometime.

I don't reply to that because what can I say? That I'm sitting here wondering if I'll ever see Gianna again? Let alone the friends we made together.

The sliding door to the pool opens, and Maria and Everly come out, obviously looking for me.

"What are you ladies doing here?"

"We came to swim with Mateo," Maria says as Sofia and Mateo follow them onto the pool deck.

The swimming playdate is a ruse that I see right through. By now, Maria has heard about what happened with Gianna, and she's here to check on me.

While the kids splash in the shallow end of the pool, Maria and Sofia stretch out on lounge chairs on either side of me.

Maria looks over at me. "How's it going?"

"Fabulous." Why should I make it easy for her to poke her nose into my business? I immediately feel shitty for thinking that way. She's here because she cares.

She lowers her sunglasses and gives me a penetrating look.

"What do you want me to say? Gianna asked me to give her some space, so that's what I'm doing."

"How much space?"

"All the space."

"And you think it's a good idea to not see her at all while she's thinking about what to do with you?"

"No, Mari, I don't think it's a good idea, but it's what she wants. End of story."

"Hmm."

On a deep sigh, I ask, "What does 'hmm' mean?"

"I just think that maybe this would be a good time to show her what life with you will be like."

"I've done that."

"When? You were either in the hospital or on a cruise since you've known her. How have you shown her what real life will be like?"

"And how do you propose I do that while giving her the space she asked for?"

"Little things. Take her a coffee at work. Send dinner to her house when she gets home. Send her flowers to let her know you're thinking of her. Write her letters and send funny cards and make your case to her."

"And that won't be a violation of the space she asked for?"

"If you're not physically present, you're not violating the space. Tell him, Sofia."

She points to Maria. "What she said."

"You guys really think it's a good idea to do stuff like that when she asked for space?"

"I do," Sofia says softly. "She's running scared, Milo. Show her she has nothing to be afraid of by trusting you."

"We saw you guys together," Maria adds. "This is not about her having a lack of affection for you. It's about her not trusting herself to let go and allow it to happen."

"I mean, her fiancé called off the wedding *at* the wedding. Imagine how traumatic that must've been." Every time I think of her showing up in her gorgeous dress, probably too beautiful for words, only to find out he wasn't going through with it, I want to kill him.

"She's probably questioning her own sanity in falling for someone else so soon after that happened," Maria says.

"Yeah, I guess."

"So show her that what she sees is what she gets with you and that she'd be lucky to have you in her life," Maria says.

"I'll think about it."

"Good," Maria says, seeming pleased with herself.

"How's Car?"

"She's sore, but on the road to recovery."

"And the baby?"

"Just fine, thank God."

"No kidding. That's a huge relief."

"It is. Car will be coming home tomorrow with orders to take it easy for a few weeks."

"I'm glad they're both okay."

"Me, too."

"Can you guys keep a secret?" Sofia asks in her usual soft tone.

Maria and I turn to her.

"I can, but I'm not so sure about her."

Maria smacks my arm. "Hush. What's up, Sofia?"

"I'm pregnant."

"Oh my God! That's amazing! All our kids will grow up together."

"I know." Sofia raises her sunglasses to wipe away tears. "I haven't told Nico yet."

"Um, why?" Maria asks, saving me from doing it.

"I'm not sure it's what he wants. I mean, we're not even married yet and—"

I reach out to her. "Sofia, he loves you with all his heart. He'll be thrilled. You have nothing to worry about where he's concerned."

"What am I going to be thrilled about?" Nico asks from across the pool deck.

"Go tell him," I whisper to her. "We'll watch Mateo."

"Thank you." Sofia gets up and tells Mateo to behave for a minute and that Maria and I are in charge.

"Okay, Mama," he says before he goes back to splashing with Everly.

"This is so exciting," Maria says as we watch Sofia go to Nico and direct him inside.

"It sure is."

I'm thrilled for my brother and Sofia even as my own heart aches with longing for the one I love and miss so much.

NICO

"What's going on?" I ask as I follow Sofia upstairs to our room.

As she gestures for me to go in ahead of her, I start to worry that something is wrong. And then she closes the door, and my anxiety spikes. The heightened state of alert I've been in for weeks has made my anxiety worse than it's ever been.

"Sofia..."

She comes to me, puts her hands on my chest and presses her sun-warmed body against me.

That's all it takes for me to want her. Actually, it usually takes much less than that.

"I'm pregnant."

I blink a few times as the words register, and then I'm whooping and picking her up and spinning her around until she begs me to stop.

"Nico! I'm going to be sick!"

I put her down and wait until she's steady on her feet to pull back so I can see her gorgeous face. "We're having a baby?"

"Yes. I know we didn't plan it so soon, and we're not even married yet—"

I kiss her. "We'll get married tomorrow."

"What?"

"Why not? It's what we both want, and now there's a baby. We can have a big celebration after the baby comes."

"You're crazy."

I kiss her until she goes weak in my arms. I'll never get tired of the way she responds to me or how I respond to her. "I'm crazy in love with you, and all I want is to be married to you and to adopt Mateo and to have more babies with you. I want us to have it all."

"I already have it all as long as I have you and Mateo and our baby."

"Then let's get married and make it official."

"Can we at least wait until the weekend, so I have five minutes to buy a dress?"

"I suppose I can wait that long, but not one minute longer."

"So impatient, my love."

"To be your husband? Yes, I am. I can't wait to have everything with you."

"I'm the luckiest to be loved by you."

"I'm the luckiest."

"We're both lucky," I tell her as I guide her to the bed. With Maria and Milo watching Mateo, we can steal a few minutes for ourselves. "And we're just getting started."

DEE

I wake up with no idea where I am, the sound of monitors beeping a quick reminder that I'm in the hospital with Wyatt, who's still asleep next to me. Probably because he's so well liked at Miami-Dade, no one objected to me sleeping at his side in the narrow hospital bed. We both sleep better when we're together, even in a hospital.

The events of yesterday and all the associated emotions come rushing back to remind me of how terrifying it was to be certain that Wyatt's heart was failing, and he might die.

I guess that's how it's going to be any time anything out of the ordinary happens with his health. I'm always going to panic and go straight to the worst-case scenario. I hate that my brain works that way, but with his situation being somewhat precarious, who could blame me?

"Why are you spinning first thing in the morning?" he asks in the gruff morning voice I love so much. More than anything, I love that I'm the only one who ever hears that version of his sexy voice.

"I'm not spinning."

"Don't make it worse by lying to me, babe."

"I'm just thinking and realizing a few things."

"Like what?"

"That I'll always be terrified at the first sign of illness in you."

His deep sigh says it all. "I wish you didn't have to live that way."

"It's a small price to pay for all the good stuff that comes with you. We have so much to be thankful for."

"Yes, we do, and I want you to stay focused on that and not always be anticipating disaster. I work in a hospital. I picked up a germ. It happens."

"We both know how those germs can be anything but routine for you."

"We do, but we can't live our lives constantly waiting for disaster to strike either."

"I don't do that. I swear I don't. I go days without even thinking about it, but when something like this happens, I can't help but be triggered."

"I know, baby, and I'm so sorry to put you through that."

"Don't be sorry. Loving you and having you love me is the best thing to ever happen to me."

"Same."

He twirls a length of my hair around his finger, something he does nearly every day. It's those little familiar things that make me feel so at home with him. "I wish more than anything that we could have all this without the black cloud hanging over us."

"The cloud is part of who we are, and I love who we are. I'm sorry if I overreacted yesterday, but it's your fault for making me so damned happy that the thought of losing you is terrifying to me."

He snuggles me into his embrace. "I'm not going anywhere except home with you later today, I hope."

"Are you sure it's not too soon to go home?"

"I'm very sure. I'm fine, Dee. I promise."

Since he knows better than I ever will about when we should be truly afraid, I take him at his word and try to relax so my own heart won't fail at the thought of life without my beloved.

NICO

In the end, it takes us three weeks to pull together a wedding that will include Sofia's newfound family in Minnesota. She recently located her father, who'd had no idea she existed, and learned she had a stepmother and three half-siblings, too. They're arriving tomorrow and staying with us, which has had Sofia cleaning every inch of the house and cooking like a madwoman. Despite my pleas to let others help her, she wants to do it herself. "This is the first time I've had my family to our home," she told me. "I want to make it perfect."

So I stood by and let her do her thing, while helping where she'd let me. I'm worried that she's going to drop from exhaustion before she says, "I do." But the funny thing is, the harder she works, the more she glows with happiness.

She has me, Mateo, my family and now hers as well as a baby on the way, and she's never seemed happier or more content as she prepares for the arrival of her father, stepmother and half siblings. Nothing pleases me more to see the change in her, from haunted and terrorized when we first met, to happy and peaceful now. That's how I want her to stay forever.

My mother and grandmothers have been cooking all week for the wedding dinner, and we're just about ready for the festivities to begin.

Milo comes downstairs, finally looking more like his old self than he has since the shooting. He rubs his hands together with glee that I can tell is manufactured. He's barely smiled since he last saw Gianna, but he's trying to rally for my bachelor party tonight.

"Ready to party, brother?"

"Ready when you are. Is this really happening at the Ball & Chain?"

"Dude… Of course it is."

"Remember… Payback is a bitch." I immediately regret the comment when his smile falters. "Sorry."

"Don't be. No worries about payback for a while."

"You don't know that for sure."

"Three weeks and hardly a word from her."

"Have you reached out to her?"

"I sent her a couple of cards and some flowers to let her know I'm thinking of her, like the girls said I should. She texts to thank me and says she hopes I'm doing well." He shrugs as heartbreak emanates from every pore in his body. I hate this for him so much.

"Well, it's her loss if you ask me."

That gets me half a smile from him. "Thanks. Let's put that aside for the night and focus on you."

"Do we have to?"

"Yes, we have to."

The front door opens as our cousin Domenic comes in, followed by Jason, Austin and Wyatt. We're so thankful he's back to full health after his bout with pneumonia and would appreciate him not scaring us—or Dee—like that again any time soon.

"You boys ready to rumble?" Dom asks.

"Ready as I'll ever be," I mutter.

"The groom thinks this isn't necessary," Milo tells the others. "We know better right, boys?"

"We sure do," Austin says, putting his hands on my shoulders to direct me to the door where they have one of my cars and drivers waiting to transport us to the party. They think I don't know about that.

"Wait. I need to say good night to Sofia and Mateo. Give me one minute."

I run upstairs to find Sofia helping Mateo change into his pajamas. He tends to be needy this time of day, and his mother is so good with him.

"Hey, guys, I'm getting ready to leave, and I wanted to say good night."

Mateo rushes over to hug me.

I'll never be able to describe what it means to me that he loves and trusts me the way he does after what he and Sofia endured at the hands of his father.

"How come I can't go on boys' night out?" he asks.

"Because it's for big boys, and little boys need to get their sleep so they can help me get married in *two* days."

I love his goofy little smile with the gap from a front tooth he lost a week ago. Shopping with him for a suit to wear to the wedding was one of my favorite things ever. I give him a big hug and then lift him so I can plop him into bed. "Sweet dreams, pal."

"Have fun tonight."

I kiss his cheek and tuck the covers in around him like I do every night. "I won't have as much fun as I do with you and Mama."

"You'd better not."

"Love you."

"Love you, too." As I start to get up, he says, "Hey, Nico?"

"What's up?"

"After you marry Mama, can I call you Papa?"

My heart nearly stops when he asks that, his little face so sweet and vulnerable.

"It would be the honor of my lifetime to have you call me Papa."

"Okay. Thanks."

"Thank you for being a son that any man would be proud of." I kiss him again, and he hugs me tightly. "Get some sleep. We've got an exciting couple of days coming up."

When I turn to leave the room, I catch Sofia wiping away tears. I follow her into the hallway and reach for her.

"Sweetest boy ever," I whisper.

"Thank you for loving him so much."

"Loving you both is the easiest thing I've ever done. Thank you for making me a Papa."

We're both battling tears when we pull back for a kiss.

"Love you forever and ever and ever, amen."

She looks at me like no one else ever has. "Love you always."

"That's all I'll ever need." I kiss her again, more intently this time, and I immediately wish I had nowhere to be.

"Let's go, Romeo," Milo calls from downstairs. "Time's a-wasting."

She gives me a stern look. "No strippers or lap dances, you hear me?"

Smiling, I kiss her again. "The only lap dance I want is from you."

"Such a charmer. Go on and have a good time with your boys."

"Enjoy your time with the girls." My sisters, mother, grandmothers, aunts, cousins and other friends are coming over to fete Sofia while I'm out with the boys.

"I will."

I tear myself away to spend a few hours without her. If I needed further confirmation that she's the one for me, it's that I've never had to tear myself away from another woman.

We head out a few minutes later, and I act surprised to see one of my limos waiting for us along with a driver who works for me. "You shouldn't have," I tell them as they crack up.

"Don't worry, we're paying Jesus tonight," Milo says as he gestures for me to get into the car.

I'm surprised to find my dad and my uncle Vincent waiting for us, champagne in hand. I thought they were meeting us there.

"Let's get this party started," Dad says as he pours champagne for the rest of us.

"Isn't this supposed to be a bachelor party?" I ask them. "Where's the whiskey?"

"We're saving that for later," Milo tells me as he hands me a glass of champagne. "A toast to the man of the hour, my big brother and best friend forever. We love you, we love Sofia and Mateo, and we're so happy for you all. Cheers!"

Damn if he doesn't nearly reduce me to tears calling me his best friend forever. Before the shooting, that wouldn't have hit me the way it does now. "Thanks, everyone. And by the way, how is it fair that Domenic got married without us even knowing it, and he didn't have to do this bachelor party bullshit?"

"You're not as clever as I am," Dom says, waggling his brows. "Where you went wrong, my friend, is in planning a big family shitshow. If you were smooth like me, you'd sneak off and do the deed without anyone knowing."

Before Sofia found her father and his family, that would've looked good to me, but now I'd never deny her the wedding she deserves.

I roll my eyes at Dom. "How's married life treating you, primo?"

"It's the best thing ever," he says, looking slightly dazzled. "How come no one told me how great it is?"

"Dude," Austin says with disdain. "We've been showing you that for a while now."

"Yes, you have, and doing a fine job of it."

"How's Carmen feeling, Jay?" Wyatt asks.

"She's much better. Tonight will be her first outing since coming home from the hospital. Viv is driving her to your place, Nico."

"Oh, good. I'm glad she's able to come. Sofia is looking forward to it."

The car pulls onto Calle Oche, home of the infamous Ball & Chain bar. I still can't believe Milo booked that place for this. Well, yes, I can. As a lifelong ballbuster, I've taught my little brother well.

The hijinks begin right away when a lightweight "iron" ball is chained to my ankle for the festivities. I'm stunned to find friends from all corners of my life waiting to greet me. High school friends I played football with, college friends I partied with, work friends and neighbors. Everyone who's anyone in my life is there.

"This is amazing, Mi," I say to my brother. "Thank you so much."

"Anything for you, bro."

After coming so close to losing him, I'm so thankful he's there to celebrate everything with, now and always. But the heartache is as plain as the nose on his face, and I'm determined to try to fix that for him before I go forth into my own happily ever after.

CHAPTER 24

GIANNA

It's been a punishing week at work, with more critical cases than we've seen all at once in quite some time. By the time the weekend rolls around, I'm ready to sleep for days. I've been so exhausted lately, and I can't help but note that the exhaustion set in shortly after I sent Milo away.

I'm enjoying my first cup of coffee in the garden patio my parents loved so much when the doorbell rings. Ugh, who's that? No one comes by without texting first, so I'm sure it's no one I want to see. But when I go to look through the peephole, I'm shocked to see Nico. I'm immediately worried that something has happened to Milo.

I open the door. "What's wrong?"

"Can we talk?"

"Um, sure." I run my fingers through my hair, which I haven't brushed yet, fearing I look as frightful as I've felt the last few weeks. "Is everything all right with Milo? He's not sick or anything, is he?"

"He's fine." Nico stops and turns to face me. "Well, that's

kind of a lie. He's not fine at all. He's been a mess since he last saw you, even if he tries to hide that from us."

My heart sinks at that news, but I also feel a tiny spark of relief at knowing he's as miserable as I am. "I'm sorry. It's all my fault. I sort of freaked out and ruined everything."

"You haven't. Ruined everything, that is. If you still care for him, I think he'd love to hear from you."

"I do care for him. I more than care for him. He's all I think about, but I just want to be fair to him. Things have been such a mess for me lately, and the last thing I want is to drag him down with me."

"I wouldn't venture to speak for him, but if I had to guess, he'd much rather be dragged down with you than be without you."

He hands me an envelope.

"What's this?"

"An invitation to my wedding. Sofia and I are getting married on Sunday at our house. We'd love it if you could join us."

"Does Milo know you're inviting me?"

He shakes his head. "It's completely up to you, but I have absolutely no doubt that he'd be very, *very* glad to see you."

"Thank you for the invite. I'll think about it."

"Okay." Nico starts to walk toward the door, but then stops and turns to me again. "The thing is, Gianna, I don't think I can be truly happy if he's hurting the way he has since things fell apart with you. If there's any chance you might feel the same way he does, then maybe you guys could figure shit out together rather than trying to go it alone?" He shakes his head, seeming to regret the outburst. "Sorry. I promised myself I wouldn't put any pressure on you. I just wanted to invite you to the wedding."

"Thank you for coming, Nico. It means a lot. Milo is lucky to have you as his big brother."

"I'm the lucky one to have him. It's always been that way.

Anyone would be lucky to have him. He's the best person I know. And now I'm pressuring you again."

I laugh even as I wipe away a stray tear. "It's fine. You're not telling me anything I don't already know."

He surprises me with a kiss to the cheek. "I really hope you can make it to the wedding. The whole family would be thrilled to see you. Take care, Gianna."

After he leaves, I open the envelope to read the invitation:

Together with their families and son Mateo,

Nico Giordino & Sofia Diaz

request the honor of your presence at their wedding

April 23, 6 p.m., at the home of

Nico, Sofia, Mateo and Milo

Reception to follow.

When I think of seeing Milo as soon as Sunday, my heart feels lighter than it has in weeks. In the kitchen, I reread the cards he's sent me for the hundredth time each. Some of them are funny, others sweet, a few as romantic as it gets. All of them bear the same message from him: *I love you and miss you.*

I've taken this time to think about what I want, and I keep coming back to him. Am I ready for what he might be to me? Maybe not. Do I care about that anymore? Not one bit. I love and miss him, too. Being without him has been a hell of my own making, and it's time to make things right. If Nico is to be believed, Milo will be happy to see me.

I hope that's still true.

After a shower, I get dressed and run downstairs to grab my

keys as I rush out the door. I need to find a showstopper of a dress to wear to a wedding.

MILO

Nico is getting married. *Today.* It's hard to believe we're at the point where we're old enough for such things, but after today, two of us will be married, one engaged and then there's me... The sad sack of the bunch, pining for a woman who may or may not feel the same way about me. Who knows what she's thinking? Not me. That's for sure. I have no idea what's going on with her.

Other than a few brief texts to thank me for the cards and flowers, I haven't heard a word from her, and I'm done reaching out. For now, anyway. A guy can only stand so much rejection before it starts to become a self-inflicted wound.

Nico comes to the doorway of my room, dressed in the sharp navy suit we picked out last weekend. "Do I look all right?"

"You look great."

"So do you."

I'm wearing a gray suit I bought to wear in a high school friend's wedding last year. It's a little loose on me thanks to the weight I lost after the shooting, but it'll work.

Nico straightens my tie, which doesn't need straightening. "I just want you to know... That if the worst had happened, I might've gotten married someday, but I wouldn't have had anyone else as my best man."

"The worst didn't happen, and I'm right here."

"Thank God for that," he says as he hugs me. "Losing you would've ruined my life."

"You would've gotten over it eventually."

"Never."

"Well, thankfully we don't have to think about that or any of the other crap. Only good things for you and Sofia and Mateo. That's what we're about today."

Nico nods. "Yeah, for sure."

"You ready?"

"Sure am. I can't wait to be married to Sofia and to adopt Mateo and to have it all. My only hope beyond that is for you to get everything you want and deserve, too."

"Today's your day. We'll worry about me another time. Let's get downstairs so we don't get accused of being late for a very important date."

As we're going down the stairs, Sofia's father, Jon, is coming up.

He and Nico embrace.

"Thanks so much for being here," Nico says gruffly. "It means everything to Sofia."

"I wouldn't have missed it for the world."

He only recently learned that Sofia existed and opened his heart, home and family to her.

"We'll see you down there," Nico says.

"We'll be right along."

"I'll be waiting."

We land in the living room, where everyone we know is waiting to hug Nico, to say congratulations and wish him well.

Abuela reaches up to put her hands on his cheeks. "Todo lo mejor de todo, mi amor."

All the best of everything, my love.

Her fiancé, Alfredo, hugs Nico next and whispers something to him that has Nico fighting tears. It's going to be that kind of day.

Nona is next to hug Nico. "I can't believe my little Button is getting married."

Nico rolls his eyes at me as she squeezes him.

"If the name fits," I say, earning a scowl from the groom.

Nona's gentleman friend, Chris, shakes hands with Nico and wishes him well.

Mom comes in from the pool deck. "There you are. Come on, boys. It's time to take your places."

"Where's Mateo?" Nico asks.

"Already where he belongs, unlike you two."

Grinning at me, Nico follows Mom outside, where another bunch of family waits to greet him. Carmen is seated under an awning, but she waves to us as we come out.

Nico blows her a kiss and hugs Aunt Viv and Uncle Vincent.

Dad is waiting for us in the front row of chairs on the deck facing an arch that Sofia, her stepmother, half sisters, Maria and Dee adorned with tropical flowers yesterday. I can't believe what they managed to put together in three weeks' time.

I return the embrace from my dad, who's an emotional mess as he hugs Nico. "My little boy is getting married."

"I'm a grown man, Dad," Nico says with his usual disdain for all things sappy.

"And you'll always be my little boy."

Mateo comes over to Nico, and he picks him up to hug him.

"I didn't get any dirt on my suit," he tells Nico.

"That's my boy."

"Where's Mama?"

"She'll be here soon."

Mom, the drill sergeant who's put herself in charge of the festivities, calls everyone out and asks them to find a seat.

I feel like I must be seeing things when Gianna steps onto the pool deck wearing a stunning red dress that looks like it was painted onto her tempting curves.

"What…" I tear my gaze off her to glance at Nico. "Why is she here?"

"You should know the answer to that question."

"But how did she know?"

"I invited her."

I can't believe he did that for me. I'm overcome with so many emotions after seeing her and knowing my brother made it happen. "Nico…"

"Hold it together for a few more minutes, and then you can go get your girl, okay?"

"Yeah. I got you, bro. No worries."

"You got the rings, right?"

"Oh shit. That was my job?"

"Seriously?"

I grin at him. "Nah. I got 'em."

"Dick."

As I lose it laughing, it's such a relief to have the old Nico back. But it's an even bigger relief to have Gianna back. I can't wait to get this ceremony over with so I can be with her.

SOFIA

I've never been more excited in my life than I am to marry Nico. Having Mateo was thrilling, but I was already having so many issues with his father that it took some of the joy out of his arrival. There's nothing but joy today. I hug my dear friend Gladys, who was so there for me and Mateo after I left Joaquín.

"Happiness always," she whispers to me before she goes downstairs, leaving me alone with the father I'd longed for all my life.

"You're beautiful, honey," Jon says. "I see my mother in you."

"Do you? I love knowing that."

"She would've adored you. I'm sorry you never got to meet her and that I've missed all the big things with you."

"Not all of them," I remind him. "This is the biggest day of my life, tied with the day Mateo was born."

He kisses my cheek. "I'll be here for everything from now on. I promise."

I made the decision not to invite my mother, who's been nothing but a source of stress and despair for me. Now that I have Jon and his family as well as Nico and his family, I have what I need. Being surrounded by positive, loving, supportive, optimistic people has made such a difference for me and Mateo.

As I curl my hand through the crook of the arm Jon offers me, I'm at peace in a way I haven't been since Milo was shot by my ex-husband. If Nico and I got through that, we can get through anything.

My father escorts me down the stairs. The French doors to the pool deck are open, and the lights Nico strung over the outdoor space are lit as the sun dips toward the palm trees. We've scored a perfect warm night, with no humidity, which is a rare thing in South Florida.

"Are you ready, sweetheart?" Elena asks when she greets us at the door.

"So ready."

"You look stunning." She kisses my cheek. "We love you and your sweet boy."

She'll never know what that means to me. "We love you, too."

At her signal, "The Dance" by Garth Brooks begins to play. Nico and I chose that song because it reminds us of how lucky we are to have found each other in this crazy world. Hearing it now reduces me to tears. I'm thankful I thought to buy waterproof mascara, especially when I see him and Mateo holding hands as they wait for me to join them.

Nico is so sexy in the suit he picked out for the wedding, and I can tell he's as emotional as I am, watching me come toward him on the arm of my father.

"Who gives this woman to be married?" the officiant asks. He's a friend of the family's and a frequent guest at the restaurant.

"I do," Jon says as he kisses me, whispers that he loves me

and joins my hand with Nico's before stepping back to sit with his wife and the rest of his family.

"You're beautiful," Nico says.

"So are you."

I hand my bouquet to Maria. She and Dee are my attendants.

Nico and I gaze at each other and recite the vows the officiant leads us through. He asked if we wanted to say our own vows, but I was afraid I'd be so nervous that I'd forget all the English I've learned at the worst possible moment. Nico and I agreed that we'd do that part in private later.

As we recite our vows, the feeling is surreal. As Nico vows to love, honor and cherish me, I believe him, because he's already shown me all that and so much more—more than I ever dreamed possible.

Milo hands him the rings we chose.

Nico slides mine on my finger, staring steadily into my eyes the whole time, almost as if he wants there to be no doubt that he's exactly where he wants to be and I'm who he wants to be with.

I don't have a doubt in my mind as I put his ring on his finger. "With this ring, I thee wed."

"By the power vested in me by the State of Florida, I pronounce you husband and wife. Nico, you may kiss your bride."

"Ew," Mateo says, making everyone laugh, including us, as Nico kisses me.

"Let's hear it for Nico and Sofia Giordino and their son, Mateo!"

Everyone is clapping and crying and whistling and celebrating our marriage. After the disaster with Joaquín, I swore I'd never get married again. I didn't want to be legally bound to a man who could control me. But then along came Nico with his beautiful family, and now I couldn't be happier to be married to him and expecting our child. I'm confident this marriage will be nothing like the first one.

This one is forever.

GIANNA

Watching Nico and Sofia exchange vows has made me an emotional wreck as I wait impatiently for the chance to talk to Milo, to *be* with Milo. During the ceremony, he didn't look away from me, except to hand the rings to Nico. Then he found me again and impaled me with his intense gaze. Every part of me wants him in a way I've never wanted any other man, even the one I was supposed to marry.

Especially him.

In the last few weeks, I've come around to the fact that I may never fully understand how I got so far down the road with a man who was utterly wrong for me. The one thing I do understand is that I love Milo and being without him has made me miserable. Maybe it's too soon after Jared, but I don't care about that or anything other than making things right with Milo.

He's the one I want, and judging by the way he's looking at me, he feels the same way.

God, I hope so.

I was so afraid I'd ruined everything until I started getting the cards and flowers from him, letting me know that he respected my request for space, but he still cared as much as always.

I've begun to believe that will never change.

He has a sister on each arm as he comes toward me. "All right, ladies, that's the end of the road. I've got important business to see to."

Both his sisters kiss his cheeks and tell him they love him.

"Love you, too. Now go away."

I giggle at the sibling banter that's so entertaining to me.

Milo steps up to me. "Fancy meeting you here."

"I was invited."

"So I heard about fifteen minutes ago."

"I hope it's okay that I came."

His entire expression goes soft with love as he takes me into his arms. "It's so okay, it's not even funny."

I cling to him, breathing in the scent that became so familiar during our time on the cruise, and release all the anxiety and fear that've gripped me since the last time I saw him. "I'm sorry. I screwed this up so badly."

"No, you didn't."

"I did, and you have to let me apologize."

"No apology needed. The only thing that matters is that you're here now, and you're back to stay." He pulls back and looks down at me, heart in his gorgeous eyes. "You are here to stay, right?"

"For as long as you'll have me."

"That's going to be a really, *really* long time."

I shrug. "So be it. You're stuck with me."

"I've never been happier in my entire life than I am to have forever to spend with you."

And just that simply, everything falls into place, and I'm certain I'm right where I belong.

CHAPTER 25

MILO

I'll never forget Nico's wedding day. Not only did his life with Sofia begin, but mine with Gianna did, too. We dance to every slow song like we're the newlyweds.

"This dress, though," I whisper to her as we sway to "Hold My Hand" by Lady Gaga. "Was it intended to stop my heart?"

"Absolutely not! I need your heart beating for many decades to come."

"Well, you almost succeeded in sending me to an early grave."

"It's too soon after the shooting for comments about you and graves."

"Sorry, love."

"Don't let it happen again."

My mother approaches us, beaming with pleasure to see us back together. She greets Gianna with a huge hug. "So good to see you, sweetheart."

"You, too, Elena."

"Are you ready to do your toast?" she asks me.

"Yep." I take Gianna's hand to keep her with me as I accept the microphone from my mother.

"Keep it clean," Mom says.

"What fun would that be?" Before she has a chance to reply, I whistle into the microphone to get the attention of the guests. "As Nico's younger brother and best man, I have a few things to say."

"Mom, take that microphone away from him," Nico says. "No one wants to hear this."

"I do," Sofia says, earning a playful glare from her husband.

The "head table" is made up of Sofia, Nico and Mateo.

Mateo moves to sit on Nico's lap.

"This is the part where Milo gets to make fun of me," Nico tells him.

"Go, Milo," Mateo says with a fist pump.

Nico tickles him until he's laughing so hard, he can't breathe.

"Nico was six when I was born, following our two sisters, who were, according to Nico, of absolutely no use to him."

Maria and Dee crack up.

"Back atcha, Nico," Maria says as Dee sticks out her tongue at him.

"They only became useful to me when they brought us Austin and Wyatt," Nico says.

Now that I've got them fighting with each other, I grin with satisfaction. "Before Sofia and Mateo came along, I was the best thing to ever happen to Nico. A baby *brother*. According to my parents, only they and Nico were allowed to hold me for the first month. Even Nona and Abuela had to wait until Nico was in bed to get a turn with me. Nico said I was his, and that was that. And it's been that way ever since. There's never been a time in my life when I didn't know I could count on Nico for anything and everything I needed. He's been my constant, my protector, my best friend, my favorite person to bicker with and the best roommate ever."

"Mostly because I won't let you pay rent," Nico says, wiping away tears as everyone else laughs.

"Well, there is that. I'm not going to revisit recent events because we've all said enough about that to last us a lifetime. What I will say is that I saw a whole other side of my ball-busting, button-pushing big brother in the last few months, and honestly? I couldn't stand him."

That makes everyone laugh hard.

"Today, when I pretended to have forgotten the rings, he called me a dick, and I was so relieved, because *that's* the Nico I know and love."

My mother shakes her head in mock disapproval as she tries not to laugh.

"And that's the Nico we all prefer. Sofia, you're perfect for my brother, and we're so glad you agreed to take him off our hands. We'll be here for you when he drives you crazy, and we'll *always* take your side against him."

"Gee, thanks, bro," Nico says as Sofia giggles helplessly.

"On a serious note, life is crazy, and knowing you have people you can count on at the best and worst of times makes all the difference. Nico, you've always been the one I could count on no matter what, and you always will be—and vice versa. I love you, and I thank you for all you've been to me since the day I came home from the hospital—the first time, that is. Sofia and Mateo, we love you so much, and we're thrilled to welcome you to the Giordino family." I hold up my glass of champagne. "To Nico, Sofia and Mateo. We wish you the best of everything."

Everyone joins me in toasting the happy new family.

"That was beautiful," Gianna says.

"Thanks. I had to bust his balls a little."

"Of course you did."

My mother invites everyone to the buffet in the dining

room. Nico rented tables and chairs for everyone to sit outside to eat.

While the guests line up for dinner, I lead Gianna inside through the laundry room and up the back stairs to the second floor.

"Um, where are you taking me?" she asks, sounding breathless and happy.

"You'll see in one second." I take her into my room, close the door and press her back against the door to kiss her. "Hi."

"Hello there."

"How're you doing?"

"So much better now that I'm with you. How about you?"

"There're no words to describe how great I feel being with you again. I thought I'd lose my mind, I missed you so much."

"I missed you, too. I've hardly slept in weeks."

I noticed the dark circles she tried to cover with makeup, but I keep that to myself. "You'll sleep well tonight."

"Will I?"

"Yep. I'll make sure you're good and tired."

"And how will you do that?"

I kiss her neck. "I'll start with this."

She shivers in my arms.

"And then, I'll do this." I unzip her dress and nudge it off her shoulders, watching it fall to the floor in a cloud of red silk.

"Shouldn't we talk first?"

"Absolutely not." I pull back from her only long enough to retrieve the dress, and then I do a double take when I see she's completely naked. "*Damn,*" I say on a long exhale. "This was premeditated."

"Just a little," she says with a nervous giggle. "You're overdressed for this party." She pushes the suitcoat off and goes to work on my tie.

I help her by pulling the dress shirt over my head and releasing my belt. "So it's a party now, huh?"

"Yep, and oh, I've missed these muscles," she says as she runs her hands over my pecs and abs. "I've missed everything about you."

"Same. I relived every second we spent together a million times, worrying that it might be all we'd ever have."

"I'm sorry, Milo."

I kiss the words off her sweet lips. "You're not apologizing for doing what needed to happen to bring you back to me. Okay?"

"Okay, but I want to tell you about it, so you'll understand."

"We have all the time in the world to talk. Right now, I just want to love you."

She reaches for me, and we meet in the middle in a collision of lips, tongues and desire so potent, it makes my head spin.

Her skin is so soft, her curves so perfect, her scent intoxicating and her kisses hot enough to start a fire that'll burn in me for the rest of our lives. Knowing that for certain makes me happier than I've ever been. I don't care that everyone I know is downstairs celebrating Nico and Sofia and probably wondering where I've gone.

Or maybe they aren't wondering at all.

I couldn't be bothered worrying about anything when Gianna is warm and soft and naked in my arms. I walk her backward to my bed, and when she's seated, I drop my pants and boxers and then come down on top of her as she wraps her arms and legs around me. Trapped in the sweetest place I've ever been, I can only breathe her in and dwell in the relief of being back with her again after fearing the worst.

But as her hands slide over my back, sending tremors through me, I want her urgently.

We both move just enough to align our bodies, and I slide into her effortlessly. "I promise we'll never skip the preliminaries again."

"We've also got all the time for preliminaries and everything else," she says, gazing up at me with so much love.

"I have one more week off from work. I want to spend that entire week in bed with you."

"I have to work."

I press my lips to her forehead. "You feel a little feverish. I assume you're not supposed to work when you have a fever."

Her smile encompasses her entire face, and it occurs to me that's the first time I've ever seen her smile quite that big. "They do encourage us to keep germs out of the hospital."

I press deep inside her, so deep I can't tell where I end and she begins.

She lifts her hips off the bed to take me even deeper and nearly finishes me off with the tight squeeze of her muscles around my cock.

"This is the best thing ever," I whisper against her lips.

"*Ever.*"

"Best day ever, too."

"No question."

"You're going to have to marry me now. You know that, don't you?"

She goes completely still under me, and I fear I might've asked for too much too soon once again. "Are you asking me?"

"Depends on what the answer would be."

"Do you mean it?"

"God, yes, Gianna. I mean it. I want to be with you for the rest of my life. If it's too soon to talk about getting married, then we'll talk about it later, but I want us to have it all."

"It's not too soon," she says. "I want us to have it all, too. So yes, Milo, I'll marry you."

"Did we get engaged on Nico's wedding day?"

"Looks that way."

"We'll get you a ring this week."

She places her hands on my face and looks at me with her

heart in her eyes. "I want you to know… I've had the big, flashy ring and planned the big, flashy wedding. But with you? All I want is the epic marriage. The rest is just details."

Smiling, I kiss her and push back into her. "I think we can do epic."

NICO

"Where do you suppose Milo and Gianna are?" I ask Sofia as we dance under the Miami moon and stars.

"Where would we be if we hadn't seen each other in weeks?"

"We're never going to go weeks without seeing each other."

"Answer the question."

Smiling, I say, "We'd be in bed."

"I bet that's where you'll find them, too." She looks up at me. "You did a good thing going to see her and inviting her."

"I told her I couldn't be truly happy unless he is, too."

"You're such a good brother."

"Not always, but I've learned not to take any of them for granted."

"I'm sorry you had to learn that the way you did."

"You're not allowed to apologize to me about that, remember?"

"I'm trying to remember that."

"Try harder. No one here blames you for what that psychopath did. Let's not even think about that today, or ever. Especially when we have so many better things to think about, such as our honeymoon."

"What honeymoon?"

"The one we're leaving on tomorrow afternoon."

"What? Where are we going?"

"To an all-inclusive resort in Jamaica."

"Oh my God! Nico! Can we afford that?"

"Nope." She knows that everything I have is invested in the business.

"But how…"

"My grandmothers gave it to us. They wanted us to get away together after everything that's happened the last few months and knew we didn't have the money for a fancy trip, so they arranged it for us."

"Stop it," she whispers. "They did not."

"They did, and Austin and Maria are taking Mateo home with them tonight for a week-long sleepover with Everly. It's all set except the packing."

"I can't believe this."

"Believe it. You're a Giordino now. You never know what's going to happen next in this family."

"I want to thank them."

"Let's go do that."

Neither of us is surprised to find them in the kitchen doing dishes.

"Ladies, you're guests at this wedding," I tell them. "Not the waitstaff."

"We tried to tell them that," one of the caterers says. "But they told us to take a break and have a bite to eat."

"They're not happy if they're not feeding people."

"We can hear you, Button," Nona says.

"Can we give that name a break on my wedding day?" I ask her.

She seems to give that some thought. "Um, no. Sorry."

They're both so funny—and so different from each other—yet their hearts are bigger than the sun. "Sofia just heard about your big surprise."

"Thank you both so much," Sofia says. "You're the most generous people I've ever known."

Nona wipes her hands on a dishtowel before she hugs Sofia. "It's our pleasure, sweetheart."

"You two deserve a break away from it all," Abuela says when she hugs Sofia. "And we couldn't think of a better wedding gift."

"I love you both so much," Sofia says. "You changed my whole life—and my son's—when you made us part of this beautiful family long before today."

"We love you, too," Nona says. "You can thank us by having the best time in Jamaica."

After we hug them both again, we go to find Mateo to tell him about the week-long sleepover with Everly. The two of them are seated on a lounge chair, watching *Dora the Explorer* on my iPad. It must've been her turn to pick, because Mateo would've chosen *Paw Patrol*. They're good about taking turns and have become more like brother and sister than cousins, which is good for them, as they have no siblings—for now, anyway.

"Mateo," Sofia says, "how would you like to have a sleepover at Everly's for a *whole* week?"

Their eyes go wide as they look at each other and then back at us.

"Will you be there, too, Mama?"

"No, sweetie. Nico and I are going on a honeymoon."

"What's a honeymoon?"

"It's a trip people take after they get married," Nico tells him.

"So I won't see you guys for a *whole* week?" Mateo asks, his little chin quivering.

"We'll FaceTime with you every day," Nico says, "and you'll see Maria and Austin, and Austin's parents, and I'm sure Milo, Dee and Wyatt will stop by and Nana and Pop, too." That's what Nico's parents told Mateo to call them. "You'll have so much fun."

Everly saves the day by hugging Mateo. "I'm so excited! We'll swim in the pool all day, and Daddy will take us to the park."

Her excitement fires his, and the two of them run upstairs to start packing.

"Thank goodness for Everly," Sofia says after they take off. "We'd better supervise the packing, or he'll get there with no underwear and ten bathing suits."

"I'll do it," I tell her. "You stay here."

"Are you trying to butter me up, husband?"

I lean in to steal a kiss. "I'm trying to get you relaxed, wife. Be right back." When I get upstairs, I realize it's a good thing I came after them, because they've already taken most of the clothes out of Mateo's dresser in the one-minute head start they had on me. "Whoa. You'd better clean that up, Mateo, or Mama's going to be unhappy."

Because he never wants his mama to be unhappy, he helps me put away the clothes he's not taking to Everly's. We pack his Spider-Man suitcase and matching backpack with a few of his favorite toys and clip the stuffed dog he can't sleep without to the backpack. "Grab your toothbrush."

I'm sitting on the bed when he returns with it and hands it to me. "Brush your teeth at least twice a day, you hear me?"

"Yes, Papa."

The word hits me like an arrow to the heart. I'm a Papa. This little boy has made me a father, and I couldn't be happier about that. I reach for him, and he comes to me like I've been holding him his whole life. "I love you, buddy."

"I love you, too, Papa."

"I'm very happy to be your papa."

"I'm happy, too."

"I'll take very good care of Mama while we're away, and I promise we'll call every day, okay?"

He nods.

"Grab your stuff, and let's get this party started."

I take the suitcase while he brings the backpack and Everly carries his pillow.

Maria and Austin are in the kitchen with Sofia when we come down.

"I can't stop yawning," Maria says. "All I want to do lately is sleep."

"You're getting close to your due date," Sofia says. "I was like that with Mateo."

"Are you kiddos ready?" Austin asks.

"Yes!" Everly responds with a fist pump into the air.

Mateo doesn't seem quite so certain.

I kneel in front of him. "You'll have a great time, and we'll talk every day. I promise."

He hugs me and then Sofia, who whispers something in his ear that makes him giggle.

We walk them out and buckle them into booster seats in the back of Maria's car. They spend so much time together that we all have two seats in our cars so we can drive them around.

Mateo's chin is quivering again when we kiss him goodbye one more time, but Austin doesn't dally. He knows to get them out of there before Mateo melts down.

After we wave them off, I walk Sofia back inside with an arm around her. "Are you okay?"

"This'll be the longest we've ever been apart."

"We don't have to go."

"Yes, we do. We need the time alone together."

"I agree, but I don't want you to be upset about leaving Mateo."

"He's in very good hands with Austin, Maria, Austin's parents and Everly, of course."

"I'll ask everyone else to check on him while we're gone."

"That'd be nice of them."

"He'll be fine, and it's good for him to do new things."

"I know."

"If you're not sure about this—"

She kisses me. "I'm sure that I want to go on the trip with you."

"Then that's what we'll do."

CHAPTER 26

GIANNA

Milo and I face each other in his bed, holding hands as we stare at each other, so relieved to be back together.

"I want to tell you what happened."

"Only if you need to talk about it. As far as I'm concerned, you being here today and telling me you love me is all I need to know."

"It's important to me that you understand why I asked you to leave that day. It wasn't because of you. It was me."

"I knew you were struggling with some things you needed to resolve before you could commit to me."

"That's it exactly. Ever since I lost my parents, I've just been flailing. I've been vulnerable and needy, and into that space came Jared, promising to make everything right for me. After years of doing battle with my brothers and coping with unbearable grief, I was so ready to let someone else carry the load. I bent myself to fit his world because I wanted so badly to be rescued. I know now that the only person who could rescue me was me. I needed to be able to trust my own judgment again before I could go forward with you."

"You've been awfully hard on yourself, love. What happened to you and your brothers was tragic, and you've done such a great job soldiering on. Your parents would be so incredibly proud of you."

"I hope so."

"I know so."

"When the news broke about Scott, it sent me down a rabbit hole of self-doubt and despair so deep, I feared I might never drag myself out of it. What helped was that my other friends felt the same way. Skylar's parents did, too. We were all shocked and devastated to know we might've been supporting the person who took her from us."

"I can see how that, on top of what Jared did, would rock your faith in all men."

"It never should've rocked my faith in you."

"It's all good, babe. I swear. I get it."

"Scott was released from jail last night, and he texted us, swearing again he had nothing to do with Skylar's disappearance, and if it takes the rest of his life, he's going to prove that to everyone. He said the new so-called evidence is bullshit, and even the judge said so when he refused to hold him."

"What do you think?"

"I want to believe him. I've talked about it with Julia and Ali, and we've decided to trust him until we have reason to believe otherwise."

"That sounds like a good plan."

"I want to tell you something else."

"I want to hear anything you have to say."

"I've come to realize that you were right. Jared was intended to show me what I don't want. Without him, I might not have taken one look at you and seen everything I *do* want. Although I have to give him credit for sending me a check for ten thousand dollars to pay off the dress I bought and to reimburse my bridesmaids for their dresses, the shower and the bachelorette party. It was a huge load off my mind to be able to pay them back for all that. He also included a note saying he was sorry for everything he put me through."

"Well, that's something anyway, and for what it's worth, I think we would've found our way to each other without you going through hell with him."

"I'd like to think so, but that relationship reset me in a way that needed to happen before I'd be ready for something like this. Before I was ready for you."

"And do you feel ready now? Really ready? Because if you aren't, I'm not going anywhere, Gianna. I'm in this for the long haul."

"I am, too, or I wouldn't be here, and I wouldn't have said yes when you asked me to marry you."

We kiss for what feels like hours.

"How about a shower before we rejoin the party?" he asks.

"Yes, please."

The shower leads to round two of the best makeup sex ever.

"We're supposed to be getting clean," I remind him as he presses me against the tile wall.

"We will. After."

"I've never done this in the shower," I tell him.

"We'll do everything for the first time together."

"I think we'd better get back to the wedding before we start a scandal."

"Oh, baby, the scandal started five minutes after we left. Why not fully enjoy it?"

"I've also never laughed like I do with you."

He holds me so close that I can feel his heart beating against my chest. "I love you so, so, so much. We're going to have the best life together."

"I can't wait for all of it."

We wash each other and nearly end up doing it again before I push him away and tell him to get dressed.

"You're staying here tonight, right?"

"If you'll have me."

"Oh, I'll have you."

"Milo."

"What, love?"

"We can't tell anyone we're engaged. Not today. This is Sofia and Nico's big day."

"I agree, but tomorrow... Tomorrow, we'll tell everyone."

NONA

After Nico and Sofia leave for the hotel they had booked for tonight, thinking that would be their honeymoon, the rest of us sit around the firepit. My sons Vincent and Lorenzo, with their wonderful wives, Vivian and Elena, my daughter, Francesca, and her husband, Domenic Senior, as well as their son, Domenic, and his new wife, Stacey, have all stayed to spend more time together. Stacey seems very nice, and I'm looking forward to getting to know her.

Our Domenic surprised us all by marrying a woman we didn't know, but he seems happy, and that's all that matters to me. His mother, on the other hand, is demanding he have a wedding she can attend. I can't say I blame her for wanting to dance at her eldest son's wedding. I'm sure he'll agree to the fuss because he's a good boy who'd never want his mother to be disappointed.

They're all good kids. We've been blessed beyond measure, and it just keeps getting better as new people join the family and bless us with more great-grandbabies on the way.

"What're you thinking about over there?" Marlene asks.

"About life and family and how blessed we are."

"Indeed we are. It was wonderful to see our Nico smiling again, like he used to before disaster struck."

"I thought the same thing." Though Nico isn't technically Marlene's grandson, you can't tell her that—and I wouldn't want to. She and I have shared everything, including our grandchildren, since her Vivian met my Vincent more than thirty years ago. That we also fight like wet cats is part of our charm, or so we like to say.

There's no one I'd rather bicker with than her. She's my best friend in the world, and she knows that as well as I do.

"I wanted to arrange it so you'd catch the bouquet," I tell her.

"Don't be silly. That needed to go to Dee, not an old fool like me."

"You aren't calling my fiancée an old fool, are you?" Alfredo asks.

"We're all old fools, and you know it," she says.

"Not me," my "boyfriend," Chris, says, making the rest of us laugh. "I'm only sixty-one."

I give him my trademarked testy look. "And you just have to keep reminding us of that, don't you?"

"I'm just saying. You may be old fools, but I'm not."

"I like him *so* much," Marlene says, with a wicked twinkle in her eye.

"You would," I retort.

I love to see Gianna sitting on Milo's lap and Dee on Wyatt's. Carmen and Jason left a while ago to get her home to rest, and the other wedding guests are long gone.

"What a day," Elena says with a sigh. "I'm so happy for Nico and Sofia—and Mateo."

"It was nice to see Nico more like his old self today," Lo says. "That's a big relief."

"Everything is finally getting back to normal," Elena says. "Thank goodness."

Her battle with breast cancer is now behind her, with her

latest scans showing no evidence of disease. Milo has made a full recovery, and if I'm not mistaken, he'll be getting married before much longer. I've never seen him look at anyone the way he does Gianna, and I'm so glad she came today and put the smile back on our Milo's face.

After coming so close to losing him, seeing him beaming with happiness and good health is all that matters to me. I love that boy with all my heart, and I'm thrilled he's found a woman who makes him as happy as Gianna does.

"I'd like to propose a toast." After the others fall silent, I hold up my glass of wine. "To family, to love, to happily ever after, to Miami, and to all good things ahead for everyone."

"Hear, hear," they say. "Hear, hear."

CARMEN

"Jason! Come quick."

He rushes into our room from the living room. "What's wrong? Are you in pain?" He's hardly left my side since I came out of surgery, down one appendix.

"No, come here."

When he's seated on the side of the bed, I take his hand and put it over my belly where I felt the first flutter of activity inside a few minutes ago. "Can you feel it?"

"What am I feeling?"

"The baby. I think I felt her move."

"Might've been gas."

"Hush! It was not gas."

His smile is one of my favorite things in the whole world. And then he gasps. "I felt it!"

"It's so amazing, isn't it? That's our baby."

"Wow."

We're quiet for a long time as we feel her movements, which send ripples across my abdomen.

"That's the coolest thing I've ever felt," Jason says, seeming as awed as I feel.

"I'm so thankful she's still in there."

"Me, too. How much longer do we have to wait for her?"

"You're the doctor. You tell me."

"About twenty more weeks." While I was in the hospital, we found out I'm further along than we first thought and that we're having a girl.

"It'll go by fast."

He kisses me and leans his forehead against mine. "I can't wait to meet her."

MARIA

"Are they finally asleep?" I ask Austin when he comes into the bedroom almost an hour after he went to tuck in Everly and Mateo.

"I think so."

"Thank you for taking one for the team."

"I'm nothing if not a team player. I can't believe you're still awake."

"I was waiting for you."

He crawls into bed and wraps his arms around me. "Here I am."

"That's what I needed." I run my hand over the colorful ink on his arm, marveling as always at the intricacy of his drawings.

"I love being what my baby needs."

"You're very good at it."

"Why, thank you."

"Today was such a great day. Nico and Sofia are so perfect

for each other, and Gianna came back. I bet we'll be dancing at their wedding before long."

"I was so happy to see her."

"Nico went to her house to invite her."

"Did he? That's awesome."

"He wanted Milo to be as happy as he is."

"Have I told you lately how much I love your family?" he asks.

"I'm so glad you do. I love yours, too."

"Nice how that worked out, huh?"

"So nice. All of it."

"Thank you for saving my Everly's life—and mine."

"That was my pleasure." I caress his sinfully handsome face. "I love everything about our life together."

"Even when I'm traveling with the team for months on end?"

"Even that, because you're doing what you love and what you're best at."

"That's not what I'm best at. I'm at my very best when I'm right here with you and our family."

"You do good work here. I still can't believe that the hottest baseball player on the planet is my husband."

"Believe it. And I still can't believe the hottest nurse in the history of hot nurses is my wife and the mother of my children—officially." My adoption of Everly was final a month ago on one of the best days of my life.

He makes me giggle whenever he says I'm the hottest nurse in the history of hot nurses. For his birthday, I bought a naughty-nurse outfit that blew his mind.

"Are you thinking about the naughty-nurse getup? Because you're not allowed to think about that unless you're going to put it on."

"That's too much work tonight, but I am feeling a little… needy."

"God, I love pregnant Maria, even more than I love not-pregnant Maria."

"Don't get used to her. Horny, pregnant Maria is temporary."

As he moves so he's on top of me, he says, "I'll just have to keep her around by getting you pregnant as much as possible."

"Easy, cowboy. But if you could take the edge off, I'd appreciate it."

He gazes down at me with so much love. Our life together is a dream come true, and it's all because of him and the way he loves me so completely. "There's nothing I'd rather do than take the edge off for my gorgeous wife."

DEE

After we get home from the wedding, I want Wyatt to go straight to bed since he's still recovering from pneumonia, but he has other ideas.

"Let's play foosball."

"I don't want to. You need rest."

"I'm not tired. Let's play."

"Why do you want to play with me when you can beat me with your eyes closed?"

"Because there's no one else I'd rather play with than you."

"Even though I'm easy to beat?"

"You're getting better all the time. Pretty soon, you're gonna beat me."

"Sure."

"You are."

"Okay, then. Two games, and then you go to bed."

"Deal."

We go outside to the pool area that we've turned into a peaceful oasis for relaxing and entertaining. Pool and foosball tables are located under an overhang that protects them from

South Florida's frequent rainstorms. Wyatt mounted a TV on the exterior wall of the house for watching Marlins and Dolphins games.

I love this space and how we've made the house our own in the time we've lived here together. The months since we bought this place have been the best of my life. Living with him, loving him, planning a future with him... I love everything about us. Except for the fear of losing it all without warning.

That hangs heavily over me, but we're starting with a therapist soon who'll hopefully help me to cope with the unknown. The recent scare still has me rattled and feeling uncertain about the future in a way that I haven't before now. Yes, I've always known his situation is precarious. But until the pneumonia hit, I hadn't had firsthand experience with how quickly his health can deteriorate.

I'll be happy to have no further proof of that until we're old and gray and cranky. That's all I want in this life—to grow old with him. And maybe have a few babies together. I'd be all for that, too.

"That was a hell of a wedding," he says as he easily scores the first point.

"Sure was. I never thought I'd see Nico settled down, but Sofia is perfect for him. She gets him."

"Yes, she does, and Mateo is adorable. They make a gorgeous family."

"Sofia told me she's pregnant. That's why they got married so quickly."

"That's exciting news. Your family is having a massive baby boom."

"We are."

"When are we going to tie the knot and add to the population?"

"Whenever you want."

"I've been ready since the day I asked you. I've been waiting for you to tell me when."

I look up at him, and he takes advantage of my distraction to score another point. Scowling at him, I say, "That was dirty."

Grinning, he replies, "All's fair in love and foosball. So when do you want to get married?"

"I told you—whenever you want."

He shakes his head. "I've never been married before—that I know of—but even an inexperienced guy like me knows who drives the wedding bus—and it ain't the groom."

"That you know of," I say with a snort of laughter. "I think you'd remember if you'd been married before."

He scores another point. "I hope so."

"Speaking of married, guess who else tied the knot today?"

"Who?"

"Marcus and Tara. I got a text from a mutual friend, asking if I'd heard. And before you ask, I'm happy for them. He's doing really well, and she seems great for him."

"No residual feelings for your old love?"

I look up at him to see if he's serious, and he scores again.

"I hate this game."

"But you love me, right?"

"Most of the time."

That shocks him, giving me a chance to score.

"And you say I'm dirty."

"All's fair," I reply with a cheeky grin. "Suddenly, I'm liking this game better, and to answer your question, I feel nothing for him except distant friendship and a hope that he continues to stay sober and finds happiness with Tara. But enough about him."

"About our wedding, and if you keep dodging the question, I'm going to think you don't want to marry me anymore."

My shock at hearing that allows him to score another point. "I quit." I walk away from the table and go to pour a glass of the

Chardonnay he keeps chilling for me in the little fridge under the bar. When I'm seated on the wicker sofa we picked out together, he sits next to me.

"What's going on, Delores?"

He calls me that only at the most important of times, usually when he's buried deep inside me and is confident I won't get mad. "Do you still want to marry me?"

"I can't believe you'd even ask me that."

"Then what's the problem, sweetheart? And don't say it's nothing. You've been as fragile as an eggshell since I got sick. I'm sorry I scared you, but I'm all better now, and there's nothing to worry about."

There's always something to worry about, but I keep that thought to myself. I promised him I could live with the uncertainty of his situation, and I'm determined to keep that promise. But recent events have rattled me. I can't deny that.

"Let's get married in September," I say.

"Yeah?"

I nod. "It's cooler then, and we can do it outside."

"Tell me when and where, and I'll be there." He kisses the back of my hand before leaning in to kiss my lips. "Everything is going to be okay. I swear."

Living with his situation is more difficult than I thought it would be, but since living without him isn't an option, I kiss him back, thankful for every minute I have with him.

NICO

"I can't believe we're married," I say to my beautiful bride.

"I know! Today felt like such a dream come true."

Her English has gotten so much better that it's almost like she's been speaking it all her life. She's worked so hard on perfecting it that I love seeing her becoming so smooth.

"Well, you can believe it, love. There's no getting rid of me now."

She raises her head off my chest. "Why would I want to get rid of you?"

"I'm not always easy to live with."

"Yes, you are."

"No, I'm not."

"Don't argue with me. I know you better than anyone."

"I love that you know me so well."

"I don't have any problem living with you. In fact, living with you in that palace you call home has been the happiest time in my life—and Mateo's."

"He's in it for the pool."

"No, he isn't, Nico. He's in it for *you*. We both are."

"I know, baby. I'm just teasing."

"You and your family... You rescued us from a nightmare, starting on the day that Jason diagnosed Mateo at the free clinic and then saved his life. The way your grandmothers swooped in and saw to our every need and then offered me an incredible job... And then there was you, their sexy grandson who came along to make me complete in a way I've never been before."

"We love you as much as you love us."

"That's the best part of it, to be surrounded by so much love. I'm not even worried about Mateo, because I know Maria and Austin love him almost as much as we do, and it's unheard of for me to not worry about him."

"I want to take away all your worries and replace them with more joy than you know how to handle."

"You've already done that. I wake up every day inside this dream we've created together. I was so afraid of losing it all after the shooting, but even then, you and your family never wavered in your devotion to me."

"None of it was your fault. We all knew that."

"We both know that some people would've blamed me anyway."

"Not people who love you, but let's not talk about that tonight when we have much better things to talk about."

"Such as?"

"Our marriage, our honeymoon, the baby we're going to have together."

"I can't believe your grandmothers are sending us on a real honeymoon. Just when I think I've seen it all from them, they go and top themselves."

"They're the best."

"They really are."

I move closer to her and wrap my arms around her before I kiss her. "My favorite part of today was that your smile never dimmed all day. I want you smiling like that every day for the rest of our lives."

"As long as I have you, I'll be smiling."

"You've got me forever."

"That's all I need."

MILO

I can't believe Gianna is sleeping naked in my arms after weeks of thinking I might never see her again. This was the best day ever, not only because my beloved brother got his happily ever after with Sofia—which was anything but assured after her ex shot me—but Gianna and I got ours, too.

My hands move over the soft skin of her back in a never-ending caress. I'm obsessed with her skin and every other part of her, too.

"Why are you still awake?" she asks in a sexy, sleepy-sounding voice.

"I don't want to miss a second with you."

"You're going to have to sleep at some point."

"Not yet."

"I'm sorry for what I put you through, Milo. I hated doing that to you."

"The only thing that matters is that you did what you needed to do and then came back to me when you were ready to."

"I was ready about five minutes after you left that day. I knew immediately that sending you away wasn't going to make anything better. It only made everything worse."

"It's all going to be better from here on out. Whatever comes up, we'll deal with it together."

"That makes everything better."

"I love you," I tell her, having no doubt that ours is a forever kind of love.

"I love you, too."

"*That* makes everything better."

EPILOGUES

Three weeks later...

MARIA

"I can't wait another minute to push," I say to my mother and Dee, who are on either side of my bed. The one person I need the most is on an airplane trying to get to me in time, but if the pressure building below is any indication, Austin is going to miss the birth of our son.

Dee looks at my phone, where I've been tracking Austin's location for hours. He pitched today in Los Angeles, and for the first time ever, I acted like the filthy-rich wife I am and had a private jet waiting to bring him home after the game, which is when he found out I was in labor. I didn't dare tell him before his start, or his concentration would've been blown to hell.

Our little guy is two weeks early. His due date had timed perfectly with almost a week between starts for Austin. So much for best-laid plans.

"He's twenty minutes out," Dee says.

I moan at the thought of having to wait even that long. An

epidural has made it so the contractions don't hurt anymore, but it can't stop the pressure, which builds with each one.

My cell phone rings.

"It's him," Dee says, handing it to me.

"Hi."

"Babe, I'm so close."

"Me, too—to having a baby, that is. I'm trying to wait."

"Don't wait if it's too much. I'll be there so soon."

"Can't wait to see you."

"Same. I'm about to go crazy from how long it's taking to get there."

"Are you triggered?" He heard about Everly's illness after a similar cross-country trek.

"Nah, I'm okay, or I will be as soon as I get to you. I can't believe he's coming today."

"I can, but I'm the one in labor."

"I'm so sorry I wasn't there."

"It's fine. You got the win. That's what matters."

"Maria, my love, you know that win has nothing on you and our son. Twelve minutes."

"I'll be here."

"Love you more than you'll ever know."

"Love you more than that."

"No way."

"Way."

"Eleven minutes."

We're still on the phone when he comes rushing in the door exactly eleven minutes later. Seventeen minutes after that, our son, Easton Giordino Jacobs, comes into the world at nine pounds, ten ounces. He's twenty-one inches long and has a light dusting of blond hair. He looks exactly like his father, minus the tattoos.

"He looks just like you, Austin," my mom says as she gazes at his sweet little face.

The next few hours are a whirlwind of grandparents, aunts, uncles and an excited big sister. I'll never forget the first minutes we spent as a family of four before Austin's parents took Everly home, promising to bring her back the next day to see her brother again.

"He's absolutely perfect," Austin says when it's just the three of us. "Thank you so much for him."

"Couldn't have done it without you."

"You did the hard part, and not for nothing, we need to talk about you keeping secrets from me when I'm on the road."

"Only this once, and it was for a good cause."

"I don't want to tell you that you were right to wait to tell me, but..."

"I knew you'd be useless on the mound if you were worried about me. By the way, the very large charge on the Amex is for the plane."

His big grin lights up his gorgeous face. "Best money we've ever spent on anything."

Four months later, this happens...

CARMEN

Labor hurts way worse than advertised. Between contractions, all I can think about is if the baby will be all right since she's arriving five weeks early. We found out a while ago that we're having a little girl, but we've mostly kept that info to ourselves. I can't wait to meet our daughter, but the fear about her early arrival and the pain of labor have my anxiety spiking.

It doesn't help that my doctor husband looks like he might pass out any second.

"You need to chill," I tell him.

"I'm chill."

Rolling my eyes, I say, "You are so far from chill, you're about to start sweating."

He grips my hand and bends his head to brush his lips over the back of it.

What does it say about the mad love I have for him that even in the throes of labor, his lips against my skin send a tingle through my entire body?

"I just want this to be over for you," he says. "I hate to see you in pain."

I'd decided to try to deliver without an epidural, but I'm already questioning the wisdom of that. The pain is *bad*. I feel like someone is wringing out my insides with a food processor, or something equally unpleasant.

"Are you scared that she's early?"

"Not really. You're almost to thirty-six weeks, when the baby's lungs are more developed. Hopefully, a little before that won't matter too much."

Hopefully. There's a lot of room for things to go wrong inside the parameters of that hope.

Another contraction requires my full attention, and how can this one be twice as bad as the earlier ones? How is that even possible? By the time it subsides, I'm crying and almost hyperventilating.

"You need an epidural," Jason says in an urgent tone. "Please, Carmen. Let them give you some relief."

"Yeah. Okay." I'm done being a supermom. This shit *hurts*.

Jason runs to alert our nurse that I've changed my mind about the epidural.

I just hope I didn't wait too long.

I'm in the throes of another vicious contraction when Jason returns with the nurse and my OB, a jovial man named Dr. Bruce, who Jason said is the best OB in Miami, and he wanted only the best for me. I've come to really like Dr. Bruce, and I'm relieved to see him.

Withstanding a full internal exam in front of your husband, even if he's a doctor, is mortifying.

"Carmen, there's good news and bad news. The good news is your baby is ready to be born. The bad news is I'm afraid you're too far along for an epidural to do much good."

I want to cry from the second part of that news.

"You've got this, Rizo."

Hearing Jason's nickname for me, the Spanish word for curly, grounds me and helps me focus. It reminds me of the circuitous journey we both took before our worlds collided in front of Miami-Dade General Hospital more than two years ago. That day changed both our lives forever, in ways too many to list, and set us on the path toward today. That we'll welcome our first child in the hospital that has played such a huge role in our love story is fitting and perfect.

I'm excited and scared and in horrible pain, but I put all my focus on the result of this ordeal—a daughter, a child who will bring parts of each of us and our families into a new life.

The next couple of hours pass in a blur of pain, pushing, tears and more pain as the pressure between my legs intensifies to the point that I fear I'll burst apart.

"You're doing great," Dr. Bruce says. "One more big push ought to do it."

"Jason." He's behind me on the bed, holding me up when I can't do it myself anymore.

"I'm right here, love. You've got this. I'm so proud of you."

Another contraction demands my full attention. I'm so exhausted and in so much pain that I'm sure I can't do this for another minute. Right when I reach my absolute limit, I hear her. She arrives with a scream of outrage that makes me laugh and then cry.

Jason is right there with me as Dr. Bruce places the baby on my chest.

"Congratulations on the arrival of your daughter."

She's here. Our daughter. And just that quickly, as if the last few hours never happened, I'm completely bedazzled by her tiny features, her feathery eyebrows, the whisp of dark hair and the olive complexion.

"She looks like her gorgeous mother, thank goodness," Jason says, sounding tearful. "She's stunning."

"What's her name?" one of the nurses asks as Dr. Bruce does something between my legs.

I couldn't care less about anything down there when my daughter is looking at me with big blue eyes. I read that almost all newborns have blue eyes, and they can't see much of anything at first. But if you ask me, she's looking right through me and touching my soul with an all-new kind of love, the kind that runs so deep as to be a permanent part of me from the first second of her life.

"Her name is Maya," I reply to the nurse. "Maya Olivia Marlene Northrup."

"That's a lovely name," she says. "Is it a family name?"

"Carmen's grandmothers are Olivia and Marlene, but Maya is an original," Jason says, looking as dazzled as I feel.

I'm a mother.

When I first married Tony, I expected to be a young mother. If our plans had come to fruition, I'd have a ten-year-old by now and probably several more. I never expected to have to wait this long, but life has a way of throwing a wrench into the best-laid plans. I also didn't expect my heart to ache for my late husband as I welcomed my first child with my second husband, but that's grief for you. It pops in at the strangest of times to remind you it's always with you.

"Are you all right, sweetheart?" Jason asks.

"I'm great. How about you?"

"Best day of my life, hands down."

"Mine, too. Isn't she so beautiful?"

Jason leans over to kiss the baby's forehead. "She is. Just like her mama."

"You'd better go get the grandparents before they spontaneously combust."

Smiling, he kisses us both again and goes to retrieve my parents and grandmothers as well as Tony's parents, who'll be extra grandparents to Maya. We'll call his mother soon to tell her she just became a first-time grandmother. Our little girl will be very well loved. That's for sure.

Jason returns with the others, who surround the bed trying to get a closer look at the new arrival.

"Meet Maya Olivia Marlene Northrup."

"Oh, mi amor," Nona says. "What an honor, and that my name comes first."

As Abuela swats at her, we laugh so hard that I moan from the pain. "Stop it. Laughing hurts." I glance up at my mother, who suffered numerous miscarriages before she had me. After having just one myself, I'm not sure how she survived that. "Would you like to hold her, Mama?"

"Oh yes. Please."

I hand her over to my mother. We've decided the baby will call her Vivi so as not to be confused with her mother, Abuela. "Maya, say hello to your Vivi, who will love you so much, you'll never want for anything."

"That's right," my mother says as tears slide down her cheeks. "You're already so loved. So, so loved."

Tony's parents, Len and Josie, lean in for a closer look.

"She's stunning, Carmen," Josie says. "She looks just like her beautiful Mom."

"Thank you for being here," I tell them.

"We're so honored to be part of her life—and yours."

"Always."

Jason brushes the hair back from my face and leans in to kiss me. "Well done, love. I'm so proud of you."

"I'm proud of us. We make pretty babies."

"Yes, we do. I think we should have a bunch of them."

I moan at the thought of more babies. "How about we talk about that tomorrow?"

Smiling, he says, "You got it."

~

I can't stop staring at baby Maya. It's all I want to do. She's so perfect and such a good baby. When I look at her, I see every dream I've ever had come true in one tiny little package. She eats, she sleeps, she pees, she poops, and then she does it all again in a cycle that has quickly taken over my life and Jason's.

She's the center of our universe.

Since her arrival, however, I've experienced odd feelings of grief for the children Tony and I never got to have. Bizarre, right? Here I finally have everything I've ever wanted, and the grief is there to remind me that it never should've been this man and this child. It should've been an entirely different life with someone else.

Jason returns from a trip to the gym and immediately comes to check on his ladies, as he calls us. "Has she spoken her first words or split an atom or done anything else I need to know about since I left?"

"None of that, but she's getting closer to being able to suck on her own toes."

"I could tell she was gifted. She's just proving it to us every day."

"I hope she gets your ability to get A's without breaking a sweat."

"I hope she gets your curls and smile as well as your sharp wit and intellect."

"Her legs are going crazy since she heard your voice."

"Let me grab a shower, and then I'll be ready for some power snuggling."

While he's gone, she keeps me entertained with the way she's constantly moving, gurgling and tooting. I'm obsessed with her eyelashes and the bow shape of her mouth. I keep trying to see myself or Jason in her, but other than the dusting of dark hair that comes from me, she's her own unique self, even if everyone else sees me in her.

Jason comes out of the bathroom wearing only a pair of formfitting boxer briefs, and as always, I take a good look at his defined chest and abs. Sometimes I still can't believe I was lucky enough to find true love twice in one lifetime.

"Quit ogling me. We have five weeks to go."

Groaning, I say, "I can't imagine doing that in five *months*, let alone five weeks." I'm so sore that I can barely sit down. Forget getting busy with my sexy husband.

"If it takes that long, it takes that long. You're still the boss."

Him calling me that goes back to the first week we met, when I used my communications and social media skills to help him restore his battered reputation so he could work as a neurosurgeon at Miami-Dade General Hospital.

"I've been thinking," he says as he stretches out next to Maya. "I should probably sell Priscilla."

"*What?*" He loves his precious Porsche almost as much as he loves me.

"We need a second car that can have a car seat. When you go back to work, we'll both be taking her to your mom's and picking her up."

My mother has insisted on watching Maya while we're at work, and I'm thrilled to take her up on that. In the last year, since Dee became the general manager, my parents have cut way back on their hours at the restaurant, and they're looking forward to being hands-on grandparents to Maya.

"Couldn't we get something else for you to use on workdays

so you can still have Priscilla for the weekends?"

"I want to be with you guys on the weekends, which makes Priscilla obsolete."

"We wouldn't even be together without her."

"You don't think so?"

"She played such a huge role in bringing us together."

"Because I had to bail you out of jail when you got accused of stealing her?"

"Hush about that!" I put my hands over Maya's ears. "She can never know about that, or we'll have teenage rebellion like you read about. She'll say, 'Mama went to jail, so why can't I?'"

He loses it laughing. "My princess will never step foot in a jail."

"That's what my father thought, too. We all know how that worked out. An hour after a smooth-talking doctor cruised into my life, I was in lockup for the first time ever."

"Admit it. I keep your life interesting."

"That's one word for it."

"Why'd you look so sad when I came back before, Rizo"

"I wasn't sad."

"I saw what I saw."

"It's the weirdest thing…" I'm appalled when my eyes flood with tears.

"What is, love?"

"Since she was born, I keep thinking about the other babies I might've had with Tony. It's like I'm grieving them or something. Like I said… It's weird."

"I think it's perfectly normal for you to be wondering what might've been with him and the kids you two would've had together."

"You do? Really? Because it feels bizarre to me. I've never been happier than I've been since she arrived, so why am I pulling the scab off that wound?"

"It's like you've said so many times—you don't get to choose when the grief resurfaces."

"Yeah," I say with a sigh, thankful that he always understands. I reach across the baby to take his hand. "You know that when it happens, it doesn't take anything away from how happy I am with you and Maya, right?"

"I know." He kisses the back of my hand. "Of course I do."

"Thank you for her, for this amazing second chance, for the life we have together, for jail, for all of it."

"Loving you and Maya is the greatest thing in my life."

Two months after that...

"I, Dee, take you, Wyatt, to be my husband..."

Three months later...

NICO

"One more big push, Sofia," the doctor says.

That's all it takes to bring our baby girl into the world, and I'm right there to watch her take her first breath as she looks around with wonder stamped onto her precious little face. "God, Sofia... She's gorgeous."

"Meet Harlow Elena Giordino," I tell the nurses and doctor.

"That's a gorgeous name for a gorgeous girl," the doctor says.

I couldn't agree more.

GIANNA

Eight years after the disappearance of Skylar Jones, a former custodian at the University of Florida is arrested and charged with her kidnapping and murder after he leads authorities to her remains. The arrest fully exonerates Skylar's boyfriend, Scott Wallace, who lived under a cloud of suspicion since her disappearance.

My friends and I are so relieved to have Skylar's case finally resolved and to have a someone charged with her death who isn't Scott. We welcome him back into our group and apologize for ever doubting him.

"I don't blame you guys for doubting me," Scott says. "But I hope you know I'll never stop loving and missing Skylar."

We won't either.

And then on Nochebuena, this happens...

"I, Marlene, take you, Alfredo, to be my husband..."

Followed a year after that by...

Dr. and Mrs. Wyatt and Dee Blake announce the birth of their twins, Alec and Alexa.

And then...

"I, Milo, take you, Gianna, to be my wife..."

Two months later...

Domenic and Stacey Giordino announce the arrival of their daughter, Francesca Rose...

And then...

Marcus and Tara have a son named Augustus, but they're going to call him Gus...

Finally...

Chris talks Livia into moving in with him.

Then they all live happily ever after in the South Florida sunshine.

And that's a wrap on the Miami Nights Series—for now, anyway. I'd love to revisit these characters at some point in the future to see what they're all up to. For now, I'll say goodbye to them and thank them for the fun I've had with them over the last few years. I'm trying not to write so many super-long series, and I feel this one is ending right where it should.

Many thanks to my editors, Linda Ingmanson and Joyce Lamb, my continuity editor, Gwen Neff, as well as my primary beta readers, Anne Woodall, Kara Conrad and Tracey Suppo. Thank you to my amazing Miami Nights Series beta readers: Dinorah Shobin, Emma Melero Juarez, Angelica Maya, Mona Abramesco, Carmen Morejon and Stephanie Behill.

A huge shout out to Dr. Sarah Hewitt, family nurse practitioner, for always checking me on the medical storylines.

As always, thank you to the "home team" that supports me behind the scenes, Dan, Emily and Jake as well as Julie Cupp, Lisa Cafferty, Jean Mello, Nikki Haley and Ashley Lopez. I couldn't do what I do without all of you, and I'm endlessly grateful for your many contributions.

To the readers who've embraced the Giordinos and the Miami Nights Series, thank you so much. It was so fun to write these characters and to set this series in a place that means so much to me and my family.

xoxo

Marie

ALSO BY MARIE FORCE

Contemporary Romances Available from Marie Force

The Miami Nights Series

Book 1: How Much I Feel *(Carmen & Jason)*

Book 2: How Much I Care *(Maria & Austin)*

Book 3: How Much I Love *(Dee's story)*

Nochebuena, A Miami Nights Novella

Book 4: How Much I Want *(Nico & Sofia)*

Book 5: How Much I Need *(Milo and Gianna)*

The Wild Widows Series—a Fatal Series Spin-Off

Book 1: Someone Like You

Book 2: Someone to Hold

The Gansett Island Series

Book 1: Maid for Love *(Mac & Maddie)*

Book 2: Fool for Love *(Joe & Janey)*

Book 3: Ready for Love *(Luke & Sydney)*

Book 4: Falling for Love *(Grant & Stephanie)*

Book 5: Hoping for Love *(Evan & Grace)*

Book 6: Season for Love *(Owen & Laura)*

Book 7: Longing for Love *(Blaine & Tiffany)*

Book 8: Waiting for Love *(Adam & Abby)*

Book 9: Time for Love *(David & Daisy)*

Book 10: Meant for Love *(Jenny & Alex)*

Book 10.5: Chance for Love, *A Gansett Island Novella (Jared & Lizzie)*

Book 11: Gansett After Dark *(Owen & Laura)*

Book 12: Kisses After Dark *(Shane & Katie)*

Book 13: Love After Dark *(Paul & Hope)*

Book 14: Celebration After Dark *(Big Mac & Linda)*

Book 15: Desire After Dark *(Slim & Erin)*

Book 16: Light After Dark *(Mallory & Quinn)*

Book 17: Victoria & Shannon (Episode 1)

Book 18: Kevin & Chelsea (Episode 2)

A Gansett Island Christmas Novella

Book 19: Mine After Dark *(Riley & Nikki)*

Book 20: Yours After Dark *(Finn & Chloe)*

Book 21: Trouble After Dark *(Deacon & Julia)*

Book 22: Rescue After Dark *(Mason & Jordan)*

Book 23: Blackout After Dark *(Full Cast)*

Book 24: Temptation After Dark *(Gigi & Cooper)*

Book 25: Resilience After Dark *(Jace & Cindy)*

Book 26: Hurricane After Dark *(Full Cast)*

The Green Mountain Series

Book 1: All You Need Is Love *(Will & Cameron)*

Book 2: I Want to Hold Your Hand *(Nolan & Hannah)*

Book 3: I Saw Her Standing There *(Colton & Lucy)*

Book 4: And I Love Her *(Hunter & Megan)*

Novella: You'll Be Mine *(Will & Cam's Wedding)*

Book 5: It's Only Love *(Gavin & Ella)*

Book 6: Ain't She Sweet *(Tyler & Charlotte)*

The Butler, Vermont Series

(Continuation of Green Mountain)

Book 1: Every Little Thing *(Grayson & Emma)*

Book 2: Can't Buy Me Love *(Mary & Patrick)*

Book 3: Here Comes the Sun *(Wade & Mia)*

Book 4: Till There Was You *(Lucas & Dani)*

Book 5: All My Loving *(Landon & Amanda)*

Book 6: Let It Be *(Lincoln & Molly)*

Book 7: Come Together *(Noah & Brianna)*

Book 8: Here, There & Everywhere *(Izzy & Cabot)*

Book 9: The Long and Winding Road *(Max & Lexi)*

The Treading Water Series

Book 1: Treading Water

Book 2: Marking Time

Book 3: Starting Over

Book 4: Coming Home

Book 5: Finding Forever

The Quantum Series

Book 1: Virtuous *(Flynn & Natalie)*

Book 2: Valorous *(Flynn & Natalie)*

Book 3: Victorious *(Flynn & Natalie)*

Book 4: Rapturous *(Addie & Hayden)*

Book 5: Ravenous *(Jasper & Ellie)*

Book 6: Delirious *(Kristian & Aileen)*

Book 7: Outrageous *(Emmett & Leah)*

Book 8: Famous *(Marlowe & Sebastian)*

Single Titles

Five Years Gone

One Year Home

Sex Machine

Sex God

Georgia on My Mind

True North

The Fall

The Wreck

Love at First Flight

Everyone Loves a Hero

Line of Scrimmage

Romantic Suspense Novels Available from Marie Force

The Fatal Series

One Night With You, *A Fatal Series Prequel Novella*

Book 1: Fatal Affair

Book 2: Fatal Justice

Book 3: Fatal Consequences

Book 3.5: Fatal Destiny, *the Wedding Novella*

Book 4: Fatal Flaw

Book 5: Fatal Deception

Book 6: Fatal Mistake

Book 7: Fatal Jeopardy

Book 8: Fatal Scandal

Book 9: Fatal Frenzy

Book 10: Fatal Identity

Book 11: Fatal Threat

Book 12: Fatal Chaos

Book 13: Fatal Invasion

Book 14: Fatal Reckoning

Book 15: Fatal Accusation

Book 16: Fatal Fraud

Sam and Nick's Story Continues....

Book 1: State of Affairs

Book 2: State of Grace

Book 3: State of the Union

Book 4: State of Shock

Historical Romance Available from Marie Force

The Gilded Series

Book 1: Duchess by Deception

Book 2: Deceived by Desire

ABOUT THE AUTHOR

Marie Force is the *New York Times* bestselling author of contemporary romance, romantic suspense and erotic romance. Her series include Fatal, First Family, Gansett Island, Butler Vermont, Quantum, Treading Water, Miami Nights and Wild Widows.

Her books have sold more than 12 million copies worldwide, have been translated into more than a dozen languages and have appeared on the *New York Times* bestseller list more than 30 times. She is also a *USA Today* and #1 *Wall Street Journal* bestseller, as well as a Spiegel bestseller in Germany.

Her goals in life are simple—to finish raising two happy, healthy, productive young adults, to keep writing books for as long as she possibly can and to never be on a flight that makes the news.

Join Marie's mailing list on her website at *marieforce.com* for news about new books and upcoming appearances in your area. Follow her on Facebook at *www.Facebook.com/MarieForceAuthor*, Instagram at *www.instagram.com/marieforceauthor/* and TikTok at *https://www.tiktok.com/@marieforceauthor?*. Contact Marie at *marie@marieforce.com*.

Made in the USA
Las Vegas, NV
08 April 2023

70321326R00187